Praise for Lee Tobin McClain

"Fans of Debbie Macomber will appreciate this start to
a new series by McClain that blends sweet, small-town
romance with such serious issues as domestic abuse....
Readers craving a feel-good romance with a bit of suspense
will be satisfied."
—*Booklist* on *Low Country Hero*

"[An] enthralling tale of learning to trust.... This enjoyable
contemporary romance will appeal to readers looking for
twinges of suspense before happily ever after."
—*Publishers Weekly* on *Low Country Hero*

"*Low Country Hero* has everything I look for in a book—
it's emotional, tender, and an all-around wonderful story."
—RaeAnne Thayne, *New York Times* bestselling author

Also available from
Lee Tobin McClain
and HQN Books

Safe Haven

Low Country Hero

LEE TOBIN McCLAIN

Low Country Dreams

HQN™

HQN™

ISBN-13: 978-1-335-01766-6

Recycling programs for this product may not exist in your area.

Low Country Dreams

Acknowledgments

Many thanks to Dony Jay, who was kind enough to help me improve accuracy of the police details (all errors are my own), and to Kathy Ayres, who read the manuscript just when I needed it done and gave many helpful suggestions. I feel like the most fortunate of writers to work with the HQN team, especially Susan Swinwood, Gloria Bairos and my wonderful editor, Shana Asaro.

Family plays a major role in all of my novels, and I'm grateful to my own small but mighty family: my sister and brother-in-law, Sue and Ron Spore; my niece, Jessica; and most of all, my daughter, Grace, my inspiration and the child of my heart.

Dear Reader,

Welcome back to Safe Haven! I love reunion romances, and since Liam is the most hearth-and-home oriented of the O'Dwyer brothers, he seemed like the perfect candidate for a second-chance hometown romance. Liam and Yasmin are very different—he struggled in school while she excelled, and he grew up in modest circumstances while she was wealthy—but they both need a helping hand from their community to overcome their family challenges to the point where they can give and receive love.

Yasmin has particular struggles because of her family's mental health issues. The latest studies show that 18 percent of adults in the US have a mental health condition. In *Low Country Dreams*, I wanted to explore the challenges families face when one or more of their members struggle with anxiety, depression or even schizophrenia... and to highlight the fact that people with mental illness are far more likely to be victims of crimes than perpetrators. I also wanted to show that a caring community—and access to mental health services—can improve outcomes and help individuals and families have better lives.

May you find a happy escape in *Low Country Dreams*... and come back to visit in October, when Cash O'Dwyer's story, *Low Country Christmas*, hits the shelves.
If you want a reminder, sign up for my newsletter at www.leetobinmcclain.com.

Be safe,

Lee

CHAPTER ONE

WORKING LATE IN a small Southern town shouldn't feel this creepy.

Yasmin Tanner looked out the office window of the church where the Safe Haven Women's Center was located. Live oaks draped with Spanish moss broke the moonlight into a crisscross pattern. Lighted upstairs windows in a few houses along the street indicated that other night owls were still awake.

Awake, although safely ensconced at home with their families.

Maybe it wasn't creepy so much as just lonely.

Yasmin turned back to the center's old desktop computer, where a spreadsheet displaying the in-the-red budget was the real scary problem she was avoiding. If they couldn't find another source of funding, the center might have to close.

The thought of all her clients who needed her—the women who showed up in a panic, often with kids—made her heart ache. No, the center couldn't provide overnight accommodations, not anymore, but they could help clients escape abusive domestic partners, help them find a place where they and their kids could be safe. If that safety net went away on her watch...

She propped her chin on her hand and stared out the dark window for another minute, then forced herself to sit up straight and study the budget again. Surely there was some way they could manage. Maybe if she let her own salary go for another month...

A loud pounding at the door made her heart jump. She stood and backed into the darkness, adrenaline rushing through her body. Abusers sometimes came to the center angry, considering it to have broken up their relationship. But women in need came at all hours, too. If she could help someone, she'd do it.

More pounding. She tiptoed to another room in the church and peeked out the window.

Her brother, Josiah? What was he doing here at this hour?

She rushed to open the door. "Joe! What's going on?" She took his hand and pulled him inside, studying the face that she used to be able to read, but that now remained an impassive mask. A symptom. But his fists were clenching and unclenching. Something had happened.

Someone was behind him... Uh-oh. Her heart gave an extra hard thump. "Rocky! Is that you?" She reached out and grasped the young teen's shoulder.

Rocky was a terrific kid who lived in a rural area about fifty miles inland. His mom kept making the wrong choices and ending up here.

But why was he here with her brother rather than with his own mother?

"Hide, hide." Josiah urged Rocky toward the church door and looked at Yasmin. "Where can we hide?"

"What happened?" Josiah had a lot of delusions that confused him, but Rocky usually knew the score. She looked from one to the other. "How'd you two meet up? Why are you wanting to hide?"

"I'm sorry, I'm sorry." Josiah kept repeating the words, looking into the center as if enemies might be hidden behind the pamphlet-holder or potted plants.

"Come on." She ushered both of them into the center, and only then did she notice the police car cruising along the street toward them.

The way her heart skittered made her mad at herself.

She was through with Liam. She wasn't going to give him another thought. She needed to focus on Josiah and Rocky, not her maddeningly attractive ex.

"Are you in some kind of trouble?" She watched her brother's nervous hands pluck at his shirt.

He didn't answer. Her Einstein-smart brother was now next to nonverbal on his bad days. She wanted to lean into his tall form, let him put an arm around her and explain the situation, tell her that everything would be okay, make high-level jokes that only the two of them would understand.

Heart aching, she turned away and studied the young teenager before them. He'd probably grown six inches since the last time she'd seen him. His hair curled messily down his neck and his shirt reeked of perspiration.

His eyes were wide and terrified.

"What's happened? What are you doing here?" She put an arm around the thirteen-year-old.

He shrugged away and brushed a fist across his eyes. Whoa. He was a tough kid, and if he was crying…

"Where's your mom?"

He hunched back, then spun and made for the door.

Josiah stepped in front of him and shook his head. "Stay here. Have to hide."

They glared at each other for a minute and something passed between them, some communication Yasmin didn't understand.

Then Rocky shoved past Josiah and looked out the door, cautiously, as if assessing whether it was safe to leave.

And froze.

Which made sense when Yasmin saw the black-and-white parked at the curb. Liam emerged and faced them, shading his eyes from the streetlight overhead.

Just looking at her former boyfriend made Yasmin's chest go tight. Time slowed down and tugged at her gut. What was Liam doing here? Had Josiah or Rocky—or both of them—done something wrong?

Liam adjusted his gun belt and clicked on his portable radio, smooth, automatic movements she'd seen him perform dozens of times, and then walked toward the church. Their eyes met and held, until Yasmin looked away, yearning gnawing at her gut like hunger. There'd been a time when she would have run to him, flung her arms around him and asked him to come help her sort out this situation, sort out all her troubles. But life's hard truths had forced her to mature and to stand her ground, solid and independent. She couldn't lean on anyone. In particular, she didn't want to lean on dark-haired, blue-eyed Liam O'Dwyer.

She glanced back. Josiah stood motionless by the church door, Rocky beside him. Neither looked ready to panic or bolt, at least not immediately. She moved down the church steps and onto the cement sidewalk, palms sweating, heart in her throat.

You're an idiot. You're supposed to be over him.

Liam spoke first. "What's going on here?"

"Nothing I can't handle." She watched as he stepped closer, alert and confident. She loved that certainty in him, had loved it since fifth grade when he'd waded into a group of kids teasing her and made them stop with a few sharp words.

Just like then, he made it clear that he could control the situation. For one thing, he was an excellent marksman and could get his Taser or gun out in less time than it would take either Rocky or Josiah—or Yasmin herself for that matter—to take a threatening step in his direction, or run away.

She also trusted that he was the kind of cop who wouldn't shoot unless it was the absolute last option, necessary to save lives.

And she didn't need to be thinking about his good character, or his protective nature, or the slight, sexy swagger in his walk. "Why are you here?"

"I got a phone call." He watched her for a moment, let his eyes travel slowly from Rocky to Yasmin to Josiah. "From your next-door neighbor." He gave a sideways nod toward old Mrs. Jackson's house.

Yasmin's shoulders relaxed a little. If Liam's visit only had to do with her nosy neighbor, then it could be quickly resolved and she could send him on his way and deal with whatever had brought Rocky and Josiah here tonight.

She could get back to her policy since their breakup: maintain distance between them.

When she saw him around town, she usually managed to ease into a different aisle at the grocery, turn down a different street. She'd locked her phone in her car more nights than one to prevent herself from giving in and texting him in a fit of late-night weakness.

In a small town like Safe Haven, avoiding your ex was difficult, but not impossible.

Except now, in the middle of the night, with a puzzling situation on your hands.

LIAM LOOKED AT the woman he used to love, standing there with her brother and some kid, and wished old Mrs. Jackson next door wasn't quite so observant and quick to leap to conclusions. When she'd called in a disturbance just a few minutes ago, said there were a couple of men skulking around the center, he'd rushed to respond, worried Yasmin was at risk.

Looked like a false alarm.

He and the other officers joked that as much as Mrs. Jackson knew about what was going on in town, they'd soon have to give her a badge. But truthfully, Liam was glad for it, glad to live in a place where people watched out for one another.

More than anything, he wanted to be appointed police chief in this place. To devote his life to taking care of it, and to show he was worthy of doing that.

But it was hard to stay focused on his goals with Yasmin in front of him. She looked like she'd lost a little weight, and even though he'd always liked her curvy figure, he had to admit she looked great. She'd taken to wearing her blond-streaked hair in long, wild curls, and even in jeans, she looked classy. Daughter of a Safe Haven blue-blooded mother and a biracial physician father who'd died young, she'd grown up with all the financial advantages, but he didn't begrudge her that, nor envy her. Her family had its share of problems.

What did make him mad was the chip on her shoulder when she was the one who'd dumped him. He gestured toward the two-story house next door. "Since Mrs. Jackson called in a disturbance, it's my job to investigate." He reached the church's front steps, tore his eyes away from her and tried to see into the building.

"Everything's fine." She glanced back at her brother and the young boy.

"Hey, Josiah, good to see you again," he said to Yasmin's brother, who was backing into the church. One of Liam's fellow officers had mentioned Josiah had gotten a little eccentric since arriving back in Safe Haven a couple of months ago, but Liam hadn't had much contact with him. There'd been no reports of his causing any trouble.

Liam focused on the kid. "Who's that?" he asked Yasmin, keeping his voice low.

She bit her lip, shook her head rapidly. "Client confidentiality. And speaking of clients, I need to take care of this one, so…"

She started to back in, letting the door close, but a loud, angry voice came from inside the center. Was that Josiah, or someone else? If there were another male visitor to the center, it would make sense of the whole "disturbance" thing. Liam climbed the rest of the way toward the church doorway and looked in.

The same voice came, less angry. It was Josiah.

Liam frowned. "You okay, Josiah?"

Josiah didn't answer, but he didn't look upset, either. Putting thoughts of Yasmin's brother and his issues aside to think about later, Liam shrugged and turned. And realized that Yasmin was only inches away.

He sucked in a breath and there it was: her musky cherry perfume. He cleared the sudden thickness in his throat. "You sure I can't help?"

"Yes!" She stepped back and lifted her hands like stop signs. "I'm fine, Liam. Go solve crimes, or whatever."

Fine, dismiss him. Maybe a cop wasn't important in the upscale world of a doctor's daughter, but let someone steal her diamond tennis bracelet and she'd call the police, all right.

Which wasn't exactly fair, since Yasmin's family money seemed to be mostly gone and she wasn't a superficial lady of leisure. He forced his mind to stay in the here and now. "Seems like there's some kind of problem."

"One I'd like to take care of." She turned away, then, as the boy scuttled past her into the church. She looked back over her shoulder. "I'll call 911 if I need anything."

Because God forbid she should call him directly. He looked at the lift of her chin, the pout of her full lips, and his body tightened. Even after everything she'd done.

She was almost inside when the boy came up

behind her. He stuck his head out the door. "You look like *him*," he said. His voice cracked, and Liam couldn't tell if it was from emotions or just the normal hormonal changes a boy's voice went through.

"Like who?" Liam asked.

The boy held out a much wrinkled and mauled business card, and Liam took it. His older brother Sean's card, for his construction business. "Where'd you get this?"

The boy cringed back, and Liam realized he'd been too abrupt, had sounded like he was making an accusation. Not to mention the fact that his uniform could be scary to a kid, especially one who was for some reason at a women's center without parents.

Kids, innocent victims of their parents' problems, always got to Liam. "Sean's my brother," he explained gently to the boy, holding up the business card. "He's on his honeymoon. Maybe I can help."

But the kid crossed his arms tight over his chest. You had to look close to see the fear in his eyes, but it was there. Liam was familiar with it—the stark "my life has blown up" terror, and the bravado that hid it—from the inside.

"If he met Sean before," he said to Yasmin, "it must have been here, at the women's center. Was he with his mom?"

She bit her lip, then nodded. Behind her, her brother ran his fingers through his hair, making it stand up on end. Had Josiah developed a drinking problem, or started using? He wasn't just nerdy and self-contained and brilliant, like he'd always been; his tension level was off the charts.

"Where's your mom now?" Liam asked the boy.

A panicked look came into the boy's eyes.

And Liam was thrown back into his past, to the day his own mother had disappeared for good. He'd been just a little younger than this kid. Why should he expect the boy to be coherent? He hadn't been.

"He doesn't have to answer your questions," Yasmin said, her voice firm. "This isn't an investigation. We've got it covered." That last was shaky-sounding, like she wasn't necessarily confident that she did have it covered.

"If there's something wrong, it would be better for us to get involved right away." He watched her lift her chin to argue, weigh the options and decide against it. She was rattled—he could tell by the way her teeth worried at her bottom lip. "I realize you're in charge of a women's center," he went on, "and you don't need men, at least men like me. But there are things I can do, like putting out a call for someone missing, that even you can't match." He heard the sarcasm in his own voice and clamped his mouth shut. It was wrong to dig up past conflicts when there was a hurting kid right in front of him.

"I'm taking him home with me," Yasmin said, lifting an eyebrow as if daring him to argue.

"Do you have his parents' permission?"

"Are you going to drag him into the station if I don't?" she challenged. "I'm a certified foster parent, remember." She turned to the boy. "Come on. Let's go where it's more comfortable and you can get some sleep."

As Yasmin gathered her things, and her brother and the boy shuffled around in the hallway, Liam debated whether to call for backup and make this a formal case. He remembered with crystal clarity what it was like to be a kid caught up in official police business when all you really wanted was your mom. Yasmin was probably taking the right approach, trying to make the boy feel better by bringing him to a home environment.

The kid was clinging on to a backpack. Had both arms wrapped around it, like it wouldn't be safe enough just sitting on his back.

The action pulled out more of Liam's memories. He knew that was why the kid was hugging it, because he'd done the same himself. His own backpack had been a treasured link to his mother, her neat "Liam O'Dwyer" written in permanent marker across the label.

So…maybe he wouldn't call this in, not unless the kid wanted him to. He cleared his suddenly tight throat. "You okay going to her house for now?" he asked the kid.

"Shut up," Yasmin's brother said.

Yasmin put her arm around him, her forehead wrinkling.

What was that about? Josiah was a couple of years older than Liam, so four years older than Yasmin, and undeniably a little odd in a chess-genius kind of way. But his social skills had always been okay.

"Shut UP!" Josiah said again, louder.

Yasmin wrapped her other arm around him in a quick hug, then said something to him and gestured back toward the church. But Josiah shook his head, his mouth tightening, eyes narrowing.

Liam left Josiah to Yasmin and knelt in front of the young teen. "If you tell us what you know about your parents, we can start looking for them."

The kid pressed his lips together and looked away.

"He needs rest," Yasmin said. "Come on, honey. I've got an extra room waiting for you."

The boy's eyes narrowed and he glanced over, his shoulders rigid, his jaw clenched.

Liam's radio crackled. "Dispatch to 33-12. Are you 10-4?"

He hesitated only a beat and then keyed his radio. "10-4, Dispatch. No checks needed." Then he turned back to Yasmin. "I'll walk you guys there."

"That's okay," Yasmin said, looking up at her much taller brother. "Josiah will be with us."

"But someone's trying to kill me," Josiah growled.

Whoa. Liam looked at Yasmin again. "What's going on?"

"He doesn't mean it," she said in an undertone.

He inhaled her perfume. "I'll walk you home," he said.

YASMIN DIDN'T WANT to be the kind of woman who needed a man's help to get along in the world. In her work, she often saw that kind of dependency go terribly, terribly wrong.

All the same, she was grateful for Liam's presence, no matter how much it hurt.

He was big and strong, knowledgeable about the town, packing heat. Safe Haven was just that, safe, but she'd had a weird feeling about tonight even before her brother had pounded on the church door and she'd opened it to see the angry, vulnerable teen he had with him.

Her heart ached for young Rocky. He'd been through so much—she knew it from his mom's frequent visits to the center, when she'd dragged Rocky along.

Yasmin hadn't been able to help them, not one bit, because his mom had always gone back to her abuser. Frustration about her center's lack of resources and about Rocky's mother's weakness threatened to overwhelm her, but she stiffened her spine.

Tonight, things were going to change. She might not be able to save the women's center, but tonight, she was determined to save this one child.

One person at a time, one good deed at a time. That was her motto ever since Josiah and his problems had come to live in her house.

"I think they're over there," Josiah said, waving

toward a row of palmettos lined up in front of some Main Street shops. "They have weapons."

"Who's over there?" Liam's voice was calm, but his eyes scanned the area Josiah had indicated. "I don't see anybody. Why do you think—"

"Shhh!" Josiah hissed.

Liam didn't react except for tensing his jaw.

In the old days, she'd have clung on to that strong, muscular arm. She'd have asked his advice about Rocky, explained her brother's diagnosis, how he now saw things that weren't there. If only she hadn't done what she'd done to push Liam away. It had been for his own good, but she hadn't known how the evenings would stretch on without his company, how she'd long for his strong arms around her. How often she'd grab her phone to text some funny detail from her day before she remembered and backspaced out the message.

"They're listening," Josiah was saying to Liam.

"Let's just get home, Joe," she said to her brother. "Then we can talk about it." She'd found that confronting Josiah about his delusions was counterproductive. Treating him with the same respect she'd held for him when he'd been well was the best way to handle his bad days.

She looked over at Rocky, who trudged half a step behind them, staring at the ground, clutching his backpack. She longed to hug him and tell him everything would be okay.

Except she didn't know that.

What she should do was to interrogate him, to find out what had happened to his mom and whether his stepdad was on the loose. But she had a good sense about kids. Rocky couldn't handle much more tonight.

Why had Josiah brought Rocky to the center? The fact that the boy had showed up there wasn't a huge surprise, since he'd come several times with his mother. And Josiah tended to wander the town, so having him arrive at the church was no big deal, either.

But for them to arrive together, and upset, and without Rocky's mom, that scared her. They didn't know each other. What had brought them together? What had they seen?

What had they *done*?

"You work at the library, right, Josiah?" Liam spoke casually, conversationally.

Josiah gave a grunt of assent, and a little of the tension tightening Yasmin's shoulders eased up. Helping Joe get a job at the library had been the best thing she'd done for him. If anything could bring reassuring normalcy to her brother's life, it was the world of books and Miss Vi, the ancient, straight-backed woman who ran the Safe Haven Public Library as carefully and firmly as if it were the Pentagon.

"That Miss Vi, she's really something," Liam continued. "She laid down the law for me and my brothers when we came to town. I was about your age," Liam added, turning back to address Rocky.

"Miss Vi is good," Josiah said.

Liam nodded. "That she is. I'll never understand why..." He paused for effect. "Why my brother Cash put a frog in the drawer where she kept the check-out stamps."

A smile tugged at Josiah's mouth, and when Yasmin glanced back at Rocky, he looked marginally less upset.

"She jumped a mile high when she opened that drawer and saw that frog. And when it hopped up onto the shoulder of her dress..." Liam chuckled.

Yasmin's heart warmed toward him. He knew how to calm people down and put them at ease.

He was good to the core, and if things were different...

"No frogs, no poison!" Josiah said suddenly, firmly.

Both Liam and Rocky looked startled. Rocky moved to Yasmin's side, putting her between himself and Josiah.

Liam looked over at Josiah with speculation in his eyes. "I'm sorry, buddy, I was just making conversation."

Josiah put both hands to the sides of his head and shook it.

Yasmin wrapped her arms around her brother from the side, her heart aching. "We're almost home." Was she going to have to put him in the hospital again? He hated that more than anything.

Just the feel and smell of her big brother brought tears to her eyes. He'd been her hero, ever since she was small. He'd protected her, taught her how to do math, taken her out to play when their mother was too stressed and depressed to deal with her. He'd been her rock through a childhood that hadn't been easy, despite the material abundance.

Now, she had to be his rock.

The trouble with tonight was, she had to take care of Rocky, too, and deal with Liam, which presented a painful challenge even in the best of times. She was being pulled in too many directions.

As they approached her house, though, Yasmin's tight muscles relaxed and she let out the breath she hadn't known she was holding. She loved her cozy little home, with its pocket handkerchief front lawn surrounded by a picket fence. Yellow coneflowers had just burst into bloom, visible even at night against the cottage's white siding.

If she could just get inside, get Rocky and Josiah settled—

"So guys." Liam stepped ahead of the group, effectively blocking their way. He looked from Rocky to Josiah and back again. "Before you go inside, could you tell me if something happened tonight I should know about?"

Rocky stopped abruptly and pressed his lips together, his whole body tensing.

Josiah put his hands on Rocky's shoulders. "No. No."

"Were there people threatening you?" Liam pressed.

"Liam!" Yasmin put a hand up, ready to physically push him away to protect her brother and an innocent child. "Everyone's tired. Leave them alone."

Liam didn't budge. "Since Josiah mentioned threats, and Rocky is out after curfew without a parent or guardian, I just want to know if something out of the ordinary happened. The safety of this town is my responsibility."

"Rocky's thirteen. You can't interview him without parental permission." Yasmin sidled past him, opened the waist-high gate and gestured for Josiah and Rocky to go through. She watched them walk to the porch and up the steps. Then she turned and stood in front of Liam, preventing him from coming into her yard.

They were so close that she could smell his aftershave, and it reminded her of the days when she'd have welcomed his help with any situation she found herself in.

But now he was dangerous to her. She had to keep her distance, to protect her own heart. To protect him.

And to protect her brother. Because she was getting a strange feeling.

Josiah's doctors had been adjusting his meds. But they hadn't gotten it right yet, because it seemed that the voices in her brother's head were getting louder, more overwhelming.

Her mother's words echoed in her head: *He gets so angry now. I'm afraid of him. He can be violent.*

She didn't believe it, couldn't. Not of the brother who'd been her idol for so long, helping her navigate life in their family and in their town.

He'd always been a good person, loving in his own way.

Mom just hadn't been strong enough to deal with the changes in Josiah, so it was better that he'd moved from Mom's little apartment in Charleston to live with Yasmin in Safe Haven.

Yasmin was glad he was here, glad to help him in his time of need.

But what if the voices had told him to do something awful?

"I'll back off for now," Liam said, still close enough to make her breathless. "But this isn't over, Yasmin."

CHAPTER TWO

LIAM WALKED INTO the Southern Comfort Café early the next morning, scrubbing a hand over his face, his head pounding from a sleepless night.

Don't check on Yasmin before 8:00 a.m., he told himself. *Just don't.*

He sat down at the counter and Rita, his favorite waitress, read his mind and poured him a cup of coffee. "Want your usual?" she asked.

He gave her a thumbs-up and was just picking up the local paper when his chief walked in.

"Need to talk to you, buddy." Ramirez patted his shoulder and then walked over to the booth in the back.

Rita lifted an eyebrow. "You in trouble?"

"I didn't think so," Liam said. Ramirez's tone made him uneasy, though.

"I'll bring your breakfast over and see if the chief wants a piece of pie," Rita said. "Pie for breakfast sweetens anybody up."

Liam hoped so, because the chief looked ready

to bite the fork in half. He sat across from the man and immediately, Rita brought the coffeepot over. "I'll be right back with some of that peach pie Abel made last night," she said.

"Do that, hon, but don't tell my wife," Ramirez said. "She's got me on rabbit food."

The chief doctored his coffee with four packets of sugar-free sweetener, not looking at Liam. Then there was an uncomfortable silence, but Liam called to mind his older brother's advice and didn't break it. "Whoever speaks first loses," Sean always said. Of course, Sean was the quiet type while Liam was normally a talker.

The chief cleared his throat, glanced up at Liam and then stirred his coffee some more.

Liam revisited his offensive guard days and kept his game face bland and unworried.

"Real sorry, Liam, but I'm putting you on day shift for a spell," the chief finally said, glancing up at Liam and then right down at the table again. "Mostly desk duty," he added, "since I cover streets during the day."

"What?" Liam put his cup down hard, sloshing coffee. Day shift was for old guys or those who preferred easy, mundane work—neighbor disputes, retail thefts, community service. Not for ambitious single guys like himself. "Why?"

The chief tore open two more packets of sweetener and stirred them into his coffee. "Mulligan's gonna be doing the evening shift for now."

Liam's muscles tensed but he bit back a sharp remark. Buck Mulligan was his rival for the opening of police chief whenever Ramirez decided to retire. Up until now, Liam had felt like he had the advantage: better college grades, academy standing and experience. That was why Liam had gotten his preference in shifts, while Mulligan had been stuck on day shift.

What Mulligan had was the social ease that came with his affluent background. He'd grown up as the son of a local successful businessman and hadn't had the rough edges Liam had brought as an angry kid in foster care.

Buck was also the man to whom Yasmin had turned when she'd decided to dump Liam. And why not? They were suited; they'd both grown up going to the country club, playing tennis and hanging out by the pool.

The real mystery was why Mulligan had taken it into his head to become a cop. Or maybe not.

It seemed to Liam that Mulligan's biggest motivation in life was to get women, and you had to face it, the badge and uniform did help with that. Liam had enjoyed the advantage a few times himself, and turned down more offers than he'd taken.

But why the chief would basically demote Liam and promote Buck...

"What's this about, sir?" he finally asked. "Did I do something wrong?"

Rita brought their breakfasts, but Liam had lost his appetite.

"Just trying out a few changes. Council's idea." The chief forked up pie.

Liam narrowed his eyes. That didn't sound like the whole story. And it didn't sound good. Safe Haven's chief of police was appointed by the city council, and to some extent Ramirez was controlled by them; they could ask him to step down at any time and appoint whomever they wanted for chief. Ramirez was a good man, but he cared about his legacy. That kept him from doing anything to antagonize the council.

If those white-collar traditionalists thought a chief was best selected from their own kind, they were out of touch.

Unfortunately, they *were* in control.

"You've always had my support," Ramirez said. "If you play by the rules, you'll continue to have it."

"Play by the rules?" What was that supposed to mean?

"Anything happen last night?" The chief lifted a hand to flag down Rita and pointed at his cup.

Liam wasn't sure whether the chief was changing the subject or implying that he knew something Liam had done wrong during last night's shift. "It was a quiet night," he said. "Helped Mindy Love change her tire. Gave the Smith girls a warning about curfew and sent 'em home. That's about it." And it was *about* it.

And keeping secrets was no way to operate. "Oh, and I investigated a disturbance Mrs. Jackson called about, over at the women's center, but nothing that needed writing up." Which was technically true. Yasmin had cited client confidentiality. The kid didn't want to talk, and he didn't have to according to the rules of the state, although the chief wouldn't see it that way. He'd bend that type of rule to get information from a kid if he felt the situation warranted that; Liam had seen him do it.

Time to change the subject. "Are you making any other changes in the shifts?" They were a four-officer department, besides the chief and a secretary. And one of the officers was a raw rookie.

"Nope. Jenkins will float to cover everyone's days off, same as now," the chief said. "And I'll still back him up and clean up his messes, in addition to working days. Mulligan will do nights, and Buddy'll continue on the graveyard shift. The switch is just between you and Buck, and it's only for a little while." The chief gulped coffee. "I hope."

At least the chief didn't seem to be behind the plan, so Liam wasn't in trouble with his boss. But if someone on council had something against him… He opened his mouth to speculate and then shut it without speaking. The chief would never talk behind people's backs. He was the soul of honor and all of a sudden, Liam wasn't in a hurry for him to retire.

Liam blew out a breath. Calm and cool. This too shall pass.

They finished their breakfasts. "Good thing is, Mulligan's starting tonight," Chief Ramirez said. "So you've got a day and night off. Report tomorrow for your first day shift."

Once outside, Liam strode through town toward his apartment. He needed a good hard run with his dog.

But being a cop in a small town meant you were never really off duty. "Liam, honey," old Mrs. Roosevelt called from her porch, "could you help me with this screen door? It's not staying shut."

"Sure." Liam wasn't a handyman, he was a police officer with a degree in criminal justice and a top-of-class citation from the academy, but truthfully, he liked being useful. He walked up her front sidewalk. Mrs. Roosevelt's screen door was, in fact, flapping in the slight breeze, and he looked it over. "You have a screwdriver?" he asked her, and then followed her through her dark, musty-smelling house to the kitchen. He waited while she dug through half her drawers to find one.

While he worked on the door, she told him about her granddaughter, who'd graduated from Howard University and was headed to law school in just a week.

"Did she stop and see you this summer?" he asked as he tightened the loose hinge that had caused the problem.

Mrs. Roosevelt clicked her tongue. "She sure did, and brought that lily-white boyfriend of hers along with her. Not that there's anything wrong with white," she added hastily. "I know the world is changing, and some of y'all are real sweet. It's just, in my day, we stuck with our own kind."

Liam wondered what Mrs. Roosevelt had thought of his relationship with Yasmin. Or who she was supposed to stick with, considering that she had both black and white in her heritage. Supposedly, there was even a little Seminole way back down the line.

"Little Miss College Graduate wanted me to serve up some soul food. That's what she called it, *soul food*."

Her indignant tone made Liam smile. "Did you do it?"

"Are you kidding me?" Mrs. Jackson let out a deep, infectious laugh. "Honey, I made spaghetti and meatballs, just to spite her."

"Good for you." He tightened one last screw and then tested the screen door. "There. That should work better."

She smiled up at him, her broad face creasing to a point where her eyes almost disappeared. "You're a good boy, Liam. Always willing to go the extra mile."

Tell that to the city council. "Happy to help, ma'am." He patted her shoulder, and she pulled him into a hug and kissed his cheek.

When he got home, Rio barked ecstatically. Good, someone was plain and simple glad to see him, wasn't going to ask for a favor or give him bad news. He snapped a leash on the Lab-rottweiler mix and headed out into the apartment building's yard.

Since his short relationship with Yasmin had ended last year, he'd put all his energy into his work, climbing the ladder. *Sublimation*, the police shrink they were all required to see had called it, when he'd heard about Liam's background. It was a good thing.

Today's demotion picked at a scab on his heart.

The wife and kids could come later. He definitely wanted that. But he'd seen the effects of poverty and desperation in his biological father, and he carried those angry genes himself. He needed a firm professional standing and money saved before he could think about a family.

Needed to get over Yasmin, too, but first things first.

Rio did his business, and Liam was picking up after him when his landlord came out of the house next door. He beckoned Liam over.

"That dog's getting too big for the place," he said.

Rio chose that moment to jump up, putting his massive front paws on Mr. Smith's shoulders. Which wasn't hard; Mr. Smith was only about five-two, but Liam snapped the leash back and made the dog sit while he apologized up one side and down the other. "He looks tough but he's not," Liam reassured the man. "He's got the Lab personality."

Smith wasn't having it, though. "Fifty-pound

limit in the lease," he said, "and that beast is push-ing a hundred pounds."

Liam drew in a breath and let it out slowly, trying to call to mind the meditation techniques they'd learned in a boring-but-required seminar last spring. "I'll work on finding another place to live," he promised.

Mentally, he was ticking off the apartment com-plexes and houses for rent in the area. Not that many were open to pets. But Liam's stomach plummeted at the thought of getting rid of the dog. He'd res-cued Rio himself, from a flood situation this spring, floating on a wooden pallet in one of the swampy rivers nearby.

Mr. Smith crossed his arms. "You broke the lease by having him here," he said. "I'm going to have to ask you to vacate within the next two weeks."

"Two weeks!" Liam frowned at the man. "You never had a problem with Rio before."

"I do now," he said in a stern voice, undoubtedly the one he used in his job as a high school princi-pal. "Two weeks. And keep the place clean. I'll be showing it."

Liam headed into town with Rio, aiming to run off his frustration, but a call from his brother Sean interrupted that plan. As he clicked into the call, a possible solution to the apartment problem came to him.

"How's married life?" he asked Sean immedi-ately. Against all odds, Sean had found love and an instant family and was making a go of it. Something none of them had expected, given the warped representation of marriage their parents had portrayed. And Liam was nothing but glad for him. Sean had taken the brunt of the heat both before and after they'd lost their mom; he had the scars to prove it. If anyone deserved a second chance at happiness, it was Sean.

"It's good, man." Sean described the fun he and his new wife and daughters were having, but he didn't go on too long. The real purpose of the call, Liam knew, was to make sure Liam was okay; Sean took his big brother role almost too seriously, given that Liam was pushing thirty. "What's new with you?"

"Everything's good," he lied—no way was he telling Sean about desk duty, his brother was too proud of Liam's rapid rise through the police ranks. "But looks like me and Rio will need a new place to stay." He explained about Mr. Smith and the two-week notice.

"Man, I'd like to help," Sean said, "but the Sea Pine Cottages are full. And Anna's and my place is getting remodeled. Workmen twelve hours a day to try to get it done before we come home." It had been the wedding gift from the guys at Sean's construction company—updating and building an addition onto one of the cottages at the rustic beach resort Sean was managing now, to make it a fit place for a family of four to live.

"You could try Ma Dixie," Sean suggested. Ma Dixie had taken Sean in when he, Liam and their brother, Cash, had been abandoned on the streets of Safe Haven as young teens.

"Not happening." Liam forced a laugh. "I ran into her at the market yesterday. She has a new foster family, three kids."

Liam was running out of options, but it was his problem, not his brother's. Sean had saved his butt plenty of times, from when they were little kids fighting on the playground to when he'd given Liam half the money to attend the police academy, as a college graduation present. Now, Sean had other priorities, and that was the way it should be. Liam reassured Sean that he and Rio would be fine and then clicked over to another call. Just before he put it to his ear, he realized who was calling him: Yasmin.

"Hey, Liam, I hate to bother you," she said in that husky voice that always drove him crazy. "But I'm worried. Rocky's taken off."

"He was here when I woke up," Yasmin said as soon as Liam arrived. Seeing him made her tight shoulders loosen, just a little, because if anyone could find the boy, it was Liam.

Never mind that her whole body warmed just at the sight of him; she was used to it, it wasn't important, and there was nothing she could do about it. "I fixed him breakfast, and he ate like a horse. I went upstairs to try to find him some of Josiah's old clothes to wear. Got caught up in a phone call. When I got back downstairs, Rocky wasn't here." Remorse battered at her: *Stupid, stupid, stupid*. She'd been a fool to leave a troubled child alone, and if something had happened to the boy, it was on her.

"So he's been gone, what, half an hour?"

"Or forty-five minutes." Despair pressed down on her like dark clouds. "I looked everywhere in the house and yard. And Josiah went down to the docks to look for him."

Liam had been scanning the yard and street, but at her words, his head snapped back and he looked at her. "Why the docks?"

"He says that's where he found Rocky last night."

"I'm going to call the department and get their help looking for him," Liam said.

Everything in Yasmin revolted against that idea. "No, Liam, let's just look a little ourselves, first, okay?" Yasmin didn't dislike the police department, but she had a funny feeling about Rocky. A protective feeling. She wished she could just put her arms around him and make the scared, trapped expression on his face disappear. "If the police find him and his mom's still missing, they might put him into the system. They could end up deciding to place him in a different home, not mine, and...well, his mom will come looking for him here. If she's able and comes back."

Liam's lips tightened, reminding her that he'd faced the same experience. His foster family hadn't been bad, but the loss of his mom had impacted him terribly, of course. She opened her mouth to say something about that, but what could she say?

"How old is he?" Liam asked.

"Pretty sure he's thirteen." Yasmin grabbed her tennis shoes and sat down on the bench beside the door to put them on.

"If he's an unattached minor, it's a status crime at most. Not even that, if his folks aren't looking for him. But what if his stepdad picked him up? He's violent, right?"

Yasmin hadn't even considered it. "Fine, call it in," she said, but just then, Josiah's face flashed on her lock screen. She clicked into the call.

"Come to the docks," Joe said, and then their connection broke.

Minutes later she and Liam were at the Safe Haven waterfront. To the right was the commercial part of town, the boardwalk where tourists liked to walk, lined by a couple of restaurants and bars. Benches dotted the area, inviting people to sit and look out into the harbor, and a couple of kiosks advertised shelling and lighthouse cruises and low country tours.

But the real heart of the town was the dock area, where shrimp boats and a seafood processing plant made mornings active and lively. Even today, a Saturday, three boats were docked and another was headed this way. The smell of fish was a given, fish and salt. For Yasmin, it was the fragrance of home.

And there was Josiah, beckoning. When they reached him, he pointed to a small shed that housed cleaning and safety equipment. "I saw him go in there. Didn't want to scare him, so I called you."

"Thanks." Yasmin gave her brother a sidearm hug, grateful that despite the lack of the smile that used to spring so readily to his face, he seemed to be better today. When he was more himself, it was impossible to believe he'd committed a crime or hurt someone.

Except his moods and emotions were so unpredictable now. Her stomach tightened as she followed Liam to the shed and peeked past him, squinting into the relative darkness.

Once her eyes adjusted, she saw Rocky, squatting behind a stack of life preservers, wiping his eyes and scowling.

Relief washed over her and she rushed past Liam to kneel beside the boy, studying his arms and legs. "Do you hurt anywhere?"

Rocky shook his head, not looking at her.

"You scared us," she scolded. "Come on home. This is no place to hang out. For one thing, it smells terrible."

She offered him her hand, but he didn't take it. He did, however, get to his feet. His clothes, the same ones from last night, were now streaked with grease and dirt, and a gray smear crossed his cheekbone.

Compassion wrapped around her heart and squeezed, tight.

Glancing back at Liam, she tried to communicate with her eyes to let her handle it. She shouldn't have called him, probably, but she'd gotten scared.

He read it—Liam was sensitive that way—and backed out of the shed. He went over to stand beside Josiah.

Yasmin put an arm around Rocky for a quick hug, then released him before he could pull away. "Let's go get you a shower, and then we can talk," she said, urging him out of the shed with a hand on his back. "What were you doing down here, anyway?"

He stared at the ground. "Lookin' for my mom," he mumbled so quietly that it took her a minute to understand.

"Is this the last place you saw her?" Liam asked. He had the sharpest hearing of anyone she knew.

Rocky stiffened, even though Liam's tone had been friendly and conversational. His face twisted into a sneer that almost hid the trembling of his chin. "What are you doing here?"

"Just giving a hand to a friend," Liam said, nodding at Yasmin. "I'm not here as a cop, if that's what you're worried about. But I'd like to help you find your mom."

Rocky lifted his chin and looked away.

"Come on back to my place." Yasmin gave Liam a headshake and then urged Rocky toward the sidewalk. Soon they were walking toward her house, Josiah and Liam trailing behind them.

She was breathing easier now that they'd found

Rocky, a little dirtier but basically safe. But as they walked, questions nudged and needled at her. How had Josiah known where to find Rocky? Why was he so interested in the boy, when these days, he spaced out on most things in life?

What had happened to Rocky's mom? And what did Josiah know about that?

They passed the women's center and Yasmin gave it a glance and a sigh. Another worry, albeit a lesser one. Fortunately, there was no one hanging around outside, which was one way clients came to her, but there was a boatload of paperwork to do inside.

"Are you working today?" Liam asked.

"I was, but…no, probably not." She was going to have to keep an eye on Rocky, and of course that took precedence over paperwork. She had to figure out what to do with the boy, but if she got him settled somehow, there might be time for an hour of catching up with correspondence and official forms. "Joe, would you mind picking up my mail and the folders on top of my desk?" She fumbled for the key and handed it to her brother. "I might do a little work at home." Truth to tell, she often took work home with her if she wasn't able to stay late at the center. It was a peril of being in charge of a nonprofit, but she didn't mind. She believed in the mission and she loved her work.

Josiah headed for the church while she and Liam and Rocky ambled on toward her place. She was still worried about what had happened last night that had gotten Josiah and Rocky so upset, and she wanted to keep close tabs on whether anyone was investigating it. "You know," she said to Rocky, "Officer O'Dwyer *could* maybe help you and your mom. Just something to think about," she added quickly, not wanting to apply too much pressure.

Rocky glanced up at her and then looked away, not speaking.

"I've got some time," Liam confirmed. "Not working tonight." He seemed like he was about to say more, but decided against it.

Josiah jogged up behind them. He had a file envelope under one arm and a letter in his hand, which he thrust toward Yasmin. "This was stuck under the door of the center."

Yasmin held up the manila envelope. Only her name was written across the front, so it hadn't come in the mail. And there was no return address.

Uh-oh. Some center client's outraged abuser, no doubt. Hate mail. Her stomach knotted. "I'll wait till I get home to open it," she said.

"Who's it from?" Liam leaned over to study the envelope.

Rocky did, too, and then he drew in an audible gasp. "That's my mom's writing!"

CHAPTER THREE

RITA TOMLINSON HAD survived amnesia, the loss of her common-law husband and a long-distance move without a job or a place to live at the other end. She'd landed on her feet, here in Safe Haven, and she thought of herself as a fairly courageous woman. But as she approached the town's little library, her heart was filled with dread.

Which was ridiculous, of course. Small-town libraries weren't scary. She'd faced a lot worse in her fifty-seven years. Even the Southern Comfort Café where she worked, as great as it was, got more low-life patrons than the library did.

The problem with the library was that it might possibly hold the key to the twenty-or-so years of her past she didn't remember.

She walked inside, relishing the blast of cold air-conditioning. After almost four months of living here, she was still getting used to South Carolina heat.

There was Miss Vi, the head librarian, showing

a flyer about a kids' chess club to a tall, thin man. It took a minute to recognize him, but she finally realized it was Josiah, Yasmin Tanner's troubled brother who'd recently moved to Safe Haven. Yasmin had become a friend since Rita had started to volunteer at the women's center, and so Rita had been privy to some of Yasmin's concerns about Josiah and his challenges.

Working at the women's center kicked up Rita's issues just a little. Which was what she wanted, she reminded herself firmly as she trudged toward the microfilm area in the back of the library. It was basically a reading room, with comfortable chairs in the middle. Books lined three walls, but the fourth held several shelves of white boxes with typed labels.

She inhaled the pleasantly musty scent of old books and approached the shelf of microfilm boxes. Lots of libraries kept old newspapers in digital form these days, but Safe Haven didn't have the budget to convert, according to Miss Vi.

She stood in front of the boxes and studied the labels, her stomach tightening. Her memories and records of her life started in Maine, in August of 1998. But when her husband had died last year, she'd learned that he'd found her just outside of Safe Haven, South Carolina. She had some kind of history here.

Which meant she needed to find out what had happened in this little town, in July of that year.

She selected three boxes and carried them over

to an old-fashioned machine. Following the instructions taped to the monitor, she located the power button and turned it on, then slid out the glass plate on the reader. Opened the box and pulled out the roll of microfilm.

She placed it on the left-hand spindle and stopped, her stomach tight, mouth dry. Her hands shook too much to continue. What if it all came back to her in a rush? What if what came back was something awful?

Drawing in slow, deep breaths, she focused on the murmur of other patrons talking behind her, a child's high, excited voice, quickly hushed by a woman who was probably his mother.

His mother.

She'd had a child, but she had no memory of it.

"Do you need help?" came a flat-sounding voice.

Rita looked up, surprised to see Josiah. "Hey there. You're Yasmin's brother, aren't you?"

He nodded, his face expressionless. "I work here."

"Do you know how to operate this thing?" *Please say no, so I can go home.*

"I think so." He leaned over to study the machine.

She scooted her chair out of the way. "Do you want to sit?"

"No." He threaded the film under a glass plate and onto the right film spool. He clicked something on the plate, and newspaper pages appeared on the screen in front of her.

"Forward," he said, demonstrating how to scroll rapidly through the pages. "Back. And, let's see…" He leaned in closer. "Focus here, zoom here." He demonstrated and then looked at her. His eyes seemed to twinkle, just a little. "Old-fashioned technology, but it works."

"Thank you." What could she say to keep this kind guy here? "How do you like your job?" she asked.

"It's good." He didn't smile, but his eyes were warm. "Do you need anything else?"

For you to distract me from this thing I don't want to do. "No, I'm fine. I've got it."

He nodded and walked away.

She scrolled through the paper quickly. It was small, only about twenty pages long. She looked at the dates on the front. Oh, right. It was only published twice a week, then and now.

A full-page ad for grocery specials caught her attention. Pop-Tarts cereal for $1.99… Oreos for 99 cents. Those were the days.

She sucked in air as she realized that she remembered those prices. Was it because she'd bought those items?

And why would you buy Pop-Tarts cereal, of all things, and Oreo cookies unless you'd done it for your kids?

She scrolled quickly away and focused on a letter to the editor about a billboard outside of town, considered an eyesore by the writer. Another deriding Bill Clinton.

Did she remember the whole of Bill Clinton's presidency, or just portrayals of it on the History channel?

She let her face sink down into her hands. This was a lot harder than she'd expected, and she wasn't even seeing anything personal.

Don't be a baby. She scrolled past an ad for a fitness center that was expanding, noting that the clunky exercise bike and the model's loose running shorts and white crew socks were not alien to her.

You have to do this.

Where was the local news? She kept scrolling until she came to the crime blotter. Heart pounding rapidly, she read the short entries. A stray dog had been found on Market Street. Three women, ages twenty-five, thirty-four and forty-one, had been arrested following a theft.

Could have been me.

A suspicious vehicle had been seen in the two-hundred-block area of Peachtree Road.

Nothing sounded familiar, but she ought to look for items about Magnolia Street, where the women's center was located. Every time she went there, she got a weird, creepy feeling, like she'd been there before.

"Josiah, did you get those books shelved?" Miss Vi's voice was stern, a little accusing. Rita liked the woman, but she couldn't be an easy boss. She glanced back to see Josiah shoving a book back into the reference section. Then he rose and walked over to a cart of books.

Miss Vi followed him, obviously scolding, although in correctly low library tones.

Focus. Rita removed the spool of microfilm and threaded in the next. Inhaling slow, careful breaths, she got the film lined up and started scrolling through the pages.

"Do you need any help?" Miss Vi asked from behind her.

She didn't ask what Rita was looking for. Rita wondered whether that was some code of librarian confidentiality, like you got at the doctor's office, or whether Miss Vi knew something about her and her search.

Should she ask her?

As quickly as that thought emerged, Rita squelched it. Miss Vi was busy. Look how upset she'd gotten when Josiah was distracted from his duty. "I'm fine. He was very helpful with this machine." She waved a hand toward Josiah, hoping to get her friend's brother out of trouble.

Miss Vi gave her a skeptical nod and moved on. Obviously, nothing Rita said would compare to what Miss Vi had observed herself.

Rita looked at the clock: 10:30. She'd planned to stay all morning, but she was feeling hungry and her eyes felt dry and hot from squinting at the screen.

She'd come back another time.

No, you won't.

She pictured her friend Norma's face—Norma, who was always nudging and pushing her to figure out the truth about her past. Norma, who was planning to move down here from Maine and who would never, no way, let Rita slack off on pursuing the truth.

And in many ways, Rita wanted the truth. The truth would allow her to get on with her life.

Maybe to get on with a decent relationship.

Right along with that thought, she pictured Jimmy's face. She definitely liked that man, even if he *was* her boss at the diner. She wanted to take him up on his invitation for a real date.

If you didn't know your own history, though, you could hardly get into a relationship. What if she uncovered something awful about herself? Something that would let her know she didn't deserve a relationship, not now, not ever?

Her fingers shaky again, she removed the second roll of film from the machine and coiled it neatly into its box. Stood up quickly, shelved the boxes and hurried out of the library.

The day's heat hit her like a steamy embrace, but she plunged into it eagerly. Just as long as she could get far, far away from those old newspapers that might reveal something about her past that she didn't want to know.

She walked rapidly, dripping sweat, needing distance from the library.

She was a coward.

She'd run smack into her own resistance and failed to beat it.

LATER THAT DAY, Liam got Rio into a sit-stay on Yasmin's porch and then knocked on her front door.

After the uproar of the letter from Rocky's mother—a letter Yasmin hadn't let him see, again citing client confidentiality—he'd gone back to his apartment to start looking online for a new place to live. There were places available, not a lot, but some.

Not a one of them allowed large dogs, though.

Yasmin opened the door, an oven mitt on her hand, looking harassed. "Just a second, Josiah," she called over her shoulder, then turned back to face him. "What's going on?" she asked, her voice cool.

Her pink cheeks and the rapid breath going through her slightly parted lips told a different story, one Liam liked better.

He wanted to help her; his arms practically ached to reach out, rub her back, squeeze her shoulders. "I have a proposal for you," he said instead.

Her eyes widened and her blush deepened. "Really, Liam, I can't deal with joking right now. I'm in the middle of trying to make pizza for two picky eaters and figure out what to do with Rocky, and I have a ton of paperwork to do for the center..."

"You can get pizza delivered, rather than make it from scratch," he suggested. "Most people do."

"True." She wiped her forehead with the back of

her hand. "But Rocky needs a real home-cooked meal, and he says pizza is his favorite. And organic ingredients help Joe with... They help Joe." She pressed her lips together as if she didn't want to reveal anything more about her brother. Then she shrugged and stretched her neck like she was trying to change the subject in her own mind. "Picky eaters, you know? Or maybe not. You never were one."

"Couldn't afford to be." Liam wanted to reach out and touch her, because he loved how hard she tried to do the right thing. But she wouldn't welcome that type of attention from him, not anymore. "You have too much on your hands," he said, "and I have an idea of how to help."

Twenty minutes later, he was arguing with her at her kitchen table while she dished up pizza and told him he was out of his mind.

"I'm not out of my mind. This will work." He took a big bite of pizza and closed his eyes. Homemade crust, spicy sausage, thick cheese...yeah, this was way better than pizza that came in a box.

Rocky and Josiah were making appreciative noises, too, while Yasmin fussed around pouring sweet tea and tossing salad.

"You don't need my garage apartment," she said. "You already have a place that's nicer."

"Not for much longer. Rio and I are getting kicked out because of how big he's growing." He glanced down at the dog, who sat attentively beside Rocky, his head moving every time Rocky's hand did, following the path of the pizza. "Speaking of the dog, are you sure you don't mind Rio being in here?"

"How can I, when he already cleaned up my floor for me?" She reached down and rubbed the dog's head, sneaked him a piece of sausage, and then went over to the sink to wash her hands. "Look, Liam, I feel like you're doing this to try to help me, but I can handle everything myself."

Maybe she could, but Liam wasn't about to relax. There was something wrong when a teenager from an abusive home showed up walking around a strange town by himself.

But you didn't convince Yasmin of things by direct force. "So the letter reassured you?" he asked.

She glanced over to the counter. There was the envelope from Rocky's mom.

Yasmin hesitated, then nodded. "I guess I can tell you this. She—Rocky's mom—she asked if I could help Rocky through the next few weeks while she straightens a few things out. We'd actually talked a little about this possibility before."

Memories caused a sick feeling in Liam's stomach. His own mother had done something similar, collecting school and doctor records for him and his brothers, sealing them into an envelope and giving them to the people at the center, in case she was incapacitated in some way.

And she *had* been; she'd disappeared. He and his brothers had never seen her again after the day that, according to Sean, their father had forced her into his truck.

Which didn't mean the same would happen to Rocky's mom. It didn't.

But in a strange way he felt like he owed this kid. Helping Rocky would be payback for all the times people had helped him. Rocky reminded him of himself at that age: the surliness, the tamped-down emotion, the hope that rose up occasionally in spite of a bad situation.

He looked over to see how Rocky was handling their discussion and was relieved to know the boy wasn't even listening. Josiah had drifted out of the room earlier, but Rocky was still there, on the floor beside Rio, playing tug-of-war with a dishcloth.

For the first time since Liam had met the child, he looked happy, carefree, like a thirteen-year-old boy should.

If he rented Yasmin's apartment, Rocky and Rio could play together. Which would benefit both of them.

"What about Rocky's father?" he asked Yasmin. "Is he a possible caregiver?"

She shook her head. "No biological father in the picture, and the stepfather would be more of a risk than a help. His mom says in the letter that he moved to California."

Rocky looked over from his tug of war with Rio. "He did?"

"Hey, kiddo, you're not supposed to be listening," Yasmin said easily. "But yeah. Does that upset you?"

Rocky snorted and turned back to the dog. "Good riddance." He started play-growling at the dog, who amicably play-growled back, tugging hard at the dishcloth.

"It would be a big help to me, and maybe to you, if I rented the apartment," Liam said quietly to Yasmin, who was watching the boy and dog, a smile on her face. "I can help keep an eye on Rocky. Couldn't hurt the kid to have another man on the scene. Maybe I can find out something, informally, that'll help him reunite with his mom. And I'll pay rent. Whatever's fair."

She met his eyes, bit her lip. "Mom's place in Charleston *is* expensive, and Josiah…" She glanced toward the kitchen door where Josiah had exited. "There are expenses there, too," she said. "But—"

"So my renting your apartment would help with money," he interrupted. "And I'll also provide a therapy dog, free." He gestured toward the floor.

Rocky chose that moment to flop down beside Rio, who was lying on his side now, chewing the dishcloth. Rio nuzzled Rocky and then went back to chewing, and Rocky threw an arm around the big dog.

Yasmin's face softened. "The therapy dog aspect is pretty compelling," she said. "This kid needs all the comfort he can get. It's just not…" She broke off, then glanced over at the clock. "Hey, your shift starts in, like, three minutes. Don't you think you'd better get to work?"

Liam's face heated. Behind the interesting notion that she knew his work schedule was the embarrassing awareness that he'd pretty much gotten demoted. Everyone in town would know it soon, but telling Yasmin was the worst by far. It seemed to highlight the fact that, at heart, he was still one of those troubled O'Dwyer boys.

"Shift change," he said. "I'm working days for a while."

She studied him for a long moment and then lifted an eyebrow. "So if you moved in," she said, "we'd all be home at the same time?"

She was so pretty that, for a moment, he couldn't think. He just looked at her slightly challenging eyes, the curve of her lips, the tilt of her head.

But after a pause, he got her drift. "You don't want me around."

She bit her lip. "It does make sense in a lot of ways, but Liam, I just don't know. How could we make that work?"

"We can do it." He stood and reached out to clasp her hand, an instinctive reaction.

She pulled her hand away. "Even if I did rent to you—and I'm not saying I will—nothing's changed between us."

"Did I say I wanted it to?" He stepped back.

She looked down at the floor and shook her head.

He wasn't sure, suddenly, whether this was a

great idea. Every time he was with Yasmin, his old feelings got stirred up.

And every time, whether openly or subtly, she rejected him.

The buzz of his phone was a welcome distraction. He saw Ramirez's name on the lock screen and clicked into the call, shrugging an apology to Yasmin as he headed out to the porch. "What's up?"

"Jenkins followed up on a sighting of a car underwater near the pier." Ramirez's voice was clipped, abrupt, different from his usual easygoing style. "Rather than following protocol, he had a couple of the shrimpers pull it out with their truck."

Liam bit back a remark about Jenkins's lack of skill. The chief knew it as well as he did.

Ramirez cleared his throat. "Putting things together, looking at security camera videos, what we could see at least, it appears the car went down on your shift last night. Did you notice anything going on at all, down by the docks?"

Liam stiffened. He hadn't, but Rocky had been looking for his mom there this morning. He glanced back through the door at the kid, who'd buried his face in Rio's side.

"I didn't see anything," he said truthfully. "What's the make of the car?" He'd check with Rocky and find out what his mom had been driving. If she'd sent her car into the tidewater, she could be disappearing on purpose.

The very thought of it stabbed him in the gut. His

brother Sean sometimes suspected their own mom had disappeared on purpose. Liam didn't want to believe it.

"It's one of those little SUVs, a Ford," Ramirez said. "White, late-model. But that's not the big news."

Something in his chief's voice made Liam turn away from the child and the house and walk out toward the street. "What's the big news?"

"When they pulled out the car," Ramirez said, "they found a body in it."

CHAPTER FOUR

SOMETHING WAS WRONG. Something that trumped her own horribly mixed feelings about renting her garage apartment to Liam, about having him around a lot more of the time.

Yasmin watched Liam click out of his phone call and carefully pocket his phone. His shoulders were a hard square, his jaw tight, the muscles in his face defined.

"What happened?" She stepped outside and closed the door behind her to block Rocky or Josiah from hearing anything.

Liam looked at her, his face unreadable. "They found a body in a car that was submerged in the bayou."

Yasmin's heart gave a great thump and then settled into heavy, continuous pounding. Dizziness had her feeling for the porch railing as she stared at him. "They found... Who is it? Do they know?" The idea of someone dying, just a few blocks away, made her stomach cramp up tight. If it were a friend...

He shook his head. "Male, Caucasian, they're guessing fortysomething. Weird thing is, he had no ID on him. Even the plates on the car were removed."

"Wow. Whew." With difficulty, she drew in one breath, then another. "Was it…a tourist? Someone drunk, who didn't know where he was going?" Awful to hope for that, except it seemed like the best-case scenario. But it didn't really make sense. "Why would he have removed his own plates?"

"He was dead before he hit the water," Liam said. "Blunt trauma to the head."

"He was *murdered*?" She stared at him. That didn't compute. Safe Haven was *safe*. "That's not what you meant, is it?"

"That's what I meant," he said grimly. "The lack of ID makes it seem like someone was covering it up."

Cold fingers of fear seemed to creep up her spine, making her so shaky she had to sit down on the top step of the porch. She tried to push aside the thought that rushed instantly into her mind.

Josiah can be violent, her mother had said.

No way, no *way* was her gentle brother capable of a crime like that.

And yet he'd been so nervous and guilty-acting the night it had happened.

Liam sat down beside her and gripped her shoulder, his touch warm and familiar. "Hey. You're upset."

But she couldn't reveal why, or not all of it. Not to a cop who was looking for a suspect. "I can't believe something like that would happen here in Safe Haven." She wrapped her arms across her stomach.

Rio came over and nudged at Liam's hand, and he moved over to make room for the dog on the step beside him. He sat at the top of the stairs with one leg tilted down, one pulled up to his chest, head tipped back against the pillar.

She wanted to touch him, to seek comfort in physical closeness. It was only natural, the same impulse that made puppies heap up together. But she didn't have that right, not after what she'd done. To stop herself, she picked up the watering can, ran water into it and started attending to the plants in her flower boxes. Between giving shots of moisture to her plants, already dry and thirsty in the heat, she studied Liam.

Why was he just sitting there, and why was he looking so discouraged? "Do they...do you...know anything more about it? Who's going to investigate?"

"For now, they're keeping it in the department. All signs point local." He frowned. "They're pretty sure it happened last night, down at the docks." His forehead wrinkled with thought. "When Josiah and Rocky came to the center last night, isn't that where they were coming from?" He nodded toward the kitchen. "Do you think he knows anything about it?"

"No! No, I don't." Too late, she realized Liam had probably meant Rocky, not Josiah.

Liam cocked his head and looked at her quizzically.

"I mean," she said, "if he'd seen something that awful, I don't think he'd have slept like a log last night and eaten like a horse today." And that was true of Josiah, too, wasn't it?

Only Josiah hadn't slept well. She'd heard him up and wandering around when she'd awakened at three.

That wasn't unusual for Josiah. But then again…

"You're probably right about Rocky," Liam said. "Although he did head for the waterfront this morning, when he ran away."

"Right, and he was looking for his mom." She blew out a breath. "Thank heavens it wasn't her they found. But if she and Rocky were down there…"

"Maybe they saw something. Or maybe Josiah did. Didn't you say he and Rocky came to the center together?"

"Yeah." She squatted near the spigot at the side of the porch and refilled her watering can, trying to think. She should probably tell Liam what Joe had said when he'd come in, how he'd insisted that they had to hide.

But if Josiah were somehow involved and the law came down on him, it would be like throwing a lamb to the wolves. She couldn't let that happen. Setting the watering can at the top of the steps, she looked at Liam. "What am I thinking? You'll be going in to work. I'll get you some coffee."

"No need for that," he said, his voice dull. "They put Mulligan on the case."

"Oh. Wow." She picked up the watering can and tipped too much water onto the big flowerpot beside the door, flooding it until the water ran out the bottom and across the porch.

Buck Mulligan. He wasn't anywhere near the cop that Liam was, so it was odd the chief would put him in charge of a murder investigation.

She'd speculate about that with Liam, except that she didn't want to open a painful wound.

Her connection with Buck came from a period of her life she'd just as soon forget. Yes, she'd needed to find a way to pull back from Liam, and telling him she didn't want to be in a serious relationship hadn't been enough to convince him. Dating his enemy had been cruel, but effective. Even now, Buck's name floated in the air between them, chilling it.

He stood abruptly and banged a fist into the porch pillar. "I know you like him, but I could do a better job."

The frustration on his face mirrored the look he'd had all the way back in fifth grade, when he'd been held back, the bigger, older kid no one wanted to be around. The one whispered about by all the over-protective mothers in town.

Not Yasmin's mother, of course, but that was another story.

"I know you could," she murmured, slipping past him to take her watering duties down to the pots that lined one side of the steps. Seeing his pain, reading that he still thought he was a no-good lowlife, made longing bloom in her chest. If only she had the right to comfort him.

If only she didn't have all these fears about her brother. About herself.

Josiah came around from the side of the house, then, carrying his portable chess set. He must be going out to play chess with Rip Martin or another of his friends. Or was he coming in? And either way, had he heard what they were talking about?

"I didn't know you were out here," she said, uneasy.

He didn't respond; he just set his chessboard up on the small table on the porch.

"Did you hear what we were talking about, Josiah?" Liam asked. "About last night?"

"What happened?" He looked from her to Liam and back again.

Liam hesitated and glanced at her, then back at Josiah. "They found a body in a submerged car. They think it went down last night."

Josiah made a little sound, kind of a yelp, but his facial expression didn't change. That was the disease; it made him look impassive.

But his hands, toying restlessly with the chess pieces, told another tale.

"Did you see anything?" Liam asked. "You're out walking a lot. Any strangers in town?" Then he shook his head. "What am I doing? This isn't my case."

Josiah tilted his head, his eyes far away, and Yasmin could tell he was hearing his voices. Her heart ached.

In fact, it ached for both men: Josiah, whose demons were too loud for him to have peace within his own mind; and Liam, who wasn't being allowed to do what he did best—protect the peace.

She heard a sound above her and looked up. Rocky's frowning face was pressed against the window.

Three men, three sets of problems, and not a thing she could do about any of them.

Except, maybe, to let Liam rent her apartment. The idea of a murder in Safe Haven shook her terribly, made her long for the safety Liam represented.

Not only that, but there was the old saying: keep your friends close and your enemies closer. If Josiah had had anything to do with what had happened down at the docks, Yasmin wanted to keep track of what Liam was finding out about it.

So maybe she *would* rent her garage apartment to him. It would be torture, a sweet kind of torture, to herself, but it might help her keep Rocky and her brother safe.

TWENTY MINUTES LATER, Liam was still pacing on the sidewalk in front of Yasmin's house, watching her putter in the window boxes. How she could find so much to do in a tiny yard was beyond him. Except that her yard was the prettiest in a block of well-kept ones. Obviously, all those flowers needed a lot of care, especially in the August heat.

He called the station and got put through to Mulligan. His stomach roiled with the crow he had to eat. "Heard Chief put you on the case," he said. "I wanted to—"

"Since it all happened on your watch and you missed it, yeah." Mulligan's tone was rich-boy sarcastic.

Liam pulled in a slow breath. Throwing the phone across the street would do nothing except cause him a big expense. "Listen, I wanted to offer my help. I know a couple of people who were out last night. I could talk to them for you."

"No, thank you. I'll do mah own interviewing." Mulligan's Southern accent had thickened.

Which usually happened when he was upset. What did *he* have to be upset about? He was the one who'd as good as stolen Yasmin from Liam, and stolen this case, too.

"Later," Mulligan said, and ended the call.

What an idiot Mulligan was. Turning down a fellow officer's offer of help. That just showed what a poor candidate for chief Mulligan was. Those in authority had to be collaborative, not trying to keep glory for themselves.

Unless the chief had told him to; unless that cut about Liam letting it go down on his watch was coming from above.

He blew out a breath, tapping the fence post by the gate with restless fingers, thinking.

He hated that this had happened when he was on duty. Intellectually, he knew you couldn't be every-where at once, couldn't prevent every crime from happening. His main activity before getting called to the women's center last night had been checking into a broken window at old Elmer Jackson's house on the other side of town, a type of crime common in small-town police work.

He'd had no way of knowing that, on the other side of Safe Haven, a murder was being committed. He itched to find out who had done such a heinous thing on a summer night in an otherwise peace-ful town.

It was more than frustrating that he couldn't in-vestigate. He was within speaking distance of a trio of people who'd been up and nearby when the mur-der had gone down, but unless the officer in charge of the case asked for his help, his hands were tied.

Two little neighbor girls, blonde look-alike sis-ters about six or seven, ran over to the fence and called out for Yasmin. That figured. She was great with kids, had wanted to be an elementary schoolteacher at one point, although that seemed to be on the back burner for now.

She'd be a great mother.

Yeah, to Buck Mulligan's kids.

Rio ran over to greet the girls, paws up on the picket fence, trampling the flowers that lined it.

"Rio!" Liam headed back into the yard and snapped his fingers. The dog turned to look at him, then back toward the little girls, giving each face one slurp of his giant tongue, making them giggle. "Rio, down."

The dog finally obeyed, doing a clumsy shuffle that ended up trampling more flowers.

Yasmin gave her garden a quick, regretful glance and then shrugged.

"Can we come in and play with him?" one of the little blondes asked.

"Only after you ask your mom and dad," Yasmin said. "And tell them the truth, that he's a big dog with muddy paws."

The sisters glanced at each other and Liam could guarantee no such message would make it to their parents' ears.

"I'll fix the flowers as best I can," Liam offered, "and do some weeding. We can keep Rio tied up."

Yasmin sank into a squat in front of Rio, kissed his nose and rubbed his velvety ears. "We can't tie this big boy up," she said, "can we? Can we?"

Rio reached for her with an enormous paw.

She blocked it, laughing. "Oh, no you don't.

You're too muddy." She stood gracefully. "It would be good if he learned some manners, though."

"I've been negligent." How was he ever going to raise kids of his own if he couldn't even teach a dog to behave?

He knelt to study the damage Rio had done to the spiky purple flowers that lined the bottom of the fence. Pink roses climbed the top in a haphazard pattern, but fortunately none of them had been trampled.

Scraping the displaced mulch back into the narrow garden beneath the fence, he mused on fatherhood, his dreams of it and the doubtfulness of it ever happening in reality. It wasn't like he'd had a great role model in his biological dad, but his foster dad had been a tough-love kind of guy, and it had mostly helped.

He tried standing up the crushed stems, shoring them up with dirt and mulch, but Yasmin leaned close and shook her head. "You'd better let me handle that," she said. "You go weed." She indicated a bed in front of the porch.

He was glad to have an understandable task. Weeding was a chore he'd been assigned as a teenager, often in punishment for some infraction of polite society's rules. He'd liked ripping out the ugly and leaving a garden looking neat.

The truth was, he was a domestic, home-focused guy. Almost twenty years ago, he'd arrived at his new foster family's place ready to break furniture and throw plates, until he'd caught his first glimpse of the bedroom that would be his. He'd never had a room to himself before, and certainly not one this bright and clean. The neatly made single bed, the poster of a University of South Carolina football player, the colorful rug over a shiny wood floor—all of it had washed over him, a wave of rest and peace. Oh, he'd done plenty of breaking and throwing after that, had plenty of anger to work out, but he'd fallen in love with the sensation of a peaceful, orderly home.

Once, he'd thought of making a home with Yasmin. She'd just bought her little cottage when they'd started dating. He'd chew nails before admitting it to his brothers, but he'd enjoyed going with her to pick out lamps and armchairs and a fancy bed.

A bed for Buck Mulligan to enjoy with her, as it turned out. Heat rose from his belly and swept through his head and hands, but he wasn't an angry teenager anymore. He breathed and loosened his fists and stole glances at Yasmin as he worked. She tilted her head as she coaxed the broken stems back upright, looking happy and in her element. He liked her looking like that.

He liked way too much about Yasmin, and that reality was coming home to him now that he was planning to live here, where he'd see her every day, where it was natural to be in the small yard together.

Once again, he wondered whether this living situation was a huge mistake.

Josiah was sitting in one of the rocking chairs on the porch, staring off into the street in some kind of a reverie. Rocky came outside and knelt next to him. "What's going on?" he asked in a whisper. "What were they all talking about?"

Obviously, Rocky hadn't seen that Liam was close enough to hear. He'd like to eavesdrop, see what he could find out, but instead he stood, intent on sharing the news in a gentle way. More than likely, Rocky had seen a lot in his life. That made news of violence extra stressful.

"Someone's dead," Josiah said before Liam could figure out a better way to phrase it.

"Is it my mom?" Rocky's tone was forced-casual, every muscle in his body stiff with tension.

"No," Liam said quickly. "It's a man."

Rocky and Josiah glanced at each other.

"Middle-aged white man," Josiah said in that flat, emotionless voice of his.

Rocky bit his lip. His eyes shifted from Josiah to Yasmin to Liam without resting on anyone.

The kid knew something. And Liam wanted to follow up, but Mulligan had nixed that idea.

Still, what could it hurt for Liam to talk with Rocky about it? If Liam learned anything important, he'd take it right to Mulligan, who could hardly turn down actual evidence. "Come help me with this," he suggested, gesturing toward the weedy flower bed. Though in truth, it wasn't *that* weedy and there was barely enough of a job for one person for ten minutes.

No matter. People talked more working side by side than being interviewed face-to-face. And if some information came out while they were working together, well, that wasn't his fault, was it? He wasn't interfering with the investigation.

"I'm not doin' that." Rocky lifted his chin and glared at Liam.

Yasmin shot Liam a quick glance, like she was worried he'd overreact to Rocky's attitude. "He's had a hard time."

"I get it." And he did. He'd gone through a long defiant stage himself, after losing his mom. Hearing about deaths or drownings in the area had shattered him for years.

Rocky sank to his knees at the far end of the flower bed and started pulling things up randomly—some plants, some weeds.

Liam opened his mouth to correct him and got a nudge from Yasmin's foot for his trouble. When he looked up at her, she shook her head marginally.

"Was he bald?" Rocky asked, so low Liam wasn't sure he'd heard it.

He rewound the conversation with the chief. "I don't know. Chief said he had a 'Bama hat floating around in the car, but there was nothing else that could identify the guy."

He glanced over at the boy in time to see him

press his lips together. His hands on the plants went still.

Yes, he knew something, all right.

"I'm going upstairs," Rocky said suddenly, and ran into the house.

Yasmin looked after him and then turned to Liam. "He's seen too much," she said.

The words brought back a memory, his older brother Sean explaining away some misbehavior of Liam's with the exact same phrase. Since studying psychology in school and talking to the evaluator during his preemployment psychological evaluation, he'd read up on the effects violence had on kids.

Liam had witnessed his first bad fight—that he remembered, anyway—when he was probably around five. A bunch of yelling and screaming had woken him up, and he'd stumbled out of his room to discover his brothers already on the stairs. He'd climbed into Sean's lap and they'd all sat and listened to shouts and shrieks and bangs, including the banging shut of the back door.

Once the silence had lasted a few minutes, they'd crept downstairs. Mom was lying on the floor, facedown, and outside they could hear Dad's truck squealing away.

Liam could still remember the way his heart had thudded and raced. He'd just wanted to get to her.

"Is she dead?" Cash had asked, holding Liam back.

Just like Rocky had asked. That kids could worry

their mom was dead—that he and his brothers had feared it—made Liam's chest feel tight and straightened his spine. Anything he could do to help fix this problem, he'd do.

Even now, he remembered how he'd been frozen with fear, how he and Cash had waited while Sean went over and shook her, got a wet bunch of paper towels and started cleaning up the blood on her face and arms, talking to her.

Pretty soon, she'd awakened, had looked around and reached toward him and Cash, forcing a weak imitation of a smile. Liam had struggled to go to her then, but Sean had made him stay back until he'd gotten her sitting up, leaning against some pillows. Then she'd beckoned him over and kissed him, held her arms out to Cash and Sean, too, and they'd all hugged.

That was the first time he'd seen how vulnerable his mother was.

He stood, wanting to escape the memories, and headed to Yasmin's tiny gardening hutch to put away the small shovel she'd given him. He leaned inside and blinked, remembering.

There in the corner was a figure made of white stone, about two feet tall: the yard angel he'd gotten for her. He'd wondered if it was tacky, not sure about his own tastes, especially buying a gift for someone who'd grown up with the best of everything.

But it looked so much like her, he'd explained when he'd given it to her. And it would look pretty in the garden of the place she was buying. She'd hugged him and said she loved it. He could still remember the happy, carefree smile on her face.

He'd imagined them putting it up together as they worked on the yard, him doing the hauling and lifting and mowing while she made it all look pretty.

That fantasy hadn't come true, obviously.

He backed out of the hutch, and turned back toward the house, thinking. She'd kept the stone angel rather than throwing it away. But she'd put it in the shed, not out on display in her garden.

What did that mean?

And what did it mean that Josiah was now going inside, following Rocky, throwing weird, fearful glances back over his shoulder?

CHAPTER FIVE

TWO HOURS LATER, after she'd gotten Rocky settled in bed and seen that Josiah was watching TV in the living room, Yasmin's shoulders relaxed a little. She wanted nothing more than to hide out in her bedroom and shut out the day, preferably with a big bowl of popcorn and a mindless movie.

She wouldn't think about Liam. His expressive face, his fatherly hand on Rocky's shoulder, the dimple that flashed when he was trying to hide his amusement.

She wouldn't think about him…except she couldn't help it. For years before they'd started dating, Liam had been the subject of her youthful romantic fantasies. They'd had that short stretch of months when those dreams had come true for her, when she'd been free to spend all the time she wanted with him, when his smile had been just for her.

Even though she'd had to break up with him, the

dreams hadn't gone away. If anything, they'd gotten more intense.

She'd just grabbed a bag of cheesy popcorn and clicked on the TV when her phone buzzed, caller unknown. She clicked on the call.

"Yasmin? It's Eldora. I own the Pig?"

"Hey." Yasmin was surprised the older woman, who managed Safe Haven's most popular dive bar, even had her phone number.

"Listen," Eldora said, "I got your number from your mom."

"My *mom*? Are you in Charleston?"

"She's here in town. Sitting at the bar."

Yasmin's mouth went dry. "I'll be right there. Thanks." She slid her feet into flip-flops and grabbed her purse and keys.

What was her mother doing at the Palmetto Pig?

Yasmin adored her mom, but not in the way some people adored theirs. She had friends who looked up to their mothers, called them for advice, respected their life wisdom. Yasmin's mom was smart in the sense of being well-read, but their role reversal had started even before that first breakdown when Yasmin was ten, and by the time she'd entered her twenties, it was complete.

Mom definitely couldn't take care of her and Josiah as kids. And recent events had illustrated that she couldn't take care of Josiah as an adult.

Yasmin often wondered whether Mom could take care of herself, but you couldn't say that to a fifty-year-old woman with a degree from Yale. Couldn't suggest that she come live with you, or at least in the same town.

Mom needed the stimulation of a bigger city, or so she always said. So Yasmin had had to be content with taking Josiah off Mom's hands and leaving her set up two hours away in Charleston, with a few friends from church and book club, a big library and quaint shopping area within walking distance, and a weekly appointment with a good therapist.

In the Palmetto Pig, the greasy smell of fried fish and hush puppies competed with a faint aroma of alcohol. Night was falling outside, but inside, the lighting level was always the same: dark, illuminated by lit-up beer signs.

And there, at the scarred mahogany bar, sat Yasmin's mother.

Her hair bounced silvery-blond, halfway down her back, and her size-four figure was accentuated by the gauzy palazzo pants and tank top she wore. Not at all to Yasmin's surprise, several of the male patrons were casting speculative glances at the pretty stranger.

Yasmin knew they were of no interest to Mom, who'd never loved anyone but Dad. In fact, their relationship had sealed Mom's fate as a Southern small-town outsider, due to his being biracial. In a bigger city, or in the North, the choice wouldn't have raised an eyebrow; Mom was pretty and fragile, the daughter of older parents in poor health.

Dad—her parents' physician and closer to their age than hers—had fallen in love, and Mom had needed someone to take care of her. The chemistry between them had been palpable even to their children.

In the conservative, upper-crust society Mom had come from, though, marrying a biracial man had marked her as an outsider, even in the 1980s.

To her credit, Mom didn't care.

As Yasmin approached her, a familiar mix of love and longing and worry tightened her stomach. She slid slowly onto the bar stool next to her mother and touched her arm featherlight, and even so, Mom jumped. "Yasmin! You scared me!"

"You scared me, too, Mom." She put a careful arm around her mother's shoulders and squeezed, lightly. "Why didn't you call? I would have come down to Charleston and gotten you."

"I just got so worried about Josiah."

That was no surprise. Yasmin was worried, too. "Did something bring that on?"

Her mother shrugged and looked away, waved for the bartender. Chip, in his twenties and eager to please, hurried over. "What can I get for you two beautiful ladies?"

"I'd like another gin fizz, honey, thank you."

Mom obviously wasn't driving back down to Charleston tonight. "Make it two," Yasmin said, and then turned back to her mother. "Did Josiah say something that got you worried?"

"No. I was looking online, reading about his condition."

"And you found out…"

"That we should maybe have him committed before he hurts himself. Or somebody else. Honey." She gripped Yasmin's hand, tight. "It's a lot on you to take care of him. I'll freely admit it was too much for me, and I'm his mother."

Everything is too much for you, Mom. But of course, Yasmin didn't say that out loud. She'd talked to Mom's doctors over the years, surfed the internet and had figured out that her mother probably had an anxiety disorder. But she was an artist, dabbled in painting and the occasional community theater production. She just thought of herself as temperamental.

"The way he sits and stares, the way he acts like he's hearing voices…"

"He *does* hear voices. That's part of his disease." Yasmin had done plenty of research herself, including watching a segment where a journalist had worn earphones mimicking what people with schizophrenia heard in their own heads. It had been awful.

Yasmin was constantly on the watch for those voices inside her own head. Whenever she scolded herself or went into an extended daydream, she worried. Was it the onset for her? Women were typically diagnosed later than men…

Their drinks arrived and they sat and sipped for a few minutes, looking in the mirrored wall at the growing number of patrons talking and laughing, listening to the country music playing.

"How has he been?" Mom asked finally.

Yasmin hesitated. "Okay."

"I can tell from how you say that that he's not."

"He *is* okay. Sometimes, he's okay." Her throat tightened and she swallowed another big swig of gin fizz. "He likes his job at the library a lot. You know how he's always loved books, and he's brilliant with the technology. And Miss Vi—remember her?—she's got him running a chess club for disadvantaged kids."

Mom bit her lip. "Is it really good for him to work?"

"It's not just good, it's crucial." Yasmin was convinced of that. "In fact, once he's in a good routine with the job, he might go for a graduate degree in library science."

"Oh, no! That would be way too much for him."

"He feels better when he has a focus like that. He's still supersmart, Mom. He has a lot to offer. And he gets so excited when we talk about him going back to school. There are all kinds of online degrees—"

Mom waved her hand back and forth, obviously done listening.

Yasmin wanted to get through to her mother, to convince her to see Josiah as himself, as a person rather than a problem. But it was hard when she knew, deep inside, that Josiah wasn't himself, not yet. And exhibit A was the way he refused to talk about what had happened the night he and Rocky had come to the center. Yasmin had asked him twice, and Rocky once. Neither of them would say anything about it.

"Hey, ladies!" A happy, hearty voice from behind them brought them both turning around on their bar stools. "Yasmin, I haven't seen you in forever!"

Yasmin couldn't help smiling at her younger friend. "Mom, this is my friend Claire. Claire, my mom, Erin Tanner."

Mom smiled and clutched Claire's hand. "Won't you join us, dear?"

"Sure, for a few." Claire looked back toward the door.

"Gin fizz while you wait for your special someone?" Yasmin teased.

"Sounds good. And I hear *you* don't have to wait. Your special someone's living in your garage apartment. True? Does your mama know?"

"Um." Yasmin tried to signal Claire with her eyes to *shut up.*

Mom giggled, obviously pleased to be included in the girl talk. "I didn't know you were seeing someone! Is it serious?"

Yasmin waved both hands, and when Chip came back, pointed to her glass for another. "I'm not seeing anyone! I have a *tenant.*"

"A hot tenant," Claire said, laughing.

Yasmin kicked her ankle.

"Who is it, dear?" Mom asked, delicately sipping the dregs of her gin fizz. Another appeared in front of her without her even having to ask.

"It's Liam O'Dwyer. One of the dreamy O'Dwyer brothers, the youngest." Claire looked off into space, smiling. "All three of those men look good enough to...well. They're handsome."

Mom frowned and tilted her head to one side. "Liam O'Dwyer? From when you were in school? I'm...surprised."

Yasmin knew why: she didn't think Liam was very smart, and had told Yasmin numerous times that he wouldn't amount to anything. "He's a Safe Haven police officer," she said firmly. "And an old friend who needed a place to stay."

"Some people have all the luck," Claire said, sighing. "We have plenty of extra room at my house. He could have stayed with me in a heartbeat."

Yasmin glared at her.

"Kidding!" Claire laughed merrily. "Hey, I also heard you have a teenager staying with you. One of the women's center kids? Listen, my folks have two of my nephews here for the summer. My sister's kids. If you're looking for some friends for your guy, bring him over. We've got the pool and a basketball hoop, and my spoiled little nephews don't fight as much if there are other kids around."

"Thanks," Yasmin said. She wondered if sulky, angry Rocky would be able to get along with

Claire's suburban nephews. That was likely to be a mismatch.

Of course, according to some, she and Liam were a mismatch, too.

Mom was frowning, biting her lip, her pleasure in the conversation obviously evaporated, her anxieties starting to kick in. "Why are all those people living at your house?" she asked Yasmin. "How can you take care of your brother?"

Yasmin sighed. Josiah had told her how Mom had infantilized him when he'd stayed with her right after his diagnosis, how she hadn't wanted him to leave the house, how she'd tried to help him make phone calls and to screen his friends. He'd made Yasmin promise not to treat him that way, and she'd agreed.

"Hey, Mom, it's okay," she said, rubbing her arm gently. "Maybe it's time to pay the tab and go back to my place."

"It sounds like you have a full house already!" Mom's eyes brimmed with tears. "I don't know what I'm going to do tonight. I don't think I can drive all the way home."

"There's plenty of room. Come on." Yasmin signaled for Chip and made a writing motion in the air. Claire said goodbye and went to meet Tony, her on-again, off-again boyfriend.

Yasmin paid the check and then put an arm around Mom and headed for the exit. She'd learned to recognize, from too-frequent experience, when Mom needed to be treated carefully.

It had happened for the first time when Yasmin was ten. Back then, in Mom's circles at least, nervous breakdowns were a thing; Mom had gone to a rehab center to get over hers. It had crushed Yasmin to spend six months without her mom, alone in the house with her dad and brother, trying to make a home, to supervise the help, arrange for groceries to be brought in and laundry sent out. Trying to be a mom, so her own real mommy could come home.

The only bright spot in that fifth-grade year had been Liam, held back a grade at the same time Yasmin had been promoted forward. They'd been the biggest and smallest kids in the class, respectively, and neither one of them had fit in.

Truth was, she'd fallen in love with him then and never fallen out of it, despite their differences.

As Mom got into the passenger seat of Yasmin's car, she gripped Yasmin's arm. "Josiah could be violent to a child," she said. "Did you ever think of that?"

"Oh, Mom, I don't think so." She hadn't even considered the possibility that Josiah could hurt Rocky; the two of them seemed thoroughly bonded.

Even so, Mom's negative attitudes about Josiah unsettled her. When Yasmin was around her beloved brother, it was hard to think of him as doing anything to hurt anyone. But what had really happened on the night of the murder? Whatever it was, it had made both Josiah and Rocky act strange.

She was pretty sure they at least knew something about the crime, even if she couldn't believe they'd participated in it.

But neither was very proficient at speaking carefully and creating a good impression. Which was why she hoped the police didn't catch wind of their possible involvement.

RITA WATCHED THE last of the burly movers head out the door of her friend Norma's beachfront condo, generous tips in hand.

"That's a wrap," Norma said, hands on hips. "Easiest move I ever did in my life. Amazing what money will do for you."

"You deserve every penny." Norma had been part of a lawsuit involving a building she'd worked in for years, unknowingly absorbing cancer-causing chemicals. She'd won her battle with breast cancer—at least, she hoped so—but the generous settlement didn't make up for the suffering she'd gone through.

The wall-to-wall windows overlooking the ocean, the rustic private balcony off the bedroom, the gleaming modern kitchen…it gave Rita a pang that just as quickly faded away. "I'm coming over here at least twice a week to see how the other half lives."

"Come every day." Norma put an arm around her. "But for now, let's hit the bar down on the water."

"Not yet." Rita flew around the kitchen, putting out dishtowels and pot holders, setting out a plant, arranging a suncatcher so that the light hit it, fracturing into rainbows. This place might be fancy, but it wasn't yet a home, and Norma deserved a home.

Norma watched her, shaking her head. "You're such a mother hen, you should've had six kids."

Rita froze in the midst of placing salt and pepper shakers in the middle of Norma's pale pine kitchen table. She looked over at her friend. Then, very carefully, she lined up the shakers and stood upright. "I'm ready when you are," she said, proud that her voice didn't shake.

Because who was to say that she *hadn't* had six kids?

Norma studied her, eyes narrowed. "Don't think I won't ask you about that," she said. "Seems like you might need a drink in front of you to answer."

"I just might." Rita forked fingers back through her hair and followed Norma down the steps that led to a private boardwalk.

At the bottom, Norma spun around like a ballerina, arms outspread. "This is mine, all mine, can you believe it?"

"Norma—"

Too late. Rita watched helplessly as her friend spun right into a tall, suit-clad silver fox.

He caught her by the upper arms and steadied her, then took a step backward. "As a matter of fact," he said in a clipped, distinctly Northern voice, "it's not all yours."

"Oh!" Norma, who was never flustered, turned pink. "Sorry to be acting like a fool," she muttered.

"Forgiven," he said, without making it at all believable.

"Do you live here?" Rita asked, because Norma obviously wasn't going to.

He indicated the condo next door. "When I'm in town." He might have been about to introduce himself, but a trio of bikini-clad teenage girls came rushing along the boardwalk, giggling over a phone, their music loud.

The silver fox stepped right in front of them, hands on hips. "Excuse me, ladies."

Their faces turned into a comical mix of fear, affronted dignity and curiosity. "What's up?" one of them asked, lifting her chin.

"There's a rule about being fully dressed on this part of the boardwalk," he said.

Their mouths hung open. "Hello?" said the bold one. "It's the beach?"

For snottiness, Silver Fox was every bit the match of a sixteen-year-old girl. "It's private property," he said, gesturing at a sign full of detailed small print. "We allow the public to use our boardwalk under certain conditions. No noise, no inappropriate attire."

"Who are you calling inappropriate?" That was Norma; she'd obviously gotten over her momentary embarrassment. "These girls are wearing what every other teenage girl wears at the ocean. Carry on, ladies," she said, waving the girls past.

"I'll be reporting this infrac—" The man choked in the midst of speaking to the departing backs of the girls.

Rita stifled a giggle at the man's expression, then made a face at Norma. "I never understood thongs."

"Doesn't seem comfortable to me, but..." Norma looked at the Silver Fox's stunned expression. "If you're going to wear one, do it when you're a teenager. Have fun, ladies!" she called after the girls, and one turned back to give her a thumbs-up.

"Completely inappropriate." The Silver Fox shook his head. "I'll speak to the board."

Rita glanced over at Norma and tried to keep a straight face. "I'm pretty sure that's what kids wear nowadays."

"And don't you have better things to do than pick on those poor young girls?" Norma asked. "Come on," she said to Rita. "I need that drink more than ever."

"Selfie first." Rita grabbed her friend's arm, and they put their heads together, laughing, ocean in the background. Rita snapped several, and they leaned over the phone together, looking through, deleting the bad ones. "There, that one's a keeper," Rita said when they found one with both of them laughing, looking happy.

She'd lost enough people that she liked to take

photos whenever she was with her friends. It was a bit of an obsession with her.

"Post it," Norma demanded. "It'll make everyone back in Maine jealous!"

"That'll be the caption," Rita decided. "Jealous yet?" She typed it in and showed it to Norma before hitting Post.

Silver Fox made a disgusted clicking sound with his mouth and started climbing the steps to his condo. Moving carefully and holding the railing, Rita noticed.

"He's handsome," Norma said, nodding in appreciation.

He was, and he seemed uptight, but if anyone could loosen him up, it was Norma. And she wanted her friend to be as happy as she was. "We didn't catch your name," she called up to the man, just to be ornery.

"That's on purpose," came his response. A moment later, his door clicked shut.

Norma rolled her eyes. "Figures."

Rita raised an eyebrow at her friend and they continued toward the upscale bar directly beside the condo complex. Her own modest little apartment complex was just fine. Peaceful, compared to this place.

Once they'd ordered drinks at a table overlooking the bay, with boat lights twinkling outside, Rita studied her friend. "Did it bother you that guy's going to be your neighbor?"

Norma waved a hand. "There's jerks everywhere."

"He was a good-looking jerk," Rita pointed out.

"Don't care. I'm not in the market."

"You can't shut yourself off," Rita protested. "You have a lot of love to give, and you're still young. And pretty."

Norma dropped her chin and glared at Rita. Then she took a long pull on her light beer and looked out across the water.

Rita knew her well enough to read her mind. She bore the scars from her cancer treatments and didn't think a man would want her.

They'd argued about it before, but tonight wasn't the time to revisit that argument.

"You're welcome to him," Norma said, gesturing back toward the condos. "Although I got the feeling your heart's otherwise engaged."

Rita pressed her lips together to keep from answering. What was happening with Jimmy was too fragile to discuss.

"Save that for later, then," Norma said. "I want to hear about your search into your past."

"I'm failing." Rita told her about her aborted trip to the library. "Freaked me out. I did a little research but had to leave before I found anything out."

"Still getting weird vibes about the women's center?"

Rita nodded. "Every time I walk by, even more when I go in to volunteer. I don't know how I would've gotten from there to the highway where T-Bone found me, though."

They ordered more drinks, and appetizers, and talked a little more. "I still feel like you're holding something back from me," Norma said.

Rita bit her lip. She wanted to confide in her friend, wanted her insight, but she *didn't* want all the pressure Norma was likely to exert if she knew everything Rita was finding out.

But knowing Norma, she'd weasel the truth out of Rita sooner or later. It was what made her a great therapist. "There's this cook at the diner—Abel?"

Before she could go on, hands on her shoulders and a familiar masculine smell made her insides quiver like she was the age of those teenage girls. "Jimmy!" She swiveled in her chair and sure enough, there was her boss, maybe her boyfriend.

"You stalking us?" Norma asked. She'd met Jimmy earlier this year and was already comfortable enough with him to tease.

"I might've seen something you posted," he admitted. Then he leaned down and growled in Rita's ear. "I couldn't just drive on by." His breath was warm on her ear.

She tilted her face sideways, wanting a little more contact. He ran a finger across her neck, under her hair, and she sucked in a breath. Then he squeezed her shoulder and they moved apart.

If someone had told her younger self she'd be this

physically conscious of a man at age fifty-seven, she wouldn't have believed it.

As he leaned over, talking to Norma now, Rita studied him. Heavy beard stubble darkened his face, even though he'd been clean-shaven at work this morning. His biceps strained the sleeves of his Charleston RiverDogs T-shirt.

"Hey," came another voice, "checking out the diner's competition?"

Rita's heart gave another big thump. "Hey, Cash," she said. He was more than twenty years younger than Jimmy, already wealthy from running his own mergers and acquisitions company, but he spoke to a restaurant manager with the same friendly attitude he could have reserved for his elite friends. Spoke to her and Norma the same way. He kept a little to himself, different from his outgoing brother, Liam, or his rough-edged older brother, Sean. But he didn't seem to have a snobbish bone in his body.

She'd be proud of him, if she had the right to be.

Jimmy and Cash said goodbye and walked off together, and Rita watched all the female heads in the room turn. Didn't matter your age: those were two fine examples of masculinity, and one or the other was sure to appeal to you.

"You said you'd gotten some inklings," Norma said. "About your past. Something about that cook, Abel?"

Rita nodded, still watching Jimmy and Cash as they exited the bar.

"Like what?"

Taking another long gulp of her Old Fashioned, Rita looked steadily at her friend. "Abel remembers me," she said. "From before."

Norma's eyes widened. "That's huge! What did he tell you? How well did he know you?"

"Not well at all. He just remembers seeing me once."

"Oh." Norma frowned. "You got me all excited there. Did he have any information?"

Slowly, Rita nodded. She hadn't been brave enough to tell anyone yet, but she had to start somewhere. "He saw me in a shop he was working at." She drew in a deep breath and added, "With three boys."

"Three *boys*?" Norma stared. "Like, kids of yours?"

Rita nodded. "He said that's how we were acting. Like mother and sons." Her throat tightened on the last words.

She picked up her drink again, but her hands were shaking and her stomach roiled, so she carefully put it back down without taking a sip. Norma was a good friend, but how would she feel about the notion that Rita might have abandoned her children? How would anyone feel?

She stared down at the table, blinking against the tears that wanted to spill out.

Norma's hand covered hers and squeezed gently. "That must be awful hard to deal with. Have you found out anything about them? Do you remember anything?"

"Like I said, I've had inklings." She looked up then, met Norma's eyes.

"Inklings like what?"

"Like that he—" she nodded toward the doorway "—Cash, that he might be one of my sons."

CHAPTER SIX

MONDAY WAS LIAM'S first day shift. He was working on some of the endless paperwork that would be way too much of his new role when their secretary-slash-dispatcher, Willa Jean, called across the office to him. "Dog attack in the park, man down. And Jenkins is…" She made air quotes. "Busy."

He was grabbing his belt when she added, "Sounds a lot like *your* dog. Big rottweiler mix, right?"

His heart lurched. "Yeah."

He jogged out to his cruiser and hit the lights. If Rio was the dog who had caused the problem, then on the one hand, that was good; although overly exuberant, Rio wouldn't hurt anyone.

On the other hand, whatever happened was Liam's fault for not training the big goof better. But how had Rio gotten as far as the park?

Minutes later he was at Safe Haven's bayfront park where several people stood around a ranting older man—who looked uninjured, thank heavens—a downcast, slump-shouldered kid and a giant, happy-go-lucky dog straining at his leash.

Rio and Rocky. Of course. He waded in and affirmed his initial observation that the older man—Mr. Long, who owned the bowling alley, the dry cleaners and a gas station out by the highway—had no visible injuries. The way he waved his arms and paced revealed that his mobility was okay. And his voice was certainly strong.

"That beast tried to kill me," Mr. Long said. "It knocked me down. It should be put down. I'll get my gun and do it myself."

"You yelled at him." Rocky's fists clenched. "It's not his fault. You were mean and you scared him."

Rio strained at the leash Rocky held, trying to get to Liam, his doggy face grinning, tongue hanging out. He had no idea he was in big trouble.

"No need to take justice into your own hands," Liam said. "That's my dog, and I apologize for anything he's done. I'll take care of it. Now, let's hear what happened, one at a time." He got Mr. Long to sit on the bench and ordered Rocky to take Rio over to a nearby picnic table and hold him or tie him up. Then he took Mr. Long's statement and those of a couple of onlookers.

What had happened was no big surprise: the man had been eating a pastry and drinking coffee, minding his own business on a park bench, when Rio had come bounding over, knocked the coffee out of his hand, eaten the pastry and, when Mr. Long stood and scolded him, knocked him down and licked his face. Fortunately, there were no burns from the coffee and no ill effects from the fall, thanks largely to the soft grass.

While Mr. Long called his wife to ask her to come and pick him up, Liam texted Yasmin. Need help with Rocky. Bayfront Park.

Sweat dripped down the middle of his back. Even summer uniforms were hot in a South Carolina August. He looked over at his dog, now lying on his back for an extended belly rub from Rocky, and sighed.

The chief would hear about this, no doubt. And Mulligan. Just another stroke against Liam: that he had an unmanageable dog.

He double-checked Mr. Long's contact information, apologized again and reassured him that they'd be in touch.

"You'd better," he said, but it was clear that he was starting to calm down. "Creatures like that shouldn't be allowed to run free." Beneath the bluster, Liam could hear the fear in his voice and the embarrassment. The man must have been humiliated to be knocked down, and at his age, a fall *could* be dangerous.

Liam walked with Mr. Long to the car where his wife was picking him up, offered more apologies. Then he turned back and headed toward the picnic table where Yasmin had just arrived—looking gorgeous in a close-fitting skirt and a red T-shirt—and was talking to Rocky.

"Is he gonna be put down?" Rocky asked as soon as Liam was in earshot.

The fear in his voice catapulted Liam back to something he'd almost forgotten: Butterscotch, the dog they'd had to leave behind when they'd run from their father. Although he hadn't thought about it in years, had been only ten when it had happened, he remembered the soft feel of the fluffy mutt's ears, the way he'd loved throwing a stick for him. Liam had been worried his father wouldn't remember to feed the dog while they were away from it, and he'd bugged their mother about it until his brother Cash had told him to shut up, that they'd never see the dog again.

That had proven to be true. The loss had paled in comparison to the loss of his mother, of course, but he suddenly remembered how he'd ached to cuddle up with the dog after losing their mom. Butterscotch was the one being who wouldn't have judged him for crying.

He swallowed hard. "No, he's not going to be put down, but we have to train him. You weren't supposed to take him off the block. What were you doing way over here?"

"I got bored, okay?" Rocky's eyes were shifting, looking anywhere but at Liam.

He was lying.

"Where were you headed with the dog?" Yasmin asked.

"None of your business!" Rocky jumped off the picnic table, thrust Rio's leash at Yasmin and took off running.

Liam stood as Rio practically pulled Yasmin off her feet, trying to run after Rocky. He grabbed the dog's leash and made him sit.

Yasmin was focused on Rocky. "I'd better see you back at my place," she called after the boy.

Rocky slowed down and looked over his shoulder but didn't stop.

"There's brownies in the kitchen," she called a little more quietly, more enticing.

Rocky picked up speed, heading out of the park.

"Clever," Liam said. "Think he'll go for it?"

"Rewards work at least as well as punishments for kids." She frowned down at Rio. "This one needs training, Liam. I'm sorry I didn't keep a closer eye on Rocky, but most dogs would be fine coming to the park."

"I know. I just haven't found time, but that's on me. I'll work out a plan tonight." He had gotten an idea of how to get Rio some training as he was talking to Mr. Long.

"He needs a bath, too," Yasmin commented. "He'd make a better impression if he didn't reek."

"True." Liam sighed and stood. "I'll do that tonight, too. Hey, do you have any idea what Rocky was really doing over here? He wasn't telling me the whole story."

"I have a good guess," she said. "A couple of times when he and his mom came to the women's center, they got sandwiches and brought them to the park. I'd bet anything he was hoping she'd show up here."

"Ouch." They'd put out a description of the woman, had reported her missing just yesterday, but there were no leads. "I'll take Rio on home and then get back to work."

"I'm going home to check on Rocky, I can take him," Yasmin said, scratching behind Rio's ears. "Bad boy that he is," she added, placing a kiss atop the shiny black head.

Liam swallowed. Yasmin had always been affectionate. And forgiving. "Thanks. That would be a big help. But how are you managing your work, being at home with Rocky so much?"

She shrugged. "I can write grants and do paperwork at home just as easily as at the center."

She made it sound effortless, but he could tell, from the tightness in her shoulders and the faint circles underneath her eyes, that it wasn't. She'd always been a hard worker, and she ran the women's center with only volunteer help. Now she'd taken on the care of a teenager, and it had to be wearing on her.

They strolled toward the parking area. Already the cars had thinned out; people tended to take their morning walks early in the August heat.

He could almost pretend that they were doing something recreational, walking the dog together, a couple. Except that she'd dumped him and made it clear she'd had no change of attitude since then. So he needed to keep his thinking practical. "I'm not surprised Rocky's searching for his mom, but is there anything else going on with him? He's acting weirder."

"I think something happened to him the night that guy went down with the car," she said unexpectedly. "I want to find out what. *You* should try to find out what."

"If he knows something, he needs to talk to the police. Mulligan, not me." Because Mulligan wasn't interested in Liam's input.

"If he won't share anything with me or you, I doubt he'll talk to a cop he doesn't know."

"Maybe *you* should talk to Mulligan." He watched her steadily. She'd think he was being hostile, and maybe he was, but he couldn't quell his curiosity about what had happened between them where their relationship stood.

"I don't want to talk to Buck," she said, looking straight ahead. "I want to check into it myself, on the down low. Figure out what happened."

Liam stared at her. "No. No way! You're not investigating a murder on your own. Why would you?"

She looked away, just like Rocky had. "No special reason."

Which meant there *was* a reason. She thought she knew something. And considering that Yasmin was one of the smartest people he'd ever met, he respected her suspicions.

But this wasn't an intellectual puzzle or a chemistry class; this was murder. And Yasmin's smarts wouldn't keep her safe. "Don't even think about it," he said, glaring at her to make sure she took him seriously.

"I won't put myself at risk. I'll just...do a little poking around."

Liam couldn't like it. Couldn't, as an officer of the law, sanction it. But he had to admit that the notion of a private, side investigation intrigued him.

Something was wrong, off, about that murder. It didn't seem like a simple robbery or a crime of passion.

They'd reached his cruiser, and Yasmin turned toward home, lifting a hand as if to say goodbye.

He took it, held it, and the simple sensation of her rough-soft hand, so much smaller than his own, seemed to send sparks through his entire body.

Her lips parted a little and she drew in a breath. Her eyes lifted to meet his, looking troubled. So she felt it, too.

He didn't let go. She didn't pull away.

"All those years of being close," he said. "We knew each other so well. Wonder why we couldn't make it work?"

She shook her head. "Don't ask that, Liam."

"Why not?"

"Just don't." She looked to the side, knelt to adjust Rio's collar. Anything, it seemed, to keep from looking at Liam.

He didn't understand why she'd ended things with him when she obviously still had feelings of some kind. Her excuse that she wasn't ready for a relationship didn't hold water. Was it that their backgrounds were so different? Was he just not good enough for her?

Was it Mulligan?

The notion burned, but he still didn't want anything to happen to her. "If you do any kind of digging around about the murder," he heard himself say, "which you shouldn't, you need to bring me along. I'll work with you."

CHAPTER SEVEN

LIAM WOULD INVESTIGATE with her. It wasn't ideal, but it did make Yasmin feel safer. And it meant she'd have control over what was found out, or at least, as close as she could get to it.

And she'd get to spend time with Liam.

She power-walked home, taking deep breaths of warm summer air, Rio leashed at her side. Maybe she and Liam could work together and figure out what had really happened to Rocky's mom and the dead man. Maybe then Josiah would be cleared. Rocky's mom would be found and reunited with her son, and Josiah's lowered stress level would help his treatment work better. She could focus better on her work at the center, try to pull it back from the brink of disaster where it had been hovering for the last few months.

Life could get back to normal.

And what then? You still can't get involved with Liam.

Not when she knew what kind of genes she carried. Even if her own mental health remained stable, she wouldn't pass along a significantly increased risk of schizophrenia as well as her mother's mostly undiagnosed issues.

Maybe sometime in the future she'd meet a man who didn't want kids. She could at least marry, right?

Of course, that kind of man had exactly zero appeal to Yasmin. She liked men who embraced their families, their kids, as her own father had done.

As Liam wanted to do.

She needed to stop thinking about Liam, but it was hard when she was walking his dog back to the home they basically shared. No, they weren't under the same roof, but the entrance to the garage apartment was a very short stone's throw from her door.

Being together this much had made hash of her efforts to forget about him and move on. Every time she saw him—which happened daily now—she wanted to touch his arm, to straighten his collar. To inhale the scent of him. To melt into his arms.

But thinking of those things she couldn't have made her heart ache, tightened her chest to where it was hard to breathe. Deliberately, trying to regain her good mood, she focused on the flowers, the sky, the birdsong. At least she'd have a little time with Liam, working with him to try to figure out what had happened on the night Rocky had arrived.

Sweet torture and a mistake for her long-term

emotional health, but it might get her through. And it would help Josiah, which was the important thing.

Josiah. All of a sudden, she realized what she'd done.

She'd left Josiah alone with Mom. And then she'd sent Rocky home into the mix.

She picked up her pace until she was almost running. Their high level of dysfunction was a big part of why Josiah was living with her now. When she'd started getting weird phone calls from both of them last year, she'd gone to Charleston to visit and realized that Mom was in no condition to care for her newly diagnosed son. Any mother would be worried about a child with a serious mental health condition, but Mom's own issues made her apprehension shoot out of control. Josiah's condition, in turn, had been fueled by Mom's anxiety, and his doctors had agreed that living with Yasmin and having some distance from his mom was a better solution.

Please, let her have gone home before he woke up. Mom had slept in today, after all the drinking last night, so she hadn't been up when Yasmin had gotten Liam's text and rushed over to the park. But Mom knew her way around town. She could have walked the few blocks to the Palmetto Pig, collected her car and headed for Charleston, all without seeing Josiah or at least, without spending much time with him. Sometimes, she was very independent.

But today was not that day. The moment Yasmin walked into her house, she discovered her mother standing over Josiah in the kitchen. Josiah sat at the table, his head in his hands. Mom was talking rapidly, her forehead lined, her fingers picking at the sweats Yasmin had given her to sleep in.

Not good. Yasmin drew in a deep breath, knowing that for her to display nervousness or upset would only make things worse. When she had herself under control, she breezed into the kitchen. "Hey, how's everyone doing?" she asked. "Where's Rocky?"

Her mother nodded sideways, at which point she saw Rocky sitting in the corner of the kitchen, playing with a handheld gaming device, his shoulders so tight they were practically glued to his ears.

When he saw Rio, his whole body relaxed. "They didn't put him down!"

"No, of course not," she said, letting the dog go. He rushed around the kitchen, bumping against her mother and doing a quick surf of the counters, then flopping down beside Rocky. Rocky wrapped his arms around the dog's big head and buried his face in his neck.

True canine therapy, and it warmed Yasmin's heart. No matter what else happened, she was glad Liam had moved into her garage apartment just so that Rocky could have the unconditional comfort Rio offered.

If only it would work for Josiah and Mom, too, but one glance at the two of them told her they weren't feeling the same warm cuddly feeling Rocky and Rio brought forth in Yasmin.

She looked through the mail as a way of avoiding the tension in the room. "Hey, here's the information we requested about Safe Haven Middle School," she commented to Rocky.

He looked at her briefly and then turned back to Rio. "I ain't going."

Mom frowned. Whether it was the sentiment or the *ain't*, Yasmin didn't know.

"School here isn't too bad," Yasmin said, trying to be reasonable.

Josiah snorted.

"It's not," Mom said without conviction. Then she sat down at the table beside Josiah.

Rocky ignored them.

"Coffee, Mom?" Yasmin picked up the coffeepot, looked at the dark brew inside. "I can make more."

"No, but thanks, honey. That's okay."

When Yasmin approached the table she thought she caught a whiff of alcohol. Was it from last night, or was Mom drinking already?

Worry gnawed at Yasmin. If her mother was drinking in the mornings, then she needed help, a lot of help. And she certainly couldn't drive home today, which meant she'd still be here and grating on Josiah for another day.

Yasmin had half a mind to take a shot of whiskey herself, but she whispered a mental prayer for strength instead.

"We'll go over to the school Monday morning and get you registered," she said to Rocky. "You'll be starting on the first day, and there will be other new kids. It'll be better than waiting."

"I'll go to school when Mom and I go home." His words were mumbled into the dog's coat.

"I'm sure you will," she said, "but until your mom's able to get back here, she asked me to take care of you. Which means sending you to school so you don't get behind." Inspiration hit, a way to distract both Rocky and Josiah from their troubles. "Just to get you back in the thinking groove after a summer off, why don't you play some chess with Josiah?"

"Don't know how," Rocky said. But something about the way he looked up suggested he might be interested.

"What do you think, Joe? Could you teach Rocky to play?"

Josiah gave the slightest of nods.

It was a start. Meanwhile, Yasmin needed to focus on finding out what had gone down that night, where Rocky's mother was. The child needed to be with her.

Why had she disappeared, anyway? The letter she'd left at the center had been completely nonexplanatory. She'd just said she'd had an emergency and asked if Yasmin could take care of Rocky.

But surely she would have come and asked Yasmin herself if it was possible. Rocky's mom was disorganized, and she'd made some bad choices in men, but she did care about her son.

But she hadn't brought him to the women's center, even though she'd sought refuge and help there in the past. Instead, Josiah had found Rocky down by the docks…at the very site where, sometime the same night, a man had been bludgeoned in his car and rolled into the bayou.

Rocky and Josiah had to know something. But neither one would talk about it to her. And when she'd suggested they go to the police, they'd both flat-out refused, even when Yasmin had told Rocky it might be a faster way to find his mom.

Now, today, Yasmin had her own mom to worry about. She needed to get Mom settled back at home, get her out of the mix and keep her from adding to Josiah's stresses. Then she'd be able to focus fully on figuring out the truth and helping Rocky.

Hopefully, clearing Josiah.

And she had to accomplish all that working with the man whom she loved but could never, ever have.

THAT NIGHT, AFTER a mind-numbing afternoon of filling out forms and answering nonessential calls, Liam arrived home to find a police car parked in front of Yasmin's house.

His heart turned over. He took her porch steps two at a time and pounded on the door. If something had happened to Yasmin…

She answered it instantly like she'd been standing right there. Forehead wrinkled, lips pressed tight.

But she looked safe, unhurt, and his heart rate settled. Until he looked directly behind her.

There was Buck Mulligan standing in the hallway, arms crossed, chin high. Looking like he ruled the place or at least, like he wanted to.

"Everything okay?" Liam kept his voice mild. He was counting on Yasmin's good Southern manners to force her to invite him in.

There was a momentary struggle in her eyes, and then she ran a jerky hand through her hair and stepped back. "Come on in," she said. "The more the merrier."

Buck frowned. "I need to conduct interviews. Is there a reason for him to be here?"

"I'm Yasmin's friend." He met Buck's eyes with a steady glare. "Looks like she might need some help."

"I'm her friend as well, O'Dwyer, but right now, I'm here on police business." Buck lifted his chin and Liam caught the unstated rest of the sentence: *and you're not.*

Ignoring Buck, Liam stepped inside just as Yasmin's mother came out of the kitchen.

"Are we finished, Buck?" Her voice, always heavy on the Southern drawl, now had a wheedling tone. "I'm just awful tired. I'd like to get a little rest… Oh." She stopped still. "Oh, my. What are you doing here, Liam?"

Like he was an unexpected bit of dirt on her shoe. "Hey there, Mrs. Tanner," he said, stepping forward and holding out a hand, not really expecting her to take it.

She didn't.

He shrugged internally. He'd tried. Something about this scene was off, and maybe it was just that he didn't like seeing Mulligan here, but he also wondered how the more vulnerable members of the household—Josiah and Rocky—were taking the day's happenings. "Is Rio here?"

"Heard he got in a little bit of trouble today." Mulligan leaned back against the wall, legs apart, still acting like he was the lord of this castle.

Liam didn't respond, just looked inquiringly at Yasmin.

"He's in the front room with the boys," she said, and stepped aside.

Liam walked past her, catching a quick whiff of her musky cherry perfume. Had she put it on for Mulligan?

The hallway was narrow, too narrow for Liam to pass the lounging figure of Buck Mulligan without jostling the man. So he did, making Mulligan straighten and glare.

Immature of him, but he couldn't help enjoying the moment.

Liam walked on into the living room. Josiah and Rocky sat at opposite ends of the couch, watching preseason football. An abandoned chessboard sat on the coffee table in front of them.

Rio bounded over, and Liam knelt to forestall the dog's leaping up on him, because that had to stop. Rio gave him a big slobbery kiss and Liam rubbed his sides.

Seeing Mrs. Tanner brought back so many memories. One in particular: the day that he'd gone home after school with Yasmin to get help with homework. That was something he'd done pretty often when they were both younger, but this day was different.

It had been awhile since he'd needed studying help, or been willing to ask for it; at sixteen, getting help from a fourteen-year-old girl was even more humiliating than it had been when they were in fifth grade. Liam had barely gotten by in school, given his spotty attendance through the crucial elementary years of learning to read and memorizing multiplication tables. Yasmin, on the other hand, was a certified genius and really did know how to do the advanced math they were being tested on.

And for once, Liam had cared about doing well. His foster dad had sat him down and explained to him the realities of becoming a cop in the twenty-first century: you pretty much had to go to college if you wanted to advance. And Liam was sold on the uniform and influence and ability to change things that came with a law enforcement career.

Yasmin had been glad to help, flattered, even.

Neither one of them had given much thought to the fact that nobody but them was home.

Not until her parents and Josiah had arrived a couple of hours later and found them sitting close together at the kitchen table, bent over a math book. Her dad had yelled and her mom had cried and it had taken him a minute to realize why: they thought her virtue was at risk from a big, older, lower-class kid who was feigning stupidity, or maybe not even feigning it, in order to take advantage of her youth and innocence.

Yasmin had been upset at the accusations, had yelled right back that they were just doing homework like a million times before. Her sassy words had gotten her sent to her room by her dad, and her mom had soon rushed upstairs, too, sobbing. That left Yasmin's father, stern, serious Dr. Tanner, to lecture Liam about appropriate rules and risks and hormonal urges, a deeply embarrassing talk not least because it held elements of truth.

Because of course, at sixteen, he'd been aware that Yasmin was blossoming and beautiful. She'd begun to acquire that hourglass figure that now made men go slack-jawed when she walked down Main Street; even back then, she'd been the subject of a few locker-room conversations.

Liam had eventually realized that they were alone in the house, and yeah, maybe he'd even imagined what he'd like to do.

But despite what her parents had assumed, Liam

had had a sense of honor. He'd known that Yasmin was only fourteen, and maybe a little naive even for that age. He'd never considered pressuring her, even touching her; that would be like throwing mud onto a beautiful stretch of pure snow.

Not only that, he actually *liked* Yasmin. She was different from other girls; she had ideas of her own, and plans; she wasn't petty and mean. She'd seen through his sullen exterior back in fifth grade, and she still knew who he was, saw his good side, despite the posturing he had to do as a bigger-than-average kid from a bad background.

He wouldn't have done anything to threaten her friendship and trust.

To then be accused of the very thing he'd fought in himself and beaten…it had burned. Especially when he realized that her parents thought of him, had always thought of him, as some kind of charity friendship for Yasmin: a person who would help her to learn compassion and kindness to the poor, to put into perspective all the advantages she had. Someone her family could maybe help, because they were good people, but who wasn't their social equal.

It had actually been Josiah who'd gotten his father calmed down, coming to Liam's defense. Liam hadn't expected help from Josiah, not that the kid was mean-hearted, but he rarely came out from behind his chessboard to get involved in life. Dr. Tanner must have known that, too, because when Josiah had strode into the kitchen and said, "Dad, back off!

He wouldn't do anything," Dr. Tanner had brought his lecture to a quick end.

The encounter and her parents' suspicions had changed the dynamics between him and Yasmin, though. He hadn't asked her for help with school-work again, and they'd drifted further apart. She'd gotten superbusy with tennis and the country club crowd, and he'd focused on beating up opposing players on the football field. He'd played offensive guard because he liked protecting people and he didn't mind getting pounded. Besides, it was a ticket to a good four-year college, something he couldn't have otherwise afforded.

Now, Liam studied Josiah, hunched at the end of the couch. He looked like he was trying to hold on to something explosive with utmost delicacy, the way he hunched over, all stiff and guarded.

"You guys talk to the officer yet?" he asked.

Josiah didn't answer, but Rocky shook his head. "Don't know why he wants to talk to us. I don't know anything about what happened, and neither does he." He nodded toward Josiah.

"You didn't see anything unusual that night you ended up at the center?"

"No," Rocky said, half-indignant.

Again, Josiah didn't answer.

But when Mulligan walked into the room, still acting like he owned the place, both Rocky and Josiah started fidgeting, looking anywhere but at him, not making eye contact.

It would take a stupider officer than Mulligan to miss the fact that they were hiding something.

"You ready to chat a little more about what happened?" Mulligan asked, stepping in front of the TV to focus on the two on the couch, ignoring Liam.

In unison, they shook their heads.

"I heard a rumor y'all were out there at the docks," he probed, taking the remote out of Rocky's hands and clicking off the television.

How had Mulligan heard that? From the shrimpers that day that Rocky had been found in the shed, maybe. Or maybe Mulligan was just fishing, but neither Josiah nor Rocky was denying it.

In the silence, Liam could hear Yasmin talking to her mother, the tread of the two women up the stairs.

"You sure you didn't see anything?" Mulligan asked, tilting his head sideways.

Rocky threw up his hands in classic annoyed teenager fashion. "Yes, I'm sure!"

Liam wondered whether Mulligan noticed how hard both men were sweating. Even though Yasmin had the AC turned pretty cool.

"Well, y'all keep thinking about it. We can put off this interview for tonight, but not forever." He turned to Liam. "Talk to you a minute?"

Liam nodded, and they walked on through the living room and stepped out on the side porch. The jerk knew the way as well as Liam did. Better.

"Hey, listen," Buck said, his voice fake-kind. "I heard you're living over Yasmin's garage and that you're goin' through a hard time. You'd do better to focus on getting back on your feet and just leave the murder investigation to me."

Liam kept his chin up, didn't show a sign that inside he was right back to his outcast years. He raised his hands, palms out. "I'm on day desk. Not my investigation." And he wasn't making any promises, but Mulligan wasn't observant enough to notice the omission.

Liam was pretty good at nuances, though, and at body language, reading people's faces. So he noticed the relief on Mulligan's, and wondered about it.

The guy liked to act like he owned the world, but he was pretty insecure about this particular case. And with good cause. He might have a lot of connections among the upper crust of the town and an in with the city council, he might have a degree in criminal justice from a more expensive college than Liam had attended, but he knew next to nothing about serious crime.

If Liam had been a better person, he'd have felt sorry for the man, but Mulligan was a jerk. If he crashed and burned trying to investigate his first homicide, it would serve him right.

The case still needed to be investigated right, though. And since he was pretty sure Buck wasn't up to the task, Liam suddenly felt more than justified in working with Yasmin on the side investigation she wanted to do. Both to help Rocky find his mom, and to keep Safe Haven safe.

CHAPTER EIGHT

YASMIN WASN'T GOING to worry about why Josiah wasn't at the house. She wasn't.

Even though his absence kicked up her anxiety big-time.

It was late morning on Tuesday, and Yasmin had just gotten back from driving her mother home to Charleston. Mom was happily settled in with a lunch from her favorite takeout and a plan to go shopping with a neighbor later that afternoon. They'd even had a nice talk on the way down, reminding Yasmin of all the things she loved about her mother—she was well-read, and funny, and had sharp insight into political and social issues of the South.

After letting Rio out to run in the yard, Yasmin sank down on the front step, watching him, thinking absently about her responsibilities.

Out of desperation, she'd taken Claire up on her suggestion that Rocky hang out with her nephews, so she'd dropped him off early that morning with Claire's parents' blessing. A discreet phone call while she was in Charleston had reassured Yasmin that Rocky was "a lovely boy" and that all three were having fun in the backyard pool.

So Mom and Rocky were both doing fine, and two out of three wasn't bad, right? Josiah was probably out walking, or maybe he'd taken an extra shift at the library. Maybe he was doing something related to the kids' chess club Miss Vi had him helping out with.

He was a grown man. She didn't need to shadow his every move. She'd promised him she wouldn't.

She went inside and studied the empty refrigerator—having a teenage boy here meant she needed to grocery shop much more often, she was realizing. She wanted to take care of Rocky, and Josiah too, but she also needed to spend the afternoon getting caught up at work. The women's center depended on her, and she couldn't let the clients down.

Her friends wished she were more fun, but how could she be? Fun had never been her forte. Or maybe it could have been, but she hadn't found the time.

"With great gifts come great responsibilities," her dad had always told her. Yasmin had been labeled gifted pretty young, and she'd helped to take the burden off her mom. She didn't expect nurturing.

Didn't expect happiness, really, not since all the news about the family genes had come into the picture. Now, with Rocky and Josiah to look out for, it had become clear that duty, caring for others, was what it was going to be.

There was no point in grieving something you couldn't change. She'd go to the diner, treat herself to a comfort-food lunch. She'd sit at the counter and have a chat with Rita if the place wasn't too busy. Maybe even do a little investigating, because she was pretty sure Rita had been working on the night that Josiah and Rocky had shown up at the center. She'd ask Rita if she'd seen anything.

And then she'd feel more fortified to get back to work.

Josiah was probably fine.

Ten minutes later, she slid into a seat at the counter in the Southern Comfort Café. She waved through the pass-through at the tall, thin cook. "Hey, Abel, what's good today?"

"Now you know every single thing is good," he said, his wrinkled face breaking into a wide smile. "But if it was me, I'd get the shrimp and cheese grits."

"Perfect," she said as Rita approached with the coffeepot. "I'll have a big plate."

"You got it, baby."

Rita poured coffee to the rim without asking. "How you doing? You know what you want?"

"Shrimp and grits, and I already told Abel," she said.

Rita leaned a hip against the counter. "You're

making my job easy." She leaned closer and lowered her voice a little. "Heard your mom was in town."

"How'd you hear that?" Yasmin took a sip of coffee and considered. "Oh. Eldora?"

Rita nodded. "Me and Norma stopped into the Pig just after you left." She studied Yasmin's face. "You doing okay? She still here?"

"Took her back to Charleston this morning." Yasmin wasn't thrilled that even Rita, who was relatively new in town, had heard about Yasmin's mom being difficult. But the sympathy on Rita's face made her let down her guard. "I love her, but... there's a little stress to it. Especially for my brother." As she said the words and thought again about the fact that she didn't know where Josiah was, anxiety tightened her chest.

"Families." Some emotion crossed Rita's face, but it was gone before Yasmin could identify it. "Abel made a couple of chocolate pies, if you need a fix."

"That'd be great."

Rita got busy with her other customers, and Yasmin leaned back, trying to relax into the comfort of her town where people knew her and supported her.

Moments later the door opened, and there came Liam, devastatingly handsome in his uniform.

And that was the disadvantage of a small town where everyone knew each other: you couldn't escape your ex.

Their eyes met as he scanned the room, looking

for a place to sit. There was an empty stool next to her at the counter.

He walked past it with a nod to her, like she was an acquaintance he didn't much want to see, and settled into a seat at the far end, next to Pudge LeFrost.

She didn't know for sure why he was acting cold, but she had a pretty good guess. Running into Buck at her place last night had probably made him mad. Probably not jealous, not anymore, but just plain mad, because he didn't like the guy.

A vise tightened around her chest, making it hard to breathe. She'd started thinking Liam liked her and wanted to be with her again, and even though it couldn't happen, she'd begun to enjoy that specialness without even knowing she was.

Now, when he'd walked right past her without a greeting, the absence of his regard almost choked her.

She didn't want to look at him, didn't want to care. But there was a mirror behind the diner counter, right in front of her. Every time she lifted her eyes, they went directly to Liam.

He'd been angry last night, that much was obvious. He'd glared at Buck like the man was poison, and understandably so. It was her own fault she'd made them into rivals.

The two men she'd treated badly, both together in one house...thinking about it had made her toss and turn all night.

She deserved it, though. Going out with Buck

had been a dumb move, but it was the only way she could think of to let Liam know she was through with him, to push him away convincingly when her heart was crying out for him.

She couldn't tell him the truth about her fears. He was a protector to the core, and would have tried to sacrifice his desire for a family if she couldn't get over her worries about what she might pass on.

And other excuses wouldn't work. Men like Liam, alpha males, didn't buy into the whole "I just need some time," or "I'm not ready for a serious relationship," or "I need to find myself." On some primitive level, to an alpha, women were property. The only way to break up with men like that was to go with another man. Which was why she'd dated Buck in the first place.

But while it had worked, it had made Liam hate her, also thanks to his alpha-male personality. The insult of her throwing him over for someone else was deep, primal.

The relationship with Buck had been brief and meaningless. He'd tried to get her into bed, of course, and for all she knew, he'd told people in town that he'd succeeded. But he hadn't. She hadn't been able to tolerate his touch because all she could think of was Liam.

And of course, Buck wouldn't put up with a platonic dating relationship for long. For that matter, neither could she. They had nothing to talk about, no basis for a friendship. Buck was good-looking and more intelligent than he let on, but he wasn't a deep thinker. Yasmin had learned long ago not to judge people on smarts; still, she found it hard to relate to a person who didn't want to learn or grow at all, who never picked up a book or read a newspaper. When she'd tried to confide in him about Josiah's diagnosis and her own fears, he'd just looked at her blankly and waved her concerns aside.

Their so-called relationship had lasted just long enough to convince Liam to leave her alone, and then they'd ended it with mutual relief.

But that was when it had sunk in, all that she'd lost. The dream of a regular life, of a husband and kids. And not just any husband, but her strong, protective, sexy childhood hero: Liam.

She swiveled in her seat to keep from staring at Liam and studied the yellowed newspaper clippings framed on one wall of the diner. A couple of minor movie stars who'd visited, local sports teams victories, and...where was it? Yes, there was the clipping about her family, back when she was nine and Josiah thirteen. Both she and Josiah had won awards in a national science competition, hence the article. Safe Haven being what it was, the paper had done a whole story about her family, her dad the doctor, her mom "active in civic affairs," which had been a stretch, but kindly meant.

How far they'd fallen. All that supposed potential had faded into nothing.

Worry for Josiah bloomed in her again. She'd

called Miss Vi on the way over, and the woman had said she'd check and see if he was anywhere in the library. But she hadn't called back, so Yasmin had to assume the answer was no.

Rita put a steaming plate of shrimp and grits in front of her. Her appetite was wavering now, but she lifted her fork and took a bite, and sure enough, it tasted good.

Josiah was probably home. She'd stop by after lunch on her way to the center.

The diner door jingled and opened, and she looked over idly, then did a double take.

Josiah was there, shaking his head, one hand braced against the door. Miss Vi had his other hand and was tugging, trying to get him to come in.

The buzz of conversation in the diner died down a little, enough that everyone probably heard Miss Vi's stern, clear words: "You worried your sister, young man. The least you can do is let her see that you're all right."

Yasmin slid off her stool and hurried over, her face heating at the way Miss Vi was embarrassing a grown man. Josiah deserved to be treated with respect. His mental illness didn't mean he should be spoken to like a child.

But to her surprise, Josiah gave Miss Vi a sheepish nod and walked into the diner.

"Come on, now," Miss Vi said, "let's go sit with your sister and get you something to eat. When was the last time you ate, anyway? You're nothing but skin and bones. Abel!" she called as she sat down one stool away from Yasmin's spot. "This young man needs a nourishing meal right away." She turned to Yasmin. "What did you order?"

"Shrimp and grits," Yasmin said faintly, and glanced up at Josiah, an apology in her eyes.

To her surprise, his lips were twitching. He sat down on the empty stool between them and folded his hands.

Something in his posture and his smile made her think of their childhood. Josiah had always been Mensa-level smart, but maybe because his mind was on bigger things, he'd disliked the mundane details of selecting clothes and washing dishes and shaving.

Having Miss Vi tell him where to go and what to eat might actually be okay with him, not because he was sick, but because he was Josiah.

Rita clipped an order on the round metal spinner and came over to them. She was smiling, too. "Coffee for you two?"

Miss Vi frowned. "I'll have coffee with some creamer, but he—" she nodded sideways at Josiah "—he should have some milk."

"Coffee," Josiah corrected.

"Two coffees it is, then," Rita said, and turned toward the coffeepot.

Once they had their coffee in front of them and Miss Vi had ordered eggs and toast, Yasmin propped her cheek on her elbow and looked at Josiah and Miss Vi. "What's going on, anyway?"

"Do you want to tell her, or shall I?"

Josiah inclined his head slightly toward Miss Vi.

She frowned at him. "Fine, then. He'd worked himself back into one of those old window seats, the ones that are shut off? With a pile of books. Today is early closing day, and we came close to locking him up in the library until tomorrow morning!"

"What were you doing, Joe?" Yasmin asked.

"Research," he said.

"Research on what?"

"How to disappear, that's what," Miss Vi said.

"Disappear?" Yasmin didn't understand. "Like, some kind of magic trick?" She remembered when Josiah had gone through a magic trick phase, but that was back when he was about ten.

"Disappear as in, get new IDs and anonymous safe-deposit boxes and remove all internet traces of you."

"What? Joe!" She grabbed his forearm. "You can never do that. Think of how much I'd miss you. Think of Mom!"

Josiah looked at her and something flashed in his eyes. He reached out and patted her arm, looking sorrowful. Then he looked away.

Yasmin's heart went straight to her throat and stayed there as she stared at her brother. Up until now, while she'd been worried about Joe and what he might have done, there had been a part of her that knew he couldn't have harmed the man in the car.

Now, suddenly, the weight of evidence shifted.

Because why would Josiah want to disappear? He'd always been eccentric, but he liked people and he loved Safe Haven. He was accepted here, admired because of his smarts, his occasional unusualness tolerated.

If he wanted to leave Safe Haven, then maybe he'd done something wrong. It hardly seemed possible, but maybe he'd actually struck the blow that had ended up killing the man in the car.

A deep chill shuddered through Yasmin. She propped her head on her hand and looked sideways at Joe. *Was* he a killer?

Do it now. Do it!

Rita drew in a breath, picked up the coffeepot and carried it over to the end of the counter. Her hand shook as she refilled Liam's coffee cup, to the point where she spilled a little onto the table. "I'll clean that up," she murmured, and made her escape.

She needed to talk to Liam. When he'd come in today and sat by himself, she'd decided she had to approach him.

Liam was the friendliest of the three O'Dwyer brothers, and the one Rita knew best due to his frequent visits to the diner. Plus, he was in law enforcement, an investigator. He was the most in tune with missing people and crime and foster care, on a professional level.

He was the one she needed to tell about the possibility of her connection to him and his brothers.

She took a couple of more breaths and returned to wipe up the coffee she'd spilled. *There's something I need to discuss with you.* No. *Do you have a minute later today?* No.

She looked at him, opening her mouth to force the words out, and then shut it again. He was staring down the counter to where Yasmin, her brother and Miss Vi from the library were having a serious conversation. Rita looked that way, too, and saw that Yasmin seemed upset. Josiah wore his usual placid expression, and Miss Vi—dear creature that she was—seemed to be in full-on lecture mode.

"Why don't you go see if she needs any help?" The words were out of Rita's mouth before she could stop and assess the wisdom of a waitress giving advice to a grown, professional man.

A grown man who might be her son, true, but he didn't know that. "Sorry," she said. "Not my business."

He smiled up at her. "Not a bad idea, though, actually." He pushed away his blue-plate special half-finished, took another sip of coffee.

The door of the diner opened and Buck Mulligan, one of the other cops and Rita's least favorite, came in.

Liam's fist tightened on the napkin he was holding, crumpling it. He glared openly as Mulligan walked over to the group at the counter.

Mulligan brushed back his hair and checked himself in the mirror behind the counter. He thought he was a ladies' man who appealed to everyone, but the truth was, he was a little too smooth and women saw that, smart women at least.

He approached the group and spoke, low. Yasmin answered, but she looked even more upset, her smile forced.

Liam stood. "Sorry I didn't drink the coffee. Okay with you if I pay at the register?"

"Sure thing. And I'll put your coffee in a to-go cup." She was ashamed of the relief that washed over her. No chance to talk to Liam today; he was in a hurry, involved in other things.

Another day would go by without Rita doing anything to discover the truth about her past. Norma would strangle her.

She needed to make progress, and the huge, obvious step was to do research and interviewing and find out whether the O'Dwyer boys were, indeed, hers. It wouldn't be an easy conversation and she didn't expect them to embrace her with open arms. After all, if they were hers, she'd walked out on them.

But she needed to know who she was, and if she'd left three boys as all the evidence suggested, then they needed to know more about their past, as well. It couldn't have been easy for them to have lost their mother.

Or been abandoned, she thought, criticizing herself. Had she abandoned her children? What kind of woman did that?

Have compassion for yourself, Norma kept telling her. Rita wasn't the kind of person to abandon a child now, and she probably hadn't been earlier, either. Something terrible must have happened to cause it.

Although her kids probably wouldn't see it that way. To a child, abandonment was abandonment.

Liam walked over to the register, right next to where Yasmin's group was sitting, and Rita followed from behind the counter to run the register. Beyond her own racing thoughts, she was fascinated by the curious drama playing out among the younger people.

Liam nodded at Buck, but the man ignored him and went back to whatever he was saying to Yasmin.

Liam's mouth tightened and he handed Rita a twenty without looking at her, still watching the conversation unfold. They could hear a few little snatches: *need to follow up* and *a few more questions.*

Yasmin looked stressed, talking past Josiah.

Rita could read the indecision on Liam's face. He wanted to get involved. And it was clear as day he had feelings for Yasmin. But it looked like Mulligan had the upper hand somehow.

Her heart squeezed. She should have known Liam enough to offer advice and counsel, but she'd missed all his growing-up years and she didn't know what he was like. She had wisdom, but not wisdom he could trust.

She'd missed out on so much. And worse, so had he.

How had he been raised? She knew all three brothers had gone into foster care, separately: how had Liam's family treated him? Had he felt loved? Pain and sorrow wrapped their tentacles around her and tightened.

She caught a signal from the corner of her eye: Jimmy, frowning at her. It took a minute for her to realize that he was frowning as a boss and not a potential romantic partner. She had customers at the counter.

She waved an apology at him and hurried over to the counter to pour coffee and take orders.

And that was one of the perils of being in a romantic relationship, or sort of, with your boss. Her personal life, her worries about her past, were affecting her work, but she didn't want to ask for lenience. It would seem like she was getting special favors.

Anyway, the drama unfolding between Liam, Mulligan and Yasmin's family—who were all arguing, more heatedly now—wasn't her business. She was just the waitress.

She wrote down orders and brought ketchup and extra cream, served up burgers and fries, poured refills of sweet tea. All of it automatic, robotic, without her usual banter with the customers. She caught Jimmy frowning at her again.

But she couldn't whip herself into anything but

rote workmanship, not today. Not given her shameful feeling that she'd evaded, once again, the truth about herself.

CHAPTER NINE

THREE DAYS LATER, on a Friday afternoon, Liam tossed a stick across Ma Dixie's yard and watched Rio run for it. He was thankful for the day off, for the cool dankness of the rich bayou air, the way it refrigerated the August heat. The chickadees' *fee-be, fee-be* sounded from the sweet gum and cypress trees, and the earthen, leafy smell tickled his nose.

"That's it, the dog needs to use up a little energy before we can work on training." Pudge LeFrost sat on a wooden chair, tilted back against one of the small cottage's stilts.

Rocky ran alongside Rio, basically chasing the stick himself. "Same principle with the boy," Pudge added, grinning his easy grin. "Fostering kids like we do, we know to keep 'em running all day. A tired kid is a good kid."

Liam nodded. "Thanks for taking the time to help us."

"Ain't me who's got a busy day," Pudge said.

"You're the one what's climbing the police department's career ladder."

"Not real fast, these days." Liam looked around at the rich, green world and his shoulders loosened. Here, he could be himself.

He hadn't grown up at the cabin belonging to Ma Dixie and now to Pudge as well, but he'd spent a lot of time here. His brother Sean was the one Ma Dixie had fostered, whereas Liam had grown up with a different family in the town of Safe Haven. But Ma's huge heart had had space for Sean's brothers, and she'd offered an open invitation for them to visit as often as they wanted. As a result, he and Cash had spent a lot of time paddling canoes in and out of the bayou, making sure they hid from Ma the fact that they were smoking cigarettes or sneaking a few beers.

He still felt welcomed by that open invitation, which was why he'd thought of bringing Rocky and Rio out here in advance of Ma's weekly Friday night supper. Pudge was a genius with animals—and kids—and if anyone could tame down Rio's wildness without breaking his spirit, it was Pudge.

He'd hesitated a bit before inviting Yasmin to join him and Rocky and Rio. Seeing Buck at her house the other night had kicked up all his old jealousies. But, he'd reminded himself, she couldn't help it that Buck was the one investigating the stranger's death.

Now, looking back through the window, he saw Yasmin and Ma talking comfortably, standing together over the counter, chopping something. The cabin was small and cooled only with fans and swamp coolers. Yasmin had grown up in so much more affluent circumstances; he liked that she was able to spend time at Ma's humble place and genuinely enjoy herself.

"Okay, boys, time to work." Pudge heaved himself upright—no easy feat, considering that he weighed more than three hundred pounds—and held up a small bag that had been tucked into the pocket of his massive overalls. "This here's the key to good training."

"What is it?" Rocky asked.

Instead of answering, Pudge held the bag out to the boy. "Smell it."

Rocky did, and then made a show of falling down on the ground and rolling around, gagging. "Ugh! That's foul! What is that?"

"Gator," Pudge said with equanimity. "Dogs like meat, and there ain't nothing tastes so good to them as gator."

He proceeded to teach them how to make Rio sit, stay and come when called. It was slow going; Rio was good-natured but almost completely without discipline. "What do you think?" Liam asked after about twenty minutes, feeling ashamed of his dog. "Is he a lost cause?"

"No animal's a lost cause." Pudge stuck a wad of chewing tobacco into his mouth. "Every dog learns at a different pace. If he's had a bad experience, he's not going to learn as fast. Same if he's scared."

He produced another bag of treats. "Tell you what. Let's run through each of his commands again and try to have him succeed once. As soon as he does, we'll give him a break."

Rocky did it, calling out commands to Rio in the firm voice Pudge had suggested. Finally, Rio went through the sequence: sit-stay-come.

"And, that's a wrap," Pudge said, rubbing Rio behind the ears. "Go throw a couple of sticks into the water, boy. Let the dog chase it. He'll love that."

As the two ran away, both Liam and Pudge watched them. "Something's happened to that boy," Pudge remarked. "He's in pain."

Liam stared at the man. "What do you mean? Physical pain?"

"No. Pain right here." Pudge gave his chest a double pat. "I can see it in his eyes. Seen it a lot, in the kids Ma fosters." Then he looked up and his face broke into a wide smile. "Well, would you look what popped up out of the swamp."

Liam looked in the direction Pudge was pointing. There, coming along the road, was a silver sports car, top down.

His brother Cash. The star of the show had made it after all.

Spectacularly successful, Cash had an easy personality and had always been the best-looking of the three O'Dwyer brothers. There'd even been a time when Liam had thought Yasmin preferred Cash to him.

That could happen again, since Liam and Yasmin weren't together. Cash wouldn't have horned in on Liam outright, but an ex was fair game.

And then Liam got a grip on himself. Jealousy and competition were something he needed to grow out of. He was genuinely proud of his brother's success. And thankful for his generosity, which had made a huge difference to Liam at an important time.

Cash bypassed the house and came around to where Pudge and Liam were. He bent down to shake Pudge's hand, then stood and held out an arm. "Little brother," he said, and they man-hugged. "You chief yet?"

"No." His answer was sharper than it had been with Pudge, but come on. Everyone kept asking him about the painful subject of his advancement—or lack thereof—at the police station. It got old.

Cash shrugged. "Being at the top can be lonely," he said. "Being one of the players instead of the manager can be a really good thing."

Both Pudge and Liam stared at Cash, clad in impeccably designed dress pants and a starched white shirt, sleeves neatly folded up, shoes that even Liam could tell were expensive leather, not made for bayou walking.

"Something you want to tell us?" Pudge asked.

"Like that you've killed off my real brother and

taken over his body?" Liam joked. "You've *always* been about success."

Cash shrugged. "It gets old," he said, and then got very focused on his phone. An action that was probably fake, because cell reception was terrible out here.

It pulled Liam right out of his own concerns. Cash had a ton of money, a revolving door of gorgeous women and an ocean's worth of pressure on him. And he'd grown up the same as Liam. Their abusive father and lost mother might have even affected him more, because he was old enough to remember more of the bad things.

Liam punched Cash lightly in the arm. "You need anything, you know I've got your back, right?"

"Thanks. I'm fine."

When they went inside to eat, some kind of conspiracy between Pudge and Ma and Cash made Liam end up sitting right next to Yasmin, so close their shoulders touched at the small wooden table. There was seafood gumbo, and pulled pork, with sides of collards and corn bread and baked mac and cheese. After eating until they were stuffed, they all somehow found room for Ma's peach cobbler. Cash told stories of his high-living business deals that had Rocky and Ma's foster son wide-eyed, and Ma and Pudge shaking their heads.

Liam watched Yasmin as she dug into the food and laughed at all the right places. There was a fine sheen of sweat on her face, which gleamingly revealed how little makeup she wore. She'd pulled her long curls back into a ponytail, with some kind of braid going along one side. It made her look more like she had in school, young and innocent. For once, the tension had left her shoulders and her eyes were clear.

He was glad he'd brought her. Ma's place was good for the soul. Yasmin carried too much and deserved a chance to kick back and relax with good people.

Only problem was, he was having a hard time keeping his hands to himself, especially when she threw her head back, laughing at one of Pudge's silly jokes. The long column of her throat seemed to beg to be kissed. When she pulled her shirt away from her chest and stomach, flapping it a little for air, he wanted to fan her, make her comfortable.

Make her happy.

And those were thoughts he didn't need to be having. She'd made it clear she wasn't interested in a relationship, and she'd dumped him for someone else, someone who was still interested if Liam could believe the evidence of his own eyes. He sucked in bayou-warm air and ate some more cobbler, trying to find another focus for his thoughts.

Ma Dixie gave it to him. "'Bout time to be thinking about school, ain't it?" She looked from her foster son to Rocky. "What grade are you in, son? My Dustin, here, is going into sixth." She ruffled Dustin's hair.

And that right there was what made Ma a great foster parent. Every kid who lived here, whether for three weeks or three years, was considered wholly hers.

"When does school start?" Cash asked.

"Starts two weeks from Monday," Pudge said. "These boys better enjoy their last couple weeks of freedom."

"Dustin's sisters, Desiree and DeeDee, they're already doing cross-country camp," Ma added. "Those girls are fast as the wind."

"You think you'll get involved in any sports?" Liam asked Rocky.

Rocky's lower lip stuck out, and his body went rigid. "I ain't goin' to school here."

Yasmin cleared her throat. "He'll be starting seventh grade. What's the school like here, Dustin?"

"I ain't goin'," Rocky said, louder.

Dustin ignored him and shrugged. "It's school. But it's not so bad. C'mon," he added, looking at Rocky, "let's get fishing poles and take the canoe out."

Rocky seemed to debate whether to stay and argue with the adults or go be a kid. Being a kid won. He stood, and both boys practically ran toward the back door.

"Don't you want to stay and eat your…" Yasmin looked at the two boys' already-empty plates. "Oh."

"Boys!" Pudge said, and there was an authority in

his usually good-natured voice that made them stop instantly and turn back. "What do you say to Ma?"

"May I be excused?" Dustin asked.

"That was a real good dinner," Rocky added.

"You boys go on out and have fun," she said, her smile wide. "But stay where you can see the lights from the house, you hear? Don't go off deep into the swamp."

"We won't," they chorused as they ran out the door.

Liam glanced over at Cash, and they grinned at each other. Liam figured Cash was remembering the same experiences he was. They'd done plenty of canoeing and fishing when they'd visited Sean out here as boys, just about Rocky's and Dustin's ages. And they hadn't stayed where they could see the lights, but the directive did keep them closer to Ma's place than they'd have stayed otherwise.

Cash's face went serious, and he put his hand over Ma's chubby, freckled one. "You were so good to us when we were that age. Still are. I want you to know I appreciate it."

Liam met Pudge's eyes. What was up with Cash? He was the least sentimental of all of them, at least normally.

Ma just smiled and turned her hand over to squeeze Cash's. "You're a good boy, Cash. You might not always show it, but there's a heart of gold in there."

Cash snorted. "You're the only one who thinks so."

Then he stood. "Here's what I think. Ma did all the cooking, and Pudge has been training that mutt of Liam's. And I'm lazy. So I think Ma and Pudge and me should go sit outside and watch the sunset while these youngsters—" he pointed at Liam and Yasmin "—do all the cleanup."

Ma opened her mouth to protest, but Pudge spoke up. "Great idea." He struggled to his feet and held out a hand to Ma. "Come on, you heard the boy."

Two minutes later, Liam and Yasmin were alone in the kitchen, with a tableful of dirty dishes.

Liam found he didn't mind at all. Even when a text from Cash pinged on his phone. You're welcome.

DON'T BE AN IDIOT, Yasmin told herself as she carried dishes from the table to the old-fashioned, white ceramic kitchen sink. *He brought you along because he knew he needed help with Rocky. That's all.*

In fact, she'd been shocked when Liam had asked her if she wanted to come out to Ma Dixie's. She'd never been, even when they'd dated; when she'd asked about it, Liam had downplayed the occasions, saying they were too casual, too country for her. She hadn't been confident enough, then, to argue, even though she'd longed for an invitation. She had heard for years about Ma and her Friday night suppers. Liam and his brothers had spent a lot of time around here. It had defined their teenage years and had been a respite from the tough love of Liam's foster family and the rigors of school.

Of course, she knew Ma and Pudge from church and events in town. But to see them in their natural element, here in the bayou, to taste that traditional cooking and to hear Pudge playing his ukulele, it was frankly wonderful.

She had been worried sick about Joe all week, ever since she'd learned that he was researching ways to disappear. Tonight, though, he was helping Miss Vi with the kids' chess club and Yasmin could relax without worries.

Thanks to Liam, who must have seen that she needed it.

Being protective, helping others, that was just who Liam was. He'd do the same for anyone; it wasn't about him inviting her out here because he had special feelings for her. That had been over long ago, if it had ever even been real. Sometimes, it didn't feel like it had.

Was it wrong to pretend, though? To allow the idea of doing dishes with him to make her happy?

If this was what she got, as happiness—and she was pretty sure that this was all she'd get—she would take it.

She carried two half-empty bowls, one in each hand, over to the kitchen counter. "Do you know where she keeps Tupperware? Or does she even have it?"

Liam laughed. "Oh, does she ever. She never

throws anything away." He opened a cupboard that was completely full of neatly stacked plastic containers, recycled from whatever they'd originally held: Cool Whip, or lard, or sour cream.

"Sweet." She pulled out containers and spooned the leftover corn pudding and gumbo into them, then found space for them in Ma's crowded fridge.

When she turned to go for another load, he was right behind her, reaching past, his cologne smelling spicy, combined with the scent of him. Liam had the image of being a good guy, almost a Boy Scout. But there was another side to him, a dark, passionate side, and she'd had the privilege and the thrill of seeing it.

Her blood pressure shot up.

Could he tell?

His eyes met hers, held. Hidden messages, nonverbal ones, seemed to pass between them.

Yeah, he could tell. No doubt about it.

She drew in a breath. "'Scuse me," she said, and sidled past him.

She tried to focus on the mismatched crockery that somehow looked perfect on Ma's rough-hewn table. Then she looked out the window, hoping the nature that surrounded them would make her feel cool and serene.

Out in the bayou, Rocky and Dustin paddled by, Rio in the middle of their canoe, mouth lolling open. They were staying close, which was good. She wasn't sure Rocky could swim.

Liam was scraping dishes and then plunking them into a sinkful of soapy water. "Sorry we're putting you to work here," he said. "No dishwasher. It's a big job."

"I'm glad to help." She scolded herself for the fact that she sounded breathless. "Let me bring you the rest of the dishes, and then I'll dry."

When she slid the last dish into the soapy water, her hands brushed against his. They were slippery with soap and the water was warm, and even that mild touch made her go soft and lazy inside. She leaned into him a little, then jerked upright, her face heating.

She who never relaxed wanted to collapse and let a man care for her.

He drew in a breath and took a step away, pulling out his hands. "Sorry."

He was protective, always had been, about anything physical. Even when they'd dated last year, he'd wanted to take care of her. He hadn't pushed her into intimacy even though she'd known he desired her. Or at least, she thought so.

She watched as he washed more dishes, whistling, ignoring her.

Maybe she'd had it all wrong.

They worked together in silence for almost an hour, getting the kitchen cleaned up and shiny, all the dishes put neatly away. She even swept the floor. But finally, it was over and there was no more to do, no more reason to be in a room alone with Liam. She sighed.

He looked over at her. "Come sit on the porch a minute?" He nodded toward the now-deserted front porch.

"Sure." Pathetic how quickly she'd responded. It must be super obvious that she wanted to be with him.

And you can't be with him, she reminded herself. She'd made her decision about kids, and she wasn't going to keep torturing herself with what she couldn't have.

She followed him out onto the moonlit porch, where an old-fashioned glider covered with flowered vinyl offered the only seating. Where could she sit, except right beside him? And it was warm—she felt *very* warm—but there was a cooling breeze.

Cash had stuck his head into the kitchen half an hour ago, saying he was leaving. Rio and Dustin and Rocky were back in Dustin's room, one of the only two rooms in the house with air-conditioning. From Ma and Pudge's open bedroom window, they could hear the sound of a television, some sitcom with a laugh track. Apparently Ma and Pudge liked it, because their real-life chuckles sounded along with the tinny canned laughs from the show.

He put his arm across the back of the glider. Not around her, she reminded herself. Across the back of the glider. "I used to sit out here every time I came," Liam said. "Listen to the bayou."

She paid attention to the nature sounds, then: the *peep-peep-peep* of frogs, the call of a night owl, the splash of flopping fish, the gentle lap of water. "I can see why you like it," she said. "Josiah would love it here."

"Should I have invited him?"

She shook her head. "Sometime, maybe. Not today." Then her face heated. She didn't mean to imply that they'd have a future in which he'd invite her relatives to his favorite places.

They didn't have that kind of future. Could never have it.

"How's he doing?" Liam turned a little to look at her, his knee brushing hers.

Something about the dark night and the friendly natural sounds of the bayou gave her the desire to confide. "He's up and down," she said. "He likes his job at the library, and he loves teaching kids to play chess. He's glad to be back in Safe Haven."

"Sounds like there's a 'but,'" Liam said.

She nodded. "At times, he's really struggling. It breaks my heart." Her throat tightened on the last word.

"It's not my business, but I've wondered whether he's in some kind of treatment." Liam leaned back and looked out at the darkening water. "Is he able to get the help he needs here?"

Yasmin drew in a breath. "I really can't tell you his diagnosis. That's his business to share. But you can probably make an educated guess after spending a few hours around him."

"Well, he hears voices and has delusions," Liam said. "Sounds like schizophrenia."

Yasmin looked down at her knees and gave a tiny nod. "There are just so many prejudices about that disease," she said. "Josiah is a good man. And yes, he has good doctors. Mostly in Charleston, since that's where he was living when he got his diagnosis. But there are good people up here as well and they're willing to consult with his primary doctors."

"Medication can help a lot, right?"

"Yes, but only if he takes it."

"Is that an issue?"

She hesitated. She longed to confide in Liam, who had such good sense and knew her family. But at the same time, he was an officer of the law. If he knew that Josiah didn't always take his meds, what kind of conclusions might he draw?

Better to focus on Josiah's good side, or one of them—he had a lot. "When he takes his meds, he's a little more, I don't know, *muted* than he would normally be. But he does really well then. He's a genius with technology. Miss Vi is thrilled to have him helping update their systems at the library."

"Figures," Liam said. "He always was crazy smart." Then he mock-punched himself in the head. "Sorry. Poor choice of words."

"It happens." Yasmin shifted on the glider, set it rocking with one foot and tucked the other foot up under her. "I think Joe wants to leave, move away," she said, surprising herself. She hadn't had anyone to talk about it with, that idea that Josiah wanted to disappear. He hadn't been willing to discuss it with her, and she was terrified of what that might mean. Was he hiding something? Trying to escape what he'd done?

"Seems like he shouldn't be away from family." Liam clasped his hands around a lifted knee. "You're really doing a great job of helping him. It can't be easy."

His praise warmed Yasmin's heart, chipping away at the hard lump of constant criticism and self-doubt that seemed to reside there. "It's an honor to take care of him. But yes, it can be hard sometimes. And he feels bad, like he's a burden."

"I'm sorry you're going through that." Around them, the sound of peeping frogs got louder and louder, swelling into a chorus. The air was cooling now, a slight breeze bringing the fragrance of oleander flowers. It only seemed natural for Liam to shuffle closer on the glider. To let his arm curve around her shoulders.

Yasmin's breath whooshed out of her. Talking with Liam about her brother had made her feel vulnerable, but also relieved. Less alone. She remembered when she could share anything with Liam, knowing that he would always have her back. Such a wonderful feeling, especially after Josiah had stopped being able to be that rock and that support to her.

Now, Liam turned to meet her gaze head-on. His hand rose to brush back a curl that had escaped her ponytail. "I like your hairstyle," he said unexpectedly, his voice a tone deeper than usual. "Reminds me of the old days, when we were in school."

"In other words, I look like a kid?" Her words came out breathy, and she couldn't take her eyes off him.

Slowly, Liam shook his head. "Oh, no, Yasmin. You don't look like a kid at all." His eyes flickered down to her mouth, then back to her eyes.

Yasmin's heart fluttered like a terrified bird. Her stomach, her chest, all that was inside her felt squeezed by warm hands, melted.

How she wanted this. This opportunity to talk to Liam in a low, intimate voice. To share the smiles and glances of lovers. To feel that sense of promise, that there was something happy and bright in their future together.

She tried to grasp on to the reasons why this couldn't happen. How she didn't dare to have children, because the risk of them developing a mental illness was so high. Not only because of Josiah, although that was the main thing, of course. But also because of her mother's issues: anxiety at the least, possibly depression and bipolar disorder, as well.

More conditions that had a genetic link.

As if all of that wasn't enough, Yasmin knew she

wasn't past the safe age herself. Women developed schizophrenia later than men in many cases. What if she got into a relationship and then started having delusions and hearing voices?

It was hard enough taking care of her brother, her blood relative. She owed him and bore the burden gladly. But she couldn't expect a romantic partner to do the same for her, wouldn't want someone to.

Wouldn't want Liam to. He had so much promise, and he had already suffered so much in life. He didn't need a girlfriend with mental health issues. That just wouldn't be fair to him.

"Hey," he said. He stroked her cheek, looking into her eyes, his own blue eyes concerned. "What sinkhole are you going down? You look like you just saw six ghosts."

"Maybe I did." Not the kind of ghosts he meant, but ghosts of a possible future.

If she let things go where they were headed right now, if she let him kiss her, she wasn't sure she would have the strength to push him away again. Doing it once had nearly killed her. Maybe she could be strong enough, but only if she put an end to this before getting closer. "I think we should go."

His head tilted to one side, his eyes steady on her. "Do you really think so?"

She hesitated, clung for just a moment to the possibility of not being the responsible one, the caretaker, the one who took charge of things and tried to make everything work out. She could let herself do

what she wanted to do every now and then, couldn't
she? She could be spontaneous, go with her emotions, her heart.

But no. Her duty was clear. Her life was about
taking care of her family, not about indulging in
something pleasurable for now, but ultimately dangerous to someone she cared about. Liam was too
good of a man, had suffered too many of life's blows
already, to be shackled with Yasmin's issues. "Yes,"
she said firmly. "I really think so."

CHAPTER TEN

SATURDAY MORNING, Liam drove around Safe Haven almost appreciating the day shift. It was 10:00 a.m. and when he stopped his car near the water, he could hear Rip Martin's harmonica playing a wild, sad tune. The man was walking along the boardwalk, probably looking for a spot to set up his bucket and try to get the tourists to give him some pity money. No permit, of course. But Liam hated to cite him. His music added to the good feel of the town.

So did the raucous, staccato sound of the seagulls, rising in intensity. He looked down the boardwalk and saw the cause: a little girl and her parents had stepped outside of Biddie's Bed and Breakfast and were throwing bread to them. They must be inlanders, unaware that their simple action would bring a cast of thousands and their accompanying mess. Biddie hurried out to warn them, wearing a big old-fashioned apron, spatula in hand. Liam smiled at the sight, but he was glad. Wouldn't want the kid to have a seagull-related trauma.

The water lapped against the dock pilings and the salt-fishy smell of the docks grounded him. He'd spent way too much time thinking about Yasmin and how she had started to let him kiss her, then pulled back, last night at Ma Dixie's.

Why did she always pull back, when he was pretty sure she was as attracted to him as he was to her? Was she still not ready for a serious relationship, the excuse she'd given before?

A call came in on his handheld and he turned it down to hear better over the static. It was Willa Jean, their dispatcher. "Robbery in progress. 10-14."

"10-14?" He couldn't have heard that right. Citizen holding suspect? On a Saturday morning?

He jogged back to the cruiser and climbed in, listening. Perp was described as a teenager, Caucasian, about five foot seven…brown hair… Liam got a sinking feeling. He knew a kid of that description.

He hit the lights and sped through town, peripherally noting a couple of dog walkers, people coming out of the grocery store, Rita and Jimmy arguing outside the diner.

Could Rocky really be stealing from the only exclusive men's store in Safe Haven? And why?

He got to Mitchell's Men's Shop, walked in and froze. There was Mitch, weapon pulled, holding it on Rocky, who was literally quaking with fear. The sight was incongruous in the midst of neat rows of folded sweaters on glossy wooden tables and a couple of serious-looking mannequins in golf attire.

"Okay, Mitch, I'll take it from here," Liam said.

"You won't let him get away?" Mitch, dressed in an impeccable white shirt and dark trousers, every hair in place, nonetheless had sweat beaded on his forehead and was breathing hard.

"Nope. You can put the gun away."

Mitch did, slowly enough to make it clear he was reluctant.

Liam's shoulders loosened. "Thanks. Now, what's this all about?"

Mitch's mouth settled into a frown. Rocky slumped against the wall of the store, his breath coming fast.

"Mitch? Rocky? Anyone want to tell me what went down here?"

"He stole two of my most expensive shirts, that's what he did!" Mitch put his hands on his hips and glared at Rocky. "Ruined them with his dirty hands. I should never have let a kid like him in."

A kid like him. Liam looked at Rocky in time to see the kid's face crumple, and his own heart squeezed. He knew what it was to be considered riffraff.

"Can you describe what you saw?" he asked. "Rocky, sit down a minute. Right there on that bench, where I can see you."

"I don't…" Mitch looked at Liam and trailed off.

He could guess what Mitch had been about to say: that Rocky was too dirty to sit on the pale canvas bench. Well, too bad: that wasn't true. The boy was a little unkempt, but thanks to Yasmin's efforts, he showered every day and his clothes were clean. Liam stared Mitch down until the other man looked away.

"I was up there working on a window display," Mitch said, gesturing toward the front of the store. "I'm pretty involved in what I'm doing, and when I look up, there's this kid running out the door. Looking a lot fatter than when he came in, so I knew he'd stuffed something into his shirt. I chased after him."

"With your gun," Liam said drily.

"Scared the socks off me," Rocky contributed. "He said he was gonna kill me if I didn't stop. For a couple of shirts!"

"Shirts that cost more than you'll ever be able to afford." Mitch crossed his arms and leaned back against the counter. "Yeah, so I did threaten him. He stole my property, from my property. And you'd better believe I'm thinking about making a full report."

Liam sighed. He'd seen plenty of teen shoplifting—though rarely from a place like Mitchell's Men's Shop—and most storekeepers were more than happy to simply lodge a complaint, scold the kid and get their items back. Mitch, though, was a different type.

He ordered Rocky to stay put and then used his tablet to get a statement from Mitch. He made sure to listen carefully and check every detail. Sometimes, just feeling heard made people drop their complaints. Not that he wanted to influence Mitch, not really; Rocky needed to face the consequences of what he'd done. But Liam definitely had a soft spot for the child and didn't want to add legal consequences to his already tumultuous life.

"Rocky, I'm going to have to take you on into the station," he said. He really ought to cuff and search the boy, too, but he wasn't going to. He was, however, going to need to call Rocky's guardian.

Yasmin.

The thought of talking with her hyped up Liam's heartbeat, which wasn't good. Especially when his news wasn't exactly what she wanted to hear.

But was Yasmin really his official guardian? Liam was pretty sure that the arrangement with Rocky's mom was unofficial, which meant trouble could ensue.

Well, they'd deal with that when it happened. This was too serious to be brushed under the rug, especially with Mitch's attitude. And even though fostering a child without official paperwork wasn't exactly kosher, it was what the Safe Haven community did. Always had, and Liam hoped it always would.

"I'm too busy to deal with this right now," Mitch said. "It's going to have to wait until my sales associate arrives at 2:00. And I'll decide then whether I want to press charges."

"Not a problem." A relief, actually, since Mitch was likely to calm down if he took a few hours to think about it. "I'll get this young man's statement once his guardian comes in, and talk to you later, and we'll figure things out. Meanwhile—" he turned to Rocky "—do you have anything you want to say?" Hopefully, Rocky knew how to apologize. The kid had decent manners overall, so Liam suspected that he did.

Rocky stood and walked toward the door of the shop. When he passed the counter where Mitch stood, he said "sorry" in a sulky tone.

Not good enough, but Liam could identify with the kid well enough not to push it.

Mitch narrowed his eyes. "You'll pardon me if I don't believe that."

"Come on," Liam said, and held the door open, putting a hand on Rocky's shoulder to make sure he didn't take off.

They drove to the station in silence. Liam resisted the urge to lecture the boy, because he could tell from his expression that Rocky was about to lose it. Nothing more humiliating than crying in front of a man you didn't know well.

He got Rocky into a holding room—the only holding room—with Willa Jean watching him. Then he called Yasmin.

"Hey, problem," he said as soon she answered. "Rocky got in some trouble. Can you come down to the station?"

"Is he okay?"

That quick question told Liam how Yasmin felt about Rocky: motherly. She was more concerned

about his well-being than about her own undoubtedly busy schedule.

"He's fine. A little upset. I'll need to release him
into your custody or keep him here, but I'd rather—"

"I'll be right there," she interrupted.

That was Yasmin, and Liam's heart seemed to
warm and reach toward her, which really wasn't
good. She had dumped him once, and she wasn't
giving him any sense now that they could have any
kind of relationship. He didn't need to be falling
for her again.

Didn't need to be thinking about kissing her
again.

He went into the holding room and told Willa
Jean she could go back to her desk. Then he sat
across the table from Rocky. He wanted to talk to
him, to treat him like a kid he cared about rather
than a criminal, but he had to follow protocol.

Besides, some uncomfortable silence might make
Rocky think. He filled out a couple of forms on his
tablet, listened to the buzz of Safe Haven's downtown outside the barred window and watched Rocky
from the corner of his eye.

The boy kept licking his lips and looking around
the barren, beige-painted room. He wiped sweat
from his forehead with the sleeve of his shirt.
Cleared his throat a couple of times.

Hmm. Trying not to cry. And Liam was glad that
Rocky took the consequences of his infraction seriously. He'd seen kids slide down in that very same

chair and fall asleep, waiting for a parent or guardian to come bail them out of trouble.

A few minutes later there was a tap on the door. Willa Jean. "Ms. Tanner is here."

"Send her in."

Yasmin burst through the door and marched over to Rocky. "Just exactly what do you think you're doing?"

"Hold on," Liam said. "I need to advise him of his rights." He did and was glad to see that Rocky was even more sobered by the official words.

As soon as he was done, Yasmin started in. "And again, I'd like to know what you thought you were going to accomplish."

"I…" Rocky shrugged his shoulders and put his head down on the desk.

"Oh no you don't." Yasmin lifted him up by the back of his shirt. "You sit up straight when I'm talking to you," she said. "This is unacceptable." Her voice was strong and stern, her stance dramatic, but Liam could see the tension in the lines bracketing her mouth. She was posturing to Rocky, but inside, she was upset.

Liam was, too. He'd thought they were making progress with the boy. "You know that stealing is a crime, right?" he asked Rocky.

"No duh," Rocky said. He was obviously going for nonchalance, but the anxiety in his brown eyes belied that effort.

Well, good. The kid needed to be scared. "Your

mom isn't here. Yasmin isn't your legal guardian. If you don't stay under the radar, you could end up in juvenile custody so fast you wouldn't know what hit you."

"No way." Rocky's head snapped toward Liam. "I ain't going to juvie. My mom couldn't find me there."

"It would be a lot harder," Liam agreed. "Not to mention a miserable experience with some of the toughest, meanest kids you've ever met. So what were you thinking, shoplifting from a store? That's not exactly keeping a low profile."

"It was just a couple of shirts," Rocky mumbled. "I didn't know the guy would see me."

"You probably didn't know he had a gun, either, or that he's quick to pull it out."

Rocky stared at the floor.

A thought flashed into Liam's mind, something Cash had said: something about how, if you love your work and do something important, it doesn't matter whether you're at the top. Well, Liam wasn't at the top in this police department, might not ever be. But he was maybe the only adult in town who could really understand what Rocky was going through. He'd spent a few uncomfortable hours in this police station, in this very holding room, when he'd been a rebellious teenager.

Yasmin sat down across from Rocky, reached out and grasped his hand. "What were you doing, anyway, stealing clothes from that pretentious store?"

"They were for school," Rocky mumbled, staring down at the table.

"For school?" Yasmin stared at Rocky, then glanced over at Liam. "You tried to steal stuff from Mitchell's Men's Shop to go to middle school?"

"I saw how nice those kids were dressed," Rocky said.

"What kids?" Yasmin tilted her head to one side, her expression puzzled.

Rocky sighed. "The ones I played basketball with."

"Oh." Yasmin looked over at Liam, understanding crossing her face. "I had him stay with Claire's nephews when I took my mom back to Charleston," she said. Then she turned back to Rocky. "Honey, those boys go to private school up North, so they wear uniforms. Even on their off days, they dress up. But nobody at the public schools down here dresses like they do."

"Dustin said the town kids make fun of how the country kids dress." Rocky's voice was defensive. "I didn't want people thinking I was a country kid."

Again, Liam could identify. Starting out in a new town, you wanted above all to fit in. To blend in, so that people didn't see you as an easy mark. If Rocky had thought he didn't have the right clothes, of course he'd try to rectify the situation. And undoubtedly, his pride wouldn't allow him to simply ask Yasmin or Liam for help. "Look," he said to the boy, "I can take you out to buy a few shirts and pairs of jeans before school starts."

"We're both glad to help you," Yasmin added, glancing at Liam. "You don't have to steal. Not ever."

An unspoken message arced between them. They'd make sure Rocky had the right clothes and backpack, whatever else he needed to make his days at Safe Haven Middle School go smoothly.

Liam had an odd sense of fate. If any two people in Safe Haven knew what it was to struggle to fit in at school, it was Liam and Yasmin. For them, it hadn't been about clothes, but the feelings were the same. They could both identify with Rocky, and moreover, identifying with Rocky, helping him, was bringing them closer together.

But he couldn't focus on that, on the appeal of it, because it was all too temporary. "We need to talk about how to handle the fact that Rocky's mom hasn't shown up yet," he said to Yasmin. "Maybe get some official paperwork started."

"She's coming to get me!" Rocky leaned forward, his voice suddenly intense. "I know she's coming to get me any day now."

"Have you had any contact with her?" Liam posed the question sharply and then watched Rocky for signs of lying.

Rocky's face fell and he shook his head. "Not since that letter. But I know she's coming back soon."

He glanced at Yasmin to find her looking at him. Once again, they communicated silently. They would work on making Yasmin his official guardian, just in case.

"In the meantime," Liam said, "we need to come up with a plan of restitution. You stole from Mitch's shop. How are you going to make that up to him?"

"I gave the stuff back," Rocky said.

"That's fine, but you still need to do something to apologize." Rocky's mouth opened like he was going to argue, and Liam held up a hand. "If you get this right, you may be able to avoid having him press charges. And that could mean you avoid the foster care system or even juvie. It's important."

"Could he do some work in the stockroom at the store?" Yasmin was frowning. "He could learn a little bit about what retail is like."

Liam looked at Rocky. Then, they both shook their heads at the same time. "I don't think Mitch is going to want help from Rocky," Liam said. "Nor that he'll be a willing mentor."

"He'll be holding a gun on me the whole time," Rocky said.

"Holding a gun on a child." Yasmin looked in the direction of Mitch's store, a murderous expression on her face.

"I talked to him some about it," Liam said, "and I'll talk some more. A gun and a temper like his don't go together. He has to get it under control."

"Good." Yasmin sighed. "Probably better for you

to talk to him than for me to try. I don't think I could stay all cool and collected." She rubbed a hand on Rocky's forearm. "He better not try anything like that again."

Rocky's eyebrows scrunched together as he studied Yasmin. Liam had to wonder whether his own mother stood up for him so staunchly. It seemed to be a surprise to the boy.

"But all that aside, we have to find a way for you to apologize. What about doing some weeding and trimming outside his store?" Yasmin looked at Rocky. "That way, you wouldn't have to be inside the store, and I know he likes the place to look immaculate."

"Or maybe hosing down the sidewalk and scrubbing it," Liam suggested.

"I don't know how to do any of that!" Rocky's fists clenched. "I gave the shirts back! Why do I have to do more?"

"It's a punishment, son," Liam said.

"To make you remember not to do anything like this again," Yasmin added.

They looked at each other, and there it was again: they were parenting Rocky together. At least for right now.

"I'll release him to your custody," Liam said, and they went out front to complete the forms, Rocky trailing behind and flopping into a metal chair. But suddenly, the door to the station burst open. Mitch marched in. "I got help at the store so I could see to this personally," he said. "I want full charges pressed against this young man. Apparently no one in town knows him. He's a drifter."

"He's *thirteen,* Mitch." Yasmin had stood and was facing Mitch while Liam kept Rocky quelled in a seat beside Willa Jean's desk. "You can't be a drifter at thirteen. He's staying with me for a little while. He's a friend of my family."

"*Your* family." Mitch rolled his eyes as if that was a condemnation in itself.

"That's right." A flash of pain crossed Yasmin's face and was gone as quickly as it had appeared.

Liam frowned. He'd always thought of Yasmin's family as upper crust, and they were definitely wealthy. Or they had been. And maybe they were a little eccentric, but he'd always thought they were respected in town.

Mitch spun on Liam. "I want to press charges against the boy."

Liam pulled out a chair. "Sit down, Mitch. Let's talk this over, and then I'll take a statement from you."

"Oh, you… Of course you'd want to do that. Always with the compromises. You're from the same low-life background yourself."

Liam's heart rate shot up and his fists clenched. He relaxed them and drew in a breath, exhaled. "Yes, I am. A lot of decent Safe Haven citizens cut me a break. That's why I'm on the right side of the law today."

Rocky stood, and both Liam and Yasmin moved to block his path of exit. But the boy squared his shoulders and faced Mitch. "I'm sorry for what I did," he said, his voice cracking a little. "I could… I could do some gardening work for you outside your store. Or wash the windows and sidewalk. To make it up to you."

Pride washed over Liam, and when he looked at Yasmin, she was nodding. "Good job, son," she said.

"You're not going to get yourself off the hook by pulling a few weeds," Mitch said. "I'm still going to press charges. I want this kid locked away. How do I start the paperwork?"

"You don't really want to do this, Mitch," Liam said.

"I sure do."

Yasmin crossed her arms over her chest, sparks seeming to shoot from her eyes. "That's gonna make a good story out at the club," she said. "Wealthy business owner refuses to accept apology from struggling teenager, presses charges for petty theft."

Mitch spun to face her. "You wouldn't dare sully my reputation."

"I'd be telling the simple truth. If it hurts, well… there's still time to change your attitude."

"You think I should accept having criminal activity against my store."

"I'm thinking you need a sense of perspective," she said. "Did you ever make a mistake? Have you ever been forgiven? Saved by a little bit of grace?"

Mitch looked from her, to Rocky, to Liam. All of them stood united against him. "I'm still going to think about this," he said, his voice as sulky as Rocky's had been earlier. "Speak to my attorney."

"That's your right," Liam said. "If you decide to press charges, you just give us a call."

"And meanwhile, he goes free?"

"With supervision," Yasmin said. "If you're not enthusiastic about his helping you out at the store, I'm sure the police station has some landscaping work that it needs done."

"A lot," Liam said. "But Mitch has first dibs on the boy's time."

Mitch glared. "I want nothing more to do with that child," he said, and spun toward the door. Just before going through it, he turned and glared at Liam. "Don't think I'll forget this when the time comes to make a decision for police chief. I have the feeling Buck Mulligan would have handled it very differently."

At which point Liam remembered: Mitch was on city council.

And he'd just become an enemy.

RITA FOLLOWED Norma into the summer madness party at Seaside Villages, face set in a frown.

She'd fought Norma on this one. She didn't like raucous events focused on drinking—which just went to show that she was getting old—and plus, it was way too hot. August in South Carolina was worlds away, hot worlds away, from summers in Maine. The little shopping area was thirty-five miles from Safe Haven, in a more touristy type of town, and Rita didn't see why they needed to come all the way out here when there were plenty of perfectly nice bars and restaurants in Safe Haven.

And besides, Norma couldn't stop bugging her about how she needed to make more progress on figuring out her past and how she needed to approach the men she suspected were her sons. She'd chickened out with Liam and she felt bad enough about that already. A whole evening of listening to why she was wrong, wrong, wrong didn't sound like a lot of fun.

But as soon as they went under the archway and inside the little complex of stores and restaurants, her spirits lifted a little. The sun was sinking lower into the sky, which meant the heat was letting up a little. A band played country music, but a peppy, modern kind Rita didn't mind.

Besides, Rita had made a plan to put Norma in her place but good, a plan to give her something to focus on aside from Rita and her issues. A plan involving a man. She couldn't wait until he showed up.

They strolled through a couple of shops that were open late, looking at the standard-issue beach art and jasmine-scented candles. Then, they came to a bohemian type of store that had all kinds of repurposed junk, the creations of local artists. The music of dozens of wind chimes set the mood for the outdoor part of the shop, while inside, incense and batik cloths and a display of brightly colored pillows and clothing created a hippie vibe that took Rita back.

Took her back, and she had the edges of a memory. But she wasn't going to try to dredge it up; she was just going to enjoy the fun, funky atmosphere. She even bought a hammered metal sun to put up on her apartment's little balcony.

In the big open area in front of the bandstand, long picnic tables encouraged everyone to mingle. Lights were strung up on poles, and people were laughing, talking and even dancing. All ages, little kids through seniors, so it wasn't actually just a bunch of wild drunks as she'd expected.

"That food smells pretty good," Norma said. "I'm going up to find me some deep-fried onions or a funnel cake before this evening is over."

"Smells to me like they roasted a pig. That's what I'm after." Rita put her hands on her hips and surveyed the food trucks in booths. "Wouldn't mind a drink, either."

"I imagine it's nice for you to be waited on instead of being the waitress." Norma gestured toward a table. "Sit down, save that spot and I'll get us some food."

"You don't have to ask me twice." Rita found a seat at the end of a long table and sat so she was facing the sunset. The sky glowed pink and orange and gold, carrying her thoughts toward the heavens.

Maybe God had brought her back to Safe Haven,

and her boys, too, so they could set things right between them. Rita didn't consider herself a good Christian, nor did she think that God rearranged people's daily lives as if He were playing a big game of chess from His seat in the sky.

Still, enough about the weird way she'd encountered the three men just when she learned she'd had three boys made her sense the movement of a force greater than herself.

Yes, she was glad the diner was closed on Mondays, and she was glad Norma had dragged her here. Maybe she could stop thinking about her sons, or possible sons, and about Jimmy, for a little while, just kick back with her friend and relax.

Norma showed up with two plates in hand, followed by a twentysomething guy who was carrying the drinks for her.

Norma put the plates down, then turned to the boy, took the drinks and handed him a bill from her pocket. "Thanks, son, I couldn't have managed that without you." She gave him her million-megawatt smile, and Rita watched him melt from the force of it.

No sooner had Rita put a big bite of pulled pork into her mouth than Norma finished crunching her own onion ring and looked at Rita, eyebrows raised. "So? Did you talk to Liam yet?"

So much for getting away from her worries for the evening. "I really don't want to talk about that."

"Hmm, still avoidant." Norma pretended to be scribbling on a psychiatrist's notepad.

"You're annoying, you know?" Rita heard a text come in, pulled out her phone and smiled. Her plan was working.

"Is Jimmy coming?"

Rita nodded. "He says so." Not that that was what she had been texting about. She felt a tiny smile curve her mouth. Norma was about to get her come-uppance.

"So how's it going with Jimmy?" Norma asked as she picked through the basket of fried veggies. "You don't sound thrilled about him coming here tonight."

She shrugged. "He's not at the top of my priority list right now. I gotta get my other stuff figured out."

Norma shook her head. "Same old thing you've been saying ever since I came and visited in the spring," she said. "Haven't you learned that you have to be who you are and open yourself to love in this world?"

Rita lifted an eyebrow at Norma. "Pot, meet kettle. You're the queen of keeping yourself closed off and pushing love away."

"Completely different situation." She looked pointedly at Rita's hands, and Rita realized she was ripping up a napkin into tiny shreds rather than enjoying her meal.

And she didn't want to talk about why she was fidgeting, so she focused on the happy environment around her. Someone was pouring something from a container into a bowl for his dog to drink—hopefully, water and not beer. On the ground beneath the table, little brown birds fought over crumbs with a *kee-WEE* sound.

She saw a familiar face, and before she could duck her head to avoid eye contact, Buck Mulligan came over, in civilian clothes, a woman with short blond hair beside him. "Hey, ladies," he said with his lazy smile. "Looks like I'm not the only person who felt the urge to get away from Safe Haven tonight."

"Pull up a chair," Norma invited, gesturing to the table beside them.

Rita restrained an impulse to kick her friend and then wondered why she felt so uncharitable. It was rare for her to take such a dislike to someone, and unfair. She didn't know Buck well enough to have formed a bad opinion of him.

"Lorraine, I'd like to introduce two of the coolest older ladies in Safe Haven," Buck said, with his trademark suave smile.

Rita glanced over at Norma, who looked amused. "Why, Buck, thank you for the compliment," she said. "Or wait, *was* it a compliment?"

Lorraine flopped down onto a bench beside Norma. "One of those backhanded ones," she said. "He's good at those."

Buck looked confused. "You guys *are* cool."

"And older. We know." Norma winked at Lorraine. "How 'bout you go buy a couple of cool older ladies another drink?"

Rita held up a hand. "One's my limit," she said. "I'm moving to lemonade."

"Buck looks to me like the kind of guy who doesn't mind standing in two different lines." Norma smiled at him.

He stood. "No, I don't mind." When Rita dug in her purse for money, he waved a hand. "It's on me."

"Thank you."

The three of them watched Buck walk briskly toward the refreshment stands. "Good-looking guy," Rita offered, trying to look at the bright side of him.

"How long have you been seeing him, honey?" Norma looked over at Lorraine.

"Oh! I'm not… We're not really seeing each other." Lorraine looked uneasy. "I'm visiting from out of town. Old friend."

"How well do you know him?" Rita was genuinely curious. Buck had come into the diner with any number of attractive women, to the point where it seemed like there wasn't a pretty, age-appropriate female in the county he hadn't dated. And he seemed willing to stretch the age-appropriate thing, too.

Lorraine yawned. "Man, I'm tired." She didn't answer Rita's question, which, admittedly, had been nosy.

"It's just that he has a bit of a reputation," Rita said. "Which could be totally undeserved."

Lorraine shrugged and looked away. "Like I said, we're not dating. And I'm not from around here."

Rita hadn't been born yesterday. She could tell the younger woman was hiding something. Maybe there was a reason she and Buck weren't supposed to be together, like that Lorraine had a husband or boyfriend already. She wouldn't put it past Buck to horn in on another man's woman.

Buck came back, handed drinks around and then sat down beside Lorraine, who shifted a little away from him.

Weird. Rita stole a glance at Norma and could tell that her friend was thinking the same thing.

"So when is Jimmy coming?" Norma asked when the silence got awkward.

"I don't know. He might not even show." As she said it, Rita's stomach jittered and jumped. She'd strung Jimmy along too long. He was a good man, and he wouldn't wait for her to figure out her life forever. He'd already been more than patient.

"Ladies." The deep voice above had a clipped Northern accent.

"Hey!" Rita couldn't believe her plan had worked. "Norma, look, it's your neighbor! Won't you sit and join us?"

He hesitated, then gingerly sat down next to Rita. He looked across the table. "I got your note," he said to Norma.

"What no—" Norma broke off as Rita kicked her ankle. "What's your problem?" she asked Rita.

"It's so nice that you're here experiencing the best our region has to offer," Rita babbled to the Silver Fox, ignoring Norma. "I don't think I caught your name. I'm Rita Tomlinson."

"Stephen Brown." He extended a cautious hand, as if worried Rita carried a contagious disease.

"And this is Norma, and Buck, and Lorraine," Rita enthused. "Guys, Stephen lives at the same condo complex as Norma does. How long have you lived there?"

Buck's sociability turned out to be an asset; he talked amiably about the town and regional sports teams and fishing hot spots. Lorraine looked at her phone and ignored them all. Norma crossed her arms over her chest and watched the flow of conversation, refusing to participate, even when Stephen glanced at her with a puzzled expression.

Rita was just leaning in, trying to draw the man out, when she smelled the faint, masculine scent of Jimmy's aftershave. She turned to see him standing above her. "You came!" She reached for his hand.

He squeezed hers briefly and then pulled his hand away. He sat down a good three feet away from her. Cold.

Stephen left to get a drink. As soon as he was out of earshot, Norma lifted her hands, palms up. "What was that all about? He acted like he didn't want to be here. So why did he come?"

Time to confess. "I might have kind of left him a note and signed your name," Rita said in a rush.

"You *what*?"

"I knew the two of you wouldn't get together if left to your own devices, and I thought he seemed… interesting." Actually, he'd seemed like one of those tough-nut-to-crack kind of guys, but Norma was the same way. Perfect.

"Now he's going to think I like him, when in fact, I think he's an uptight old man. Besides, he's all good-looking and then there's me."

"You're pretty," Buck, Lorraine, Rita and Jimmy said simultaneously.

Norma flushed and glanced down at herself, and Rita knew exactly what she was thinking. Her double mastectomy had made her feel permanently flawed and unwomanly. She'd tried for reconstructive surgery, but complications had made it impossible.

It was hard to get past those negative voices in your head, even if you were a therapist accustomed to helping other people get over their hang-ups.

"You gotta be open to love," Rita urged her friend.

"*You* seem plenty open to that guy," Jimmy said to Rita. His voice had an edge to it, one she'd never heard before.

The hairs on the back of her neck rose. "You accusing me of something?" She frowned at him. That sense of possessiveness struck something deep and painful inside her. She didn't even know what it was. It was lost in the amnesia years.

"I have no claim on you," Jimmy said. "You've made that real clear. But that doesn't mean I want to sit around and watch you flirt with someone else." He stood. "Later, folks." Then he walked away, back straight, shoulders squared.

Rita stared after him, her chest tight. "The nerve of him."

Norma and Lorraine didn't look sympathetic, and Buck was just staring off into space.

"Maybe you're just trying to avoid getting involved," Norma said. "Maybe you're scared."

"Like you know it all," Rita snapped, and then felt bad. "Sorry. I just… I don't know. I guess it's time to go home."

"Maybe what I said rang true," Norma said. "Seems to me you need to take a look at yourself before you go trying to fix up other people."

Rita sighed, looking off in the direction Jimmy had gone. "You could be right."

CHAPTER ELEVEN

"I'M JUST FRUSTRATED." Liam leaned into Cash's refrigerator, scouring the offerings. "Don't you have anything to drink except…" He pulled out a slim, colorful plastic bottle and studied it. "Ion-infused vitamin water with a hint of pomegranate?"

"You should have brought a six-pack if that was going to frustrate you." Cash took another big bite of pizza and grinned at Liam. "My beverage offerings are all healthy."

Liam snorted and twisted the bottle open. He took a long swig and shrugged. "Tastes about like water from my tap. And that's not why I'm frustrated."

"Why, then?"

"Because my hands are tied in a murder investigation in my own town."

Cash wiped his mouth and looked at Liam. "That dude found in the car? Why are your hands tied?"

"Not my case," Liam said. "The chief gave it to Mulligan. Something about city council."

"Mulligan couldn't find a pickup truck in a Walmart parking lot," Cash said. "And I'm guessing your chief knows it. Why don't you investigate anyway?"

Liam blew out a sigh. "Seems like every time I look into anything it disturbs something else. Like Rocky. He was right in the area when it happened, and his mother is missing, but if I call attention to him, he might get taken away from Yasmin, put into the system. And…he's already sort of bonded with her."

"So you leave the kid out of it," Cash said. He didn't question the validity of prioritizing Rocky over justice. Although they'd had decent experiences in foster care as teenagers, they all knew that staying with family or close friends was best.

They ate in silence for a few more minutes. They were in Cash's condo, impeccably but impersonally decorated. Cash rarely spent time here, but he'd been staying in Safe Haven for almost a week now. Liam wondered why, but Cash wasn't talking.

He finished his slice, wiped his mouth and thought out loud. "Yasmin's brother, Josiah, was somewhere in the vicinity of the murder, too," he said. "But interviewing him is a challenge. Interviewing either of them is a challenge. Mulligan tried, but he didn't have any success."

"Of course he didn't have success, he's an idiot." Cash dismissed the other officer with a wave of his hand. "Does he have any background in homicide?"

"Not much. Less than I do, and I'm no expert." Liam had spent a year working in a department just outside Atlanta, and he'd helped on a few investigations. Other than that, what he knew came mostly from college classes and the academy.

Still, it was more than Buck knew, and certainly more than the other two Safe Haven officers. The chief had some long-ago experience as a detective, but his focus was the community and good leadership. As it should be. That had always been enough in Safe Haven, until now.

Cash sat forward, elbows on knees, hands clasped. "How would you manage an investigation, if you *could* investigate?"

"I'd hunt the waters, the eddies down below where the car was found. Interview Josiah and Rocky and the fishermen. Try to find Rocky's mom in an unofficial way, see if there's a connection to her disappearance. Get in touch with Rocky's step-dad, who's somewhere in California." He sighed. "Buck's told me he doesn't need my help and doesn't want me involved."

"What does the chief say?"

Liam shrugged. "I can't question his decision of who to assign. I know Buck's reporting his findings to the chief, but they're playing it close to the vest. And the chief's been taking a lot of sick days, so Buck's really on his own."

Cash leaned back on his leather couch, frowning. "Why doesn't he want you involved, is the question," he said. "He's political, right? Solving a murder case himself will make him look good for the chief job."

"Yeah." Liam's gut twisted.

Cash slapped a fist into his other hand. "I don't like it. You'd be better at the murder investigation, and better as chief. Do they know who the guy is, even? The victim?"

Liam shook his head. "It's strange. No identifying information on him, and the vehicle was stolen from a parking lot, so they must be working with prints. Which, if he's never been arrested, may not be on anyone's radar."

Talking about the case with his brother lit a fire in Liam. No progress was being made on a murder in his town, and it made Safe Haven seem less safe. Even if the victim was just a drifter, a drifter was a person.

Cash stood up at the same time Liam did. "Are you thinking what I'm thinking?"

"Nothing to stop us doing a little fishing at Bonita Point, where the water might've spit something up."

"Makes sense. I'll come along," Cash said. "I always liked that place."

"You might get your fancy shoes dirty. I'm talking about walking around in the marshland."

Cash punched his shoulder. "Maybe I've changed a little, okay? Can't a guy change?"

"You better change those shoes." Liam looked

scornfully down at Cash's Italian leather loafers. "You got any boots around here?"

"Nope. Running shoes."

"Yeah, those'll protect you from a copperhead," Liam said sarcastically.

"You suck."

Twenty minutes later, Liam had grabbed evidence-collecting supplies and they were out in the marsh-land below the bay where the body had been found. All Liam's years of fishing had made him familiar with the swirls of water where flotsam gathered. And yeah, it was a place that had a personal history to him, but it was no big deal.

At least he didn't think so until Cash brought it up. "Hey, isn't this where you beat up some guy who was assaulting Yasmin?"

"Yeah." Liam didn't want to talk about it.

"I was already gone. How'd you happen to be in the right place at the right time?"

"Night fishing." Being in nature by himself had always calmed Liam. He and his foster dad had had their struggles, but Liam couldn't be anything but grateful that he'd passed along his love of fishing, and the skills to go with it. "One night when I was down here," he said, "I heard a car in the woods. At first I was mad because I wanted to be alone. But it wasn't long before I heard a woman scream-ing for help."

"Yasmin?"

Liam nodded. "That entitled bozo had ripped off

her shirt and was getting ready to do more. I pulled him out of his car and…" He didn't need to go into it. Cash had been in plenty of fights himself, a couple of them protecting women. It was something in their DNA, or at least from their childhood. They'd let their mother be lost, and granted, they'd just been kids, but it had haunted all three of them. "Then I took his car and drove her home in it." He'd taken off his own shirt and given it to Yasmin to cover up with, but it had been impossible to forget that glimpse of her breasts he'd seen, which made him feel like a complete dog.

"Bet her parents freaked."

"They blamed me at first." Liam remembered the bitter taste of that, but he also remembered the way Yasmin had pulled herself out of her own misery to defend him to her parents. To explain that he had saved her. "Once they figured out the truth, her dad was grateful. He took care of that rich kid's family trying to get me arrested for assault and car theft, and he set up a scholarship for me to go to college up at UNC, where he'd gone." No coincidence that the scholarship had also taken him far away from Yasmin. Liam couldn't fault Yasmin's dad about that. He'd never even dared to have the dream of being with her, and he hadn't blamed her father for being protective of her, not wanting her to get caught up in a relationship with Liam out of gratitude. He'd just been thankful for the opportunity her dad had dropped in his lap.

"Heavy, man." Cash was texting and Liam rolled his eyes. Here he was spilling his thoughts to his brother and Cash wasn't even listening.

They came to the series of eddies where all kinds of things gathered from the surf. He found a big stick and started poking around. Bottles and empty Valvoline cans, a kids' plastic lunchbox.

"See anything?" Cash was looking into the brackish water with distaste. "Man, it sure does stink down here."

"Wimp." Liam saw something red and stirred the water, fished up a red rubber shoe.

Now, where had he seen one of those recently?

He squatted down, studying it, and then it came to him. There'd been one hanging off Rocky's backpack that night when he'd first come to the center. Only one, which had struck him. But he'd never asked the kid about it.

He pulled it closer and dropped it on the ground to study.

"What do you make of that?" Cash knelt beside him.

"Rocky had one," he said slowly. "Guess there's all kinds of reasons a kid's shoe could end up in the water, huh?"

But he had an uneasy feeling about it. If Rocky's shoe had floated down here—and there was no evidence that it was Rocky's, there were probably a hundred pairs of these shoes along this stretch of coast—it meant Rocky had been near the water that night. He'd copped to hanging around the docks, but he'd vehemently denied getting anywhere near the water.

Rocky was a strong kid, and he was angry.

Liam couldn't believe he'd bludgeoned the un-identified victim and then sent him driving off the dock in his car. But he was secretive about what had happened that night. Could he have been some-how involved?

YASMIN LOOKED AT the text from Cash again as she climbed out of her car in the Chaloklowa Nature Reserve, shuddering as memories assailed her. He'd said Liam needed her. It seemed a little odd.

"Bad place," Josiah said.

She nodded. It hadn't seemed bad, not until she'd made the mistake of parking here with Lenny Ekstrom and nearly gotten herself assaulted. Truth to tell, she hadn't been back here since then.

"Thanks for coming with me, Joe," she said. Her brother might have his problems, but he was big and strong and protective. She stepped a little closer to him.

Sounds rose up around them, the marshy alive-ness of the bayou: frogs, and chattering squirrels, and birds. The lapping of the water a made a con-stant, rhythmic backdrop. It reminded her that she had loved this place once.

Instinctively they started on the trail toward the

water, and soon enough, they heard voices. She put a hand on Josiah's arm.

He stopped, glanced over at her, and listened. "Liam and Cash," he said.

So that was all right. Yasmin started along the path again, and within two minutes, they came out of the wooded section and into the view of the bay. And there they were, two of the best-looking men this side of the Mississippi River. Even though she and Joe were walking quietly, Liam caught sight of them, or maybe just sensed them. He was a great police officer that way.

He tilted his head to one side, looking confused.

Cash said something to him, and his eyes widened. "Really?" she heard him say.

So maybe Liam didn't want her here. She'd have turned back if it wouldn't have been so awkward. But with Joe here, she just plunged forward.

"Hey," she said to the two of them. "Cash, I got your text. What's up?"

Cash smiled his easy smile. "Just thought you two might have a few things to talk about. Josiah, if you want, I can take you home." He grinned at Yasmin. "That is, if you can take Liam home."

Yasmin didn't get it. "But why—"

Josiah was making a noise in his throat, high-pitched and creepy. She looked at him, and then looked in the direction of the item he was staring at.

A red shoe? Why would he be freaked out by a red shoe?

"That shoe look familiar, Josiah?" Liam asked. Subtly, he shifted from friend to police officer, watching every nuance of Josiah's expression and body language.

Josiah stared at Liam, then knelt and looked at the shoe.

"Does it mean something to either of you?" she asked Liam and Cash, partly to take the spotlight off Josiah.

"Maybe." Liam studied it steadily. "I think it's Rocky's."

"Rocky's?" Yasmin looked from the shoe to Liam and back again. "Why would Rocky's shoe be here?"

"That's what I'm trying to figure out," he said. "I think he lost it on the night of the murder."

Those few words made everything shift inside Yasmin. Did Liam suspect Rocky of murder? It didn't seem possible. The boy was just thirteen.

But if Rocky had done something, and Josiah had witnessed it… That would put the night's events in a whole new light.

"But the murder happened in Safe Haven," she said. "We're at least two miles downstream."

"The pattern of the tides," he said. "Lots of stuff from there ends up here."

"Are you going to turn it in as evidence?"

"I don't think they'll take it."

She looked at him steadily. "So this is the start of our investigation."

"I suppose it is," he said. He took a plastic evidence bag from his pocket and used a stick to pick up the Croc and drop it inside. "Exhibit A, if anyone wants to see it."

Josiah grabbed for the bag, but Liam had extremely fast reflexes, and pulled it away. "Hey, buddy, I need that."

"I have to have it," Josiah said. "I have to take it to them."

"Take it to who?"

Yasmin's heart sank. This was a new development in Josiah's illness. He talked about "them" a lot. People who were giving him orders. He felt like he was on some kind of a mission. Apparently, it was a classic symptom. She put a hand on her brother's arm. "Joe," she said, keeping her voice low and soothing. "Joe, I think it's the voices."

"No, I really need it!" Joe grabbed for the bag again.

"Afraid I have to take it, buddy," Liam said. "But if you go with Cash, he'll help you figure out a different plan. He's good at that."

Cash's eyebrows drew together. He obviously wasn't in on the nuances of Josiah's illness. But to his credit, he played along. "Come on, pal," he said to Josiah. "Let's go talk about it at Liam's place. I know he's got a cold one in the fridge with your name on it."

Josiah was puzzled by that comment, given the

expression on his face, but when Cash took his arm and urged him along, he didn't resist.

Yasmin and Liam watched the two of them disappear up the trail.

"Do you think he's getting worse?" Liam asked her.

"Not exactly. It's just, some things bother him. Something about that shoe triggered something in his mind. And it's like older voices drop off and new ones come in. Right now, he thinks he's on a mission."

Liam put an arm around her and tugged her next to him. The gesture was completely friendly, but still, it made Yasmin's heart beat a little faster. "I'm sorry, babe," he said. "That must be tough on you to see him like that."

She nodded and blinked as tears pushed against the backs of her eyes. She wasn't going to cry.

"Any ideas on what he was seeing when he looked at the shoe?" he asked.

She shook her head. "No idea."

"You don't think it's Rocky's, then?"

"I know boys are wearing those shoes now, but I've never seen a pair—or just one—among Rocky's stuff." She looked out across the black water, listened to the rise and fall of the night frogs and tried to let her shoulders relax. Not easy to do with Liam's arm still around them, because really, she wanted to turn into him, put her arms around him, feel his strength and relax into it.

That, obviously, would be a mistake.

"I'm sorry Cash called you here," Liam said.

She glanced over at him, but he was looking out across the water, not at her.

"I think he's trying to push us together."

"Why?"

"Your guess is as good as mine. I never saw Cash as a matchmaker before, but he's been acting a little weird lately. Like he's changing."

The thought of Cash pushing them together made Yasmin's skin heat all over. If only things were different. If only she could be the woman who would make Liam happy.

But she couldn't. "That's nice Cash is changing. But he really doesn't need to interfere like that."

"Look, Yasmin," Liam said, his arm tightening on her shoulders. "I know you said you weren't ready for a serious relationship before. But we've both changed. Maybe now, we could give it another try."

His words stoked a longing in her. She looked up. His face was just inches away from hers. She could feel the rise and fall of his chest, feel his breathing against her cheek, smell his faint cologne blended with the slight, sweet sweat that was his own indefinable masculine scent.

She'd always loved how he smelled.

Standing this close together, looking out at the romantic, moonlit water, wasn't a good idea. But her brain had gone too foggy to remember why.

She lifted a hand to push him away, but seemingly of their own volition her fingers stroked his cheek instead. Rough stubble. "You need to shave," she murmured.

A half smile quirked his mouth. "True, if we were going to kiss. Then, I might scratch you with this beard. But we're not going to kiss." His eyes never left hers. "Are we?"

"We shouldn't," she whispered.

"Shouldn't we?" He stepped around to fully face her, his other arm coming up to touch her chin. "Would it really be such a bad thing?"

Her breathing got away from her, running fast, like she'd been working out. She couldn't take her eyes away from his. "Yes. It would be a bad thing."

"We wouldn't want to do a bad thing." His voice was smoky and husky, promising tantalizing pleasure. It sent a tingle through Yasmin's very core.

His hands splayed across the back of her head, fingers forking through her hair. "Thing is," he said, "I really want to kiss you."

Her body was throbbing and she wished he would just do it. But his lips hovered a few inches from hers, and she realized that he wouldn't. He was too honorable. He was waiting for her to say yes.

And that made all the sense in the world, given where they were, given that once in this very same spot, a boy had tried to take away her right to choose.

And this man, who had been a man, even back

then, had saved her. Had she ever properly thanked him? All she remembered was a continued sense of devastation as she'd recovered from the horror of the assault. When she'd gotten her head back above water and looked around, Liam was away at college.

Now, he was here with her, and he wanted to kiss her, but he was leaving it up to her.

Wisdom dictated that she pull away, because she knew that she wasn't right for him, that she couldn't give him what he needed long-term, that she was too much of a risk.

But with the night warm around them, with the water lapping gently against the shore, with the stars twinkling overhead, she didn't seem able to do the wise thing. She rose up on her tiptoes, shoved her fingers into his soft dark hair and kissed him.

She started it, but she didn't have to work to keep it going. Liam took over, at first gently, brushing his lips across hers. Then with a playful nip and growl that sent shivers down her spine.

And then with the passion that had been building during all these hurtful months when they hadn't been together but had been 100 percent aware of each other. He deepened the kiss and pulled her hard against him, and her breathing went ragged.

She'd blocked this out, how well they fit together, how their kisses seemed to have a rhythm all their own.

Finally, he lay his cheek against hers. "Did I

scratch you after all?" he asked, his voice husky, deep, impossibly sexy.

She reached up to run a shaky finger down his cheek. "I didn't mind."

He caught her finger in his hand and brought it to his lips, his eyes hot on hers. "We're playing with fire."

The words, meant to ignite, threw cold water over Yasmin's passion. They *were* playing with fire. Liam didn't know the half of it. Yasmin couldn't take this relationship anywhere. And though Liam was good-looking and could have any number of women for a night or a month or a lifetime, Yasmin knew his secret: at heart, he was a one-woman man who wanted nothing more than a family.

It wouldn't be fair to pursue their feelings for each other, physical or emotional. She pulled away. "We should go," she said, hearing the shakiness in her own voice, her heart breaking for what she was giving up, throwing away.

He narrowed his eyes, studying her. "You sure?"

No.

"I'm sure," she said.

He nodded once, took her hand and led her to the car. Drove her home without talk. Walked her to her door, and once there, put his hands on her shoulders. "We started something up again," he said, "and I want to see where it goes." Then he kissed her fast and hard, turned and strode to his apartment without looking back.

CHAPTER TWELVE

THE NEXT DAY, Liam walked through town with his brother Sean, who had just returned from his honeymoon the previous day. It was the end of a twelve-hour shift, and all was right with the world.

He'd kissed Yasmin and she hadn't pulled away. She'd been into it in a way that you couldn't fake. And though they hadn't made plans to see each other again, he was hoping she was home and that, after he got a shower and walked Rio, they could spend a little time on her porch.

That was what mattered to him, what he liked: hanging out with the woman he cared about, on her porch.

"Hey!" Sean nudged him with an elbow. "You're out of it."

"Sorry."

"Check it out." Sean scrolled through his phone and showed Liam picture after picture of the honeymoon. It was kind of funny. Sean was a big, quiet hulk normally, but now he couldn't shut up about his family.

"Did you and Anna get any alone time, with the twins there?"

"It's Disney, man. There's babysitting. Ma and Pudge paid for a couple of nights of it as a wedding present and we made good use of the time."

Sean looked so happy that Liam envied him, wondered why he couldn't seem to find the relationship and the happiness his brother had. Mostly, though, he was just glad for Sean. As the oldest, he had struggled the hardest over losing their mom, and he'd felt a big weight of responsibility for Liam and Cash. He deserved happiness.

"Wish we'd been able to go to Disney with Mom, way back when," Sean said. "She would've loved it. Loved taking us there."

Liam shook his head. "I don't remember her well enough." The truth was, he remembered his foster parents much better than his mom, but they'd never have taken the kids to Disney. Too far, too expensive, too much chaos. They'd liked things controlled and predictable.

"She'd have loved it," Sean repeated. It seemed like his happiness as a family man had made him mellow toward the mother they'd lost. At other times in the past, Sean had suspected their mom to have abandoned them on purpose, but these days, he focused on the good times of their childhood.

"Well." Liam checked up and down the street

and then urged Sean on. "C'mon, I'm on patrol. But I'm glad one of us did it. Found someone, I mean. Made a family."

"You can do it, too," Sean said. "I'm not gonna lie, figuring out how to be with a woman isn't easy with how we grew up. But man, it's worth it."

"I can see that." Liam nodded at Sean's phone full of pictures. It *would* be worth any amount of effort to make that happen, to get that happy.

They came to the section of the boardwalk where a few rowboats were docked, glanced at each other, and stopped by unspoken agreement, looking across the bay and into the bayou.

"Think the twins have forgotten?" Liam asked. Their biological father had kidnapped them here and gone off into the swamp, and it had taken everything Sean, Cash and Liam had—and a lot of help from the community, and a lot of prayer—to get them, and Anna, safely home.

"They've started forgetting. Anna and I never will."

All the more reason Sean and Anna deserved happiness. They'd been through a lot, both of them.

They walked past Rip Martin, who was leaning against the wall of Jones Drugstore, playing a mournful tune on his harmonica. A hat was beside him, and he started to hold up a sign with his free hand—veteran, four kids, it said, only half of which was true—but then when he saw Liam, he put the sign facedown over the hat and continued playing, not meeting Liam's eyes.

"Did I hear right, that the city council passed an ordinance against panhandling?" Sean asked. He reached into his pocket and dropped a ten on top of Rip's sign, giving the old man a smile and a wave. Rip returned a salute.

"Yeah, they passed it," Liam said. "Way it came out, they made it illegal to give to anyone within ten feet of a road. Good thing I happened to be looking the other way."

"Rip's been here forever. He doesn't cause any trouble."

"You and I both know that. But there are those who say he scares off the tourists."

As if on cue, a group of people came out of La Florentine, the only truly fancy restaurant in Safe Haven.

They were talking and laughing loudly, and one of the women stumbled, then caught herself on the arm of the man beside her.

"I better leave you to do your job," Sean said.

"Later." Liam waved and then walked toward the crowd, not aggressive, not like they were in trouble, just checking things out.

At the center of the crowd was Buck Mulligan. Great.

And now that Liam was close enough to recognize people, he realized that most of the group belonged to the city council. Even better.

He turned back and took a few long steps to where Rip sat. "You best be moving on," he said.

"Wha—" Rip looked to the noisy group on the street and nodded. "Thanks, bro."

Liam held out a hand and helped Rip climb to his feet. The man was in his sixties and had lived a hard life, and it showed. But he'd also served in Vietnam, which was almost certainly why Sean, also a veteran, gave him money every time he passed by.

After Rip was steady and gathering his things, Liam turned back toward the crowd outside La Florentine, which didn't seem to be breaking up. Except the woman who'd been stumbling; she and a well-dressed man were climbing into a car.

"It's Mr. Shoe!" Buck yelled, looking toward Liam.

There was an outburst of laughter, abruptly shushed. As if they were all in on an ongoing joke, and Liam knew exactly what it was about: the red shoe he had turned in as evidence earlier this morning, after a lot of wavering. He didn't want to involve Rocky, but he couldn't in good conscience hold on to something he knew intuitively had some bearing on the case. He'd swallowed his pride and explained to Buck that the shoe was similar to one Rocky had, one that Josiah recognized. That he might want to talk to them both again about whether they'd been near the water on the evening the car had gone off the dock.

He didn't know what spin Buck had put on the

story, but obviously, no one was taking it seriously. Taking *him* seriously. Liam's chance to become police chief was slipping away.

His face felt hot, but there was no time for embarrassment. The woman who'd been stumbling around was now behind the wheel. "Hey!" he yelled, and ran toward the group and the diagonally parked Audi.

Which backed out with a screech and...*bang*! Promptly hit the car parked across the street.

The Audi rebounded a few feet and jerked to a stop. The man in the passenger seat got out, yelling.

By now Liam was close enough to see that the driver had put her head down on the steering wheel. Her shoulders were shaking. Laughter or tears?

A few people from surrounding restaurants and shops were outside now, looking at the two cars.

Liam went directly to the drivers' side and rapped on the window.

The woman's head was still down, shoulders still shaking.

"Open the window!" her passenger, presumably her husband, bawled into the car.

The woman jolted upright, looked at her husband and then, probably based on his excited gesticulations, looked over at Liam and then opened the window.

"Ma'am," he said, "step out of the vehicle." He opened the door and, when she didn't show signs of obeying, he took her arm and gently pulled. "Come on, ma'am, I don't want to have to cuff you but I will."

"Get out, Misti, geez!" The husband came around and tugged at her, too, much more roughly than Liam had.

"Get her over to the curb," he said to a couple of the bystanders who appeared to be her friends. Then he assessed that the husband was sober. "Let's get this vehicle out of the middle of the street, and then we'll talk."

The husband squealed into the parking space, making his friends laugh. Someone had even brought out drinks for the crowd.

Liam sighed. This was his least favorite type of police work. And it was almost worse when it was neighbors rather than folks from out of town. They didn't even have the excuse that they were on vacation.

Buck strolled over and put a patronizing hand on Liam's back. "I'll handle it from here," he said. He wore civilian clothes, a sport coat and dress pants, and he smelled of alcohol.

"No problem," Liam said. "I've got it."

"You tend to overreact. I'll handle it."

Liam restrained his impulse to slug the jerk. And since when did Buck have that kind of authority? "There's physical damage. There's going to be paperwork and insurance companies involved. You've been drinking."

The husband came over. "Let's just handle this

quietly," he said. "No need to do a report. I'm going to pay for any repairs."

"When an accident happens, sir, we need to file a report."

"Look," Buck said, "we all bend the rules a little." He looked pointedly down the street toward where Rip had been sitting. "You take care of your friends. Let me take care of mine."

Which sounded just like a corrupt small-town department. He opened his mouth to protest.

The restaurant's doors opened. Yasmin and a couple of her friends came out.

At the same moment, Tom Turner, head of city council, walked over and patted Liam on the back. "I'll fix it with the chief, if you're worried about that," he said.

Yasmin wore an old-fashioned dress, black-and-white polka dots. It hugged her figure where it mattered and ruffled out at the bottom and the top. She looked girly, more so than usual.

And utterly gorgeous.

The three women stopped, and it didn't take long for a couple of men from Buck's group to go over and start talking. Undoubtedly explaining what had happened.

The explainer was laughing, and one of Yasmin's friends chuckled.

Yasmin didn't laugh. Instead, she looked his way, her expression concerned.

"See? There's no more to do here." Buck waved a hand. "Carry on with your beat."

"Great idea," Tom said, slapping Buck on the back. "I'll fix it with the chief."

"And I'll make sure *he*—" he pointed at the husband "—pays for the car," Buck said. He looked directly at Liam. "Sometimes, we handle our cases a little on the down low, right?"

Liam clenched his teeth to keep himself from calling them all on being jerks. His heart raced with anger and apprehension, too. Pretty likely Buck was referring to the night of the murder, when Liam hadn't reported his suspicions.

Tit for tat. But Liam didn't like it one bit.

He documented everything and then phoned the chief. Ramirez sighed heavily into the phone. "Let her go," he said finally.

"Yes, sir." Liam clicked off the call, told the drunk woman she was free to go and headed back to the station with a very sour taste in his mouth.

YOU'RE WORTHLESS.

It was the middle of the night, and Yasmin tossed and turned in the grips of a vivid dream.

No one believes anything you say.

She sat up in bed, heart racing so fast she thought she might explode or pass out. She looked around her bedroom, moonlight streaming in through the open window. All the familiar shapes slowly came into focus.

It had just been a dream.

She hugged her knees to her chest. That voice had seemed so real, so terrifying. She hated nightmares. And even knowing that Josiah and Rocky were both in the house, and Liam was just across the yard, she still felt scared.

You're fat and worthless. You should quit your job. Send Rocky and Josiah away.

She sucked in an audible gasp. Pinched the backs of her hands. Was she still asleep?

Stay away from Liam. No one will ever believe you.

Yasmin pressed her hands to her mouth and pulled her knees tighter, a ball of a person.

She was hearing voices. Having delusions. And it was terrifying.

Oh Joe, I'm sorry for not understanding before.

The voice sounded so real.

She sat for a long time, but the voice didn't replay. A huge stone pressed down on her. She could barely summon the strength to go get a glass of water.

When she finally did, she found Josiah in the kitchen, opening and closing cupboards. He turned when she came in, looked at her and tilted his head to one side. "You okay, sissy?"

"Not really." She went to him, wrapped her arms around him, and he submitted to it, even patted her back a little. When she let go, he sat down so he was more on her level. "What's wrong?"

"What do your voices sound like, in your head?"

He stared at her. "They don't want me to talk about them."

"Is it real? Something you can actually hear?"

He nodded. "Sometimes they argue. Sometimes they won't shut up."

This was hard. "Do they tell you what's wrong with you?"

"Like what?"

She bit her lip, hard enough to hurt. "Did they ever say you were ugly and worthless?"

Surprise registered on Josiah's usually impassive face. "No, never," he said slowly. "My voices are good. Or just…loopy."

That was a relief, at least. "I'm glad your voices are good," she said. "Because you're good." She gave him another hug and then headed upstairs to her room.

That voice had been so audible. She could swear there was someone in the room with her, but no one had been there.

She was starting to develop Josiah's condition herself. Not only that, but the voice in her head had told her no one would believe her. About what?

She got into her room, closed the door quietly, sat down on her bed. Her breath came in shorter, faster bursts. Her hands gripped and ungripped the sheets, and she realized she was fidgeting just like Josiah so often did.

Would she hear it again?

Right now, she didn't feel compelled to do what

the voice had told her to do. Quit her job? Send Rocky and Joe away? She wouldn't even consider it.

Thankfully, the voice had only spoken a couple of times, and now was silent. But that could change. Maybe this was how it started.

She grabbed her phone, Googled "How does schizophrenia start?"

Withdrawal from friends and family. When was the last time she'd done something with her friends? Well, last night, actually. But before that, hadn't she been pulling back?

Drop in performance at school or work. Hmm. She'd just finished writing a major grant proposal for the women's center, but it had been an uphill climb. She hadn't felt her usual enthusiasm, and she didn't feel at all confident that they'd get the grant.

Trouble sleeping. Well, considering that it was 3:00 a.m. now and there wasn't a chance she'd go back to sleep tonight—check.

Irritability or depressed mood. Anyone, especially Josiah or Rocky, could attest that Yasmin was plenty irritable.

Lack of motivation. She blew out a breath. There'd been a time when she was brimming with energy to accomplish great things at the women's center. Before that, she'd been the head of the education club in college, and involved in volunteer outreach to poor kids in Charleston.

Now…even the thought of that kind of involvement made her tired.

Strange behavior…well, that was a matter of opinion. And she definitely wasn't abusing substances. But she'd checked yes to five of the seven symptoms. And she'd heard voices. A voice. Telling her to do something clearly awful and wrong.

Her shoulders were tight, practically up around her ears, but she tried to get a grip on herself. *Take action,* her father had always said. *It'll make you feel better, whatever the problem.*

Take action. Later today, she'd go to the library and find out more. Get Miss Vi to help her. Knowledge was power.

Her dreams of having a husband and child had already burst and disappeared, like soap bubbles. She'd been sad.

But there must have been a tiny part of her that had hoped she was wrong, hoped she could build a family life. Now that hope was gone.

She lay down on her side, buried her face in her pillow and wept.

THE NEXT MORNING, after a sleepless night, Liam washed his face and took a cup of coffee out on the porch. He couldn't believe what he'd seen last night, and yet there it had been.

There had been someone in Yasmin's bedroom. Someone who had climbed down the rose trellis.

After the encounter with Mulligan and the city council, he'd been wakeful, and he'd slipped out onto the little stoop outside his apartment, late, being quiet so as not to wake up Rio. He'd seen Yasmin's lights go on at 3:00 a.m., had seen her silhouette downstairs, moving around her kitchen.

And then he'd seen a shadowy figure climb down out of her bedroom, half illuminated in the cloudy moonlight. He'd tried to hold back the sick feeling inside himself, but he was pretty sure the man had been Buck Mulligan. Meaning, Buck and Yasmin were involved again.

Liam kicked hard at a stone, and it went flying up to ping against one of the porch steps of Yasmin's house. Good. Hopefully it had dented it, ruined the paint.

How could she do it? How could she go back with a suave dingbat like Mulligan? Only days after she'd kissed Liam like she meant it?

She'd made a fool of him for a second time, and he felt like giving her a piece of his mind. But even more than Yasmin, he mostly blamed Mulligan. Him, Liam would like to punch.

Put that together with how arrogant and sure of himself Buck had acted last night outside the restaurant, and Liam's chances of building himself a decent life here in Safe Haven were getting more and more slim.

His chances of being police chief, of keeping Safe Haven a safe place, especially for women at risk, was pretty much biting the dust.

He chugged the rest of his coffee and brought Rio out. He'd like to go for a run, avoid people and lick his wounds in privacy. But he'd promised to spend the day with his brothers, getting breakfast and then fishing out at Ma Dixie's.

Rocky was in Yasmin's yard, looking at something on the ground. The boy wore an old T-shirt and jeans, the clothes he'd come in. He definitely needed to do some shopping before school started.

"Hey, buddy," he said, strolling over. "What's up?"

"There was someone in the house last night," Rocky said. "I'm looking for footprints. And I found one. Look!"

Rocky studied the plain tread, a man-size boat shoe, most likely. Liam studied it, too, just to be companionable.

"Do you think it was a thief?" Rocky asked eagerly.

"I doubt it, son." Liam blew out a sigh. No reason for Rocky to hear the details of why a man might visit a woman in her bedroom at night. And it was a little weird that Buck was climbing out Yasmin's window instead of using the stairs and front door like a normal, adult man. Maybe they got off on that. Or maybe they were trying to hide their relationship from Josiah and Rocky.

Yasmin and Josiah came out the front door then, and although they glanced over toward Rocky and Liam, they didn't stop to chat. Which shouldn't be a surprise. Yasmin was probably preoccupied thinking about her new boyfriend. Her new-old boy-friend.

He kicked at the soil, defacing a couple of foot-prints. Rocky sidestepped away from him.

Cash pulled up and tooted on the horn of his Lexus. Liam started toward the car and then stopped, turned back to Rocky. "We're going fish-ing later," he said. "Want to come? We can stop back and pick you up."

"Yasmin said we have to go shopping for school clothes today." Rocky made a face.

Liam considered. "That shouldn't take long. I can stop by the mall and pick you up, if you let me know where you're going to be. I'll bet you'll be allowed." Even though Yasmin had moved on from him, with breathtaking speed, she probably still needed, or wanted, his help with Rocky.

"Okay, I'll tell her!" The boy's face was sunny, and Liam was glad to have invited him.

Rocky went inside and Liam got into the car. Cash called Sean, who'd been supposed to meet them for breakfast before going fishing but was run-ning late. "I'm a newlywed, man!" he said. "I'll meet you guys out there."

Cash started up the car and headed for the diner, giving Sean a hard time on the speakerphone. Liam tried to participate, but he couldn't muster up any energy for it. Sean was happy, home in bed with his woman on a Saturday morning, and even more than last night, Liam was just plain jealous.

CHAPTER THIRTEEN

WHENEVER YOU DIDN'T want to run into someone you knew, that was when you were guaranteed to have it happen. Rita knew this, so she actually had put on a little makeup and a decent-looking pair of jeans before heading to the outlet malls thirty minutes away from Safe Haven, up on the other side of Myrtle Beach.

She wandered through stores, getting more and more blue. There was a shirt she would've liked to wear, her favorite shade of green, but the lower neckline just wouldn't look good on a woman of her age. She said as much to a gray-haired woman who was rifling through clothes on the same sale table.

"Honey, I don't even bother to look for nice clothes for myself these days. I'm shopping for my granddaughter. Come on over here, Courtney, I want you to try this on."

As the woman and her granddaughter argued, Rita left the store in a hurry. She'd been running away from her own problems, but her problems were chasing her; everything she saw and heard made her think of the emptiness of her past.

If what she suspected about the O'Dwyer boys was true, then she had grandchildren—not biological, not yet, but kids her son was fathering. But she didn't know them. Could she ever be close enough to take them shopping, fuss at them about what was appropriate to wear? Or was that opportunity simply lost, lost forever because of whatever had happened in her shadowy past?

She wandered into a store that carried a lot of jeans and pants she liked, but it was the same situation. She could hear a mother arguing with her son over the number of rips in the jeans he wanted to buy, and the appropriate tightness of them.

"What do you care? You're not my mother."

Oh. So she'd been idealizing; it wasn't a mother-son duo. But the voices did sound familiar. She peeked around a rack of boys' jeans, and there was Yasmin and that kid she seemed to be fostering, Rocky.

It was back-to-school time. Lots of families shopping together, and Rita wondered if she had done that type of shopping for the three boys that Abel claimed she'd been with right before losing her memory. Had they gotten along well, or poorly? Had she been able to afford nice things for them?

"Look," Yasmin was saying with that quiet tone that meant she was deeply irritated, "you need a couple of pairs of jeans and at least five shirts. I know you'd rather shop with Liam, but since he's not here right now, let's get started picking things out."

Rocky slumped, staring miserably at the shelves of polo shirts. A fresh splotch of acne had sprouted on his cheek, and his hair stuck up in a way that Rita found adorable, but Rocky himself probably didn't.

They looked like they could use a little support. "Hey, Yasmin," Rita said, coming out into the aisle of the store. "And you're Rocky, right? Are you guys looking for school clothes?"

"Trying to," Yasmin said. "Apparently, I'm totally out of touch with what middle-schoolers wear around here."

Rita thought about kids who came into the diner. "I bet they don't wear these dressed-up type of shirts," she said. "I mean, these are nice, but I see a lot of kids wearing T-shirts."

"Thank you!" Rocky threw up his hands. "That's what I've been trying to tell her."

She was smiling sympathetically at Yasmin when Liam approached them. Her heart lurched a little.

Oh, how she wanted to talk to him about the possibility that she was his mother. Her heart ached with the desire but fluttered with cowardice at the same time. If she told him the truth, would he reject her outright?

"There you are!" Yasmin put her hands on her hips and smiled at Liam. "It's about time. Rocky is pretty fed up with me. I think he needs a man to shop with."

"Sorry," Liam said. There was no trace of a smile on his normally friendly face. "I was planning to take him fishing, but I can help him shop first."

"Oh." Yasmin's eyebrows drew together, the skin between them pleating. "Um, okay, as long as you keep an eye on him."

"Will do," Liam said. "Come on, Rocky."

"Sure!" Rocky spun away from Yasmin, and Liam turned, then looked back.

"Hey, Rita," he said. Then he and Rocky walked off down the aisle.

Yasmin stared after them, for a long time.

"You okay?" Rita patted Yasmin's shoulder. "Want to get a coffee or something?"

"Do you know anything about mental illness?" Yasmin posed the question out of nowhere, not looking at Rita.

"Not much," Rita said. "Why?"

Yasmin bit her lip. "I don't know. My brother, Josiah, has some problems, and sometimes, I worry that I do, too."

"You could talk to Norma. She knows a lot about mental health, with her counseling background." And as such, she had a lot of wisdom backing her up when she kept urging Rita to get out there and figure out her past and tell the truth to people. It wasn't just Norma being pushy. It was the best path to psychological health.

Too bad it was so hard to do.

"Your having issues wouldn't be the first thought that came to my mind about you," Rita said. "I think you're a pretty great person, taking on the care of a teenage boy. That can't be easy."

Yasmin shrugged. "His mother bailed. I'm the only option he has right now."

Tension clawed at Rita's stomach. How many people had said the exact same thing about her when she'd disappeared, leaving behind her children?

She cast about for something to say. "Is his mom a friend of yours?"

Yasmin tilted her head, her eyes squinting a little. "I wouldn't call Lorraine a friend, exactly. But we've known each other awhile, and I'm glad to help out for Rocky's sake. He's a great kid."

Lorraine. She'd just met a Lorraine. She thought back and remembered that was the same name as the woman Buck had been with at the sunset party.

When you were blue, the best way to feel better was to help someone else. "Come on," she said. "Let's at least get out of the men's department. We should either shop, or eat, or get a glass of wine, don't you think? I'd love to talk to you about the women's center. Maybe I could do more to help you. I have a few ideas."

"That would be great," Yasmin said. "Great to hear your ideas, and…and great to hang out some, today."

And Rita got the feeling that, in some ways, Yasmin was just as lonely as she was.

"I DON'T WANT to go stupid fishing!" Rocky's arms crossed and his face twisted into a classic middle-school sneer.

Liam narrowed his eyes at the kid. "You wanted to go when we asked you this morning."

It was later the same afternoon, and they were standing at the little dock behind Ma Dixie's place. Liam's brother Sean was showing honeymoon pictures to Ma Dixie, and Cash was dumping ice into a cooler. Rio ran back and forth between all of them, barking madly.

After a morning of shopping for school clothes with Rocky—and seeing Yasmin—Liam had to reach pretty deep for patience. "How come you don't want to go now?"

"I thought we could bring Rio with us!" Rocky's stance was still defiant.

Cash meandered down. "You done much fishing before, Rocky?" he asked.

"No, because it's stupid!"

Cash nodded slowly. "I guess it is, kind of."

Rio chose that moment to knock over Pudge's toolbox, so they all went back up to where the older man was sitting. Rocky ran ahead, probably as much to get away from Liam as to help Pudge.

"He's scared," Cash said in a low voice, nodding at Rocky. "Can he swim?"

That hadn't even occurred to Liam, and he felt like an idiot for it. "Don't know."

"Remember how close to the shore they stuck

the other night when we were here? There's a reason for that."

Liam nodded. "Makes sense."

"Thank you kindly," Pudge was saying as Rocky
picked up the toolbox that Rio had knocked over
and knelt to organize the tools that had spilled out.
"Seems to me that dog needs some more training.
If young Rocky, here, would stay and work on that
with me, you three could get your fishing jones
taken care of yourselves."

"Yeah!" Rocky pumped his arm in the air.

Truthfully, that sounded like a relief to Liam. But
he hated to seem to buck his responsibility. Rocky
would report to Yasmin on his day, and she'd learn
that Rocky hadn't spent the time with Liam after
all, but rather with Pudge.

"Sounds like a win-win," Sean said. "You get
your dog trained, *and* a fishing trip with your bros.
What's not to like?"

"I'm supposed to be taking care of him," he tried
to explain. "I asked Yasmin if he could come with
us, so he's my responsibility."

"Me," Pudge said, "I was planning to have him
take care of me, fetch and carry for me since Dustin
and his sisters are off on a visit."

Rocky was kneeling now, burying his face in
Rio's side. "Can I stay here with Pudge?" he muttered in a voice Liam had to lean in to hear.

Being here with him and Cash and Sean, doing
something unfamiliar, must be just too much for

Rocky. That was understandable. "Okay, sure," he said. "We'll be a couple of hours, max."

"Take your time," Pudge said. "This dog needs a lot of training."

"Well…"

Cash and Sean looked at each other. Then they each grabbed one of Liam's arms and one of his legs and started carrying him down toward the water.

Liam struggled madly, but a minute later he was in. Dunked. He sputtered to the surface, shaking bits of plants and algae out of his hair. He scrambled up through the mud to where his brothers stood laughing. Cash had been the ringleader—and he was smaller—so Liam ran at him first, caught his midsection like a charging bull and hurled him into the water.

He and Sean both laughed as Cash emerged looking furious. He was the one who wore only expensive clothes. Cash started for Liam, but Liam held up a hand. "Only one of us not wet yet," he said.

Cash gave a quick nod, and they both took Sean together. Each grabbing one of his arms, they threw him into the water.

Farther up on the grassy area, Pudge and Rocky were laughing. Rio ran down and started splashing around in the water, too, so Liam threw him a couple of sticks and he chased them, swimming back to shore like a crocodile. Ma Dixie came bustling down with towels, threw one to each of them, and scolded. "That water is full of snakes," she said.

"You're setting a terrible example. Rocky, don't go near that water, and don't let the dog do it either."

Horsing around with his brothers, being scolded by Ma, Liam felt like a kid again.

They all dried off and got in the boat. Liam's clothes clung to him, wet and clammy, and the brackish water made him feel itchy. All the same, his mood had lifted. Hot August sun sparkled on the water. Off through the reeds, a couple of white egrets cried out, seeming to complain to each other. The rich, dank smell of the bayou filled his senses: neither pleasant nor unpleasant, exactly, just home.

Once they were out near a favorite fishing hole, Sean turned off the motor. "Don't know why you were so set on bringing the kid."

"I wanted to ask him about something I found," Liam said. Though that hadn't gone well; Rocky had denied having a pair of red Crocs. But Liam knew what he'd seen.

"That shoe?" Cash had taken off his designer sneakers and was wringing out his socks.

"Yeah."

"Any more information about that?" Cash asked.

Liam's face heated remembering how Buck had mocked him for bringing in that particular bit of evidence. "They weren't interested," he said, "or rather, Buck wasn't, even though I explained that Rocky might've lost it that night."

"Aren't you supposed to be interested in any-thing related to the case, if you're a cop?" Sean dipped a hand into their minnow bucket and baited his hook.

"Not if you're Buck Mulligan." Liam's jaw clenched. The man was more concerned with cozying up to city council then with solving a murder.

Murder anywhere was a horrible thing, but murder in Safe Haven felt ten times as bad, at least to Liam.

"How's the path to becoming chief going?" Sean asked.

Liam shrugged a shoulder. "Not great."

"Why not? What happened?"

"Don't bug him about it," Cash said. "Being chief isn't the be-all and end-all."

Even Liam stared at Cash for that one.

"What? It's not. Money and power…they don't solve your problems."

"It's not the power or the money," Liam said. "I don't care about that stuff, but this town is important to me."

Both of his brothers concentrated on their fishing, but he could tell they were listening. Curious.

"Look, I just don't want what happened to our mom to happen to anyone else. Ever. I think I'm the person who can fight it, at least in this town. Mulligan isn't."

Both of Sean's eyebrows lifted, and then he gave a slow nod. "Makes sense."

All of a sudden Cash's rod arced and line started

running out. "Fish on," he said, and whipped his arm back to give out line.

"Nice job, man." Sean leaned forward. "Oh, yeah. That a channel cat?"

Cash was spinning and pulling, spinning and pulling. "Come on," he crooned, "Come on in."

Liam lifted half up to watch the water. "I really don't think he knows he's hooked yet."

"Feels kinda like a flounder." Cash tugged some more. "Like a real big flounder."

The fish was within sight now, and Liam recognized it. "Redfish!"

"Yeah," Sean said, "that's a nice little redfish. Who'd have pegged Cash for the first catch? In the marsh, yet."

"Come on out here, baby." Cash was netting the fish now, grinning, looking completely different from the high-powered businessman he was.

"What do you think," Liam asked, "eight, ten pounds?"

"It's not even the flood tide yet," Sean crowed. "Redfish loves the tide and the freshwater. I'm going to catch me a bigger one."

It wasn't long before Liam got a bite, hooked it and pulled in a fine mullet. Then Cash caught another one. Then they both had to give Sean a hard time, because they all knew he was the best fisherman among them, but he hadn't had a nibble.

Liam held a cold can of soda to his forehead. The hot humid air, the sun filtered through the bayou's thick leaves, the fishy smell of his hands and clothes, his brothers' laughter... Liam wanted to open his hands and grasp it all and hold on.

It was a moment like they'd had when they were teenagers. And Liam hoped they'd still be doing this when they were older than Pudge.

Out here in the low country marsh, you knew that God was in His heaven. And you could at least pretend that all was right with the world.

They fished and joked and talked for another hour or so before they turned the boat back toward Ma Dixie's place. When they got close, Sean turned off the motor and they just drifted, looking toward the shore.

Pudge still sat in his same chair, and Rocky ran back and forth, chasing Rio. It was good to hear the boy's happy shouts. For once he sounded like a kid. And Rio was loving it, barking madly.

"Grandfather figure," Cash commented.

Liam opened his mouth to argue that Pudge was more like a father than a grandfather. But then he watched as Pudge heaved himself out of his chair and hobbled down toward the dock.

He was getting older. They all were.

Out of nowhere, Liam flashed back to the day he graduated from college. To the surprise of everyone, including himself, he'd graduated from UNC with honors. He'd known he wouldn't have anyone there at graduation, since his foster family had moved down to Florida by then. They'd been older and not in the best of health. Sean was overseas, and Cash was in New York. And it had stung a little to see all the other graduates with their families, but Liam was used to being different and he still felt good. He'd achieved more than anyone had ever expected.

Then his name was called and he walked to the stage and there was crazy loud cheering, louder than for almost anyone else in the whole graduating class. It turned out that Sean took leave and Cash flew in from his hotshot job, and Ma Dixie and Pudge had driven up from Safe Haven. And yeah, Liam might've gotten something in his eye that caused it to water a little, but he got it under control. They'd all gone out for a big celebration dinner. During that, his brothers had presented him with a graduation present: a check for his police academy tuition. And Liam had known that even though his family was a little different, it was a family, and he'd felt surrounded by their love.

Now, Liam looked at Rocky, running carefree with the dog, and he thought about how what had happened to Rocky wasn't his fault. In the same way, what had happened to him and Cash and Sean hadn't been their fault.

Rocky couldn't change what his parents did, and he could still become a great person. Liam believed the same of his brothers: Sean and Cash were both good men despite their miserable excuse for a father.

What about him? Could he give himself the same opportunity, forgiveness and grace as he gave to others?

THE NEXT TUESDAY, Yasmin opened the door of the women's center at lunchtime, thinking she'd eat her sandwich outside, only to discover Rita and Norma standing there, arguing.

"Hey, girls," she said, trying to infuse some energy into her voice.

That was how it had been with her for the last couple of days: trying to muster energy she didn't have. A dark cloud seemed to press down on her, making every movement and activity a huge challenge.

In her mind, a continual refrain chanted: *schizophrenic, schizophrenic.* It was so persistent that she wondered if it, too, was part of the voices that would plague her more and more as her condition worsened.

"We're here to drag you away from your work." Rita held out a hand. "Come on, you have some sneakers in there, right? Let's go for a walk."

Yasmin tried to smile. "Thank you guys, so much, but I just can't. I have a ton of paperwork to do." Even as she said it, she felt a kind of hopelessness descending over her. How could she get everything done? Even now, Rocky was at home playing video games under Josiah's half-baked supervision. No telling what trouble or conflicts might arise between them. She should really be there. But she had a responsibility to her board of directors and especially to her clients. She couldn't let them down, even though she was increasingly aware that the job was too much for one woman to do.

"You look awful." Norma put her hands on her hips. "A little fresh air will make you do better work, faster."

Probably true. And of course she looked awful. She'd just started experiencing symptoms of a severe and lifelong mental illness.

"We won't take no for an answer," Rita said.

They wouldn't, either. She could tell. "It's too hot," Yasmin said weakly. But she waved them into her office and hunted under her desk to find her shoes.

When she sat up, Rita was looking around the room, her face pale, a fine sheen of sweat on her forehead. "I feel it, more than ever. I've been here before."

Her tone was odd. "Where, in this back office? I don't think so." Rita volunteered at least once a week, but Yasmin discouraged volunteers from coming into her office. Partly because there were sensitive records here, but also because she was embarrassed about the stacks of files she never had time to put away.

"A long time ago." Rita looked around. "In this room."

"You mean, before you moved here? Did you travel through?"

Norma waved her hand in Yasmin's direction, a "be quiet" gesture. She touched Rita's arm, studying her intently for a few seconds. And then she turned back toward Yasmin. "Did this office used to be more central to the center's operations?"

"I think so, before the church was renovated." Yasmin watched Rita, concerned. She seemed close to hyperventilating.

"Do you have any old records from the center? Any intake forms, that kind of thing?"

"There are a bunch of files in the basement, but I'm not sure what kind of shape they're in. We had some water damage a few years ago." She tilted her head to the side, distress for her friend pushing aside her own worries. "Rita? Are you okay? Do you want something to drink? Want me to look something up?"

Rita waved a hand. "I'm fine. No need to look at old records." She stood up quickly. "I'll be outside." She hurried out of the office.

Yasmin stuffed her feet into sneakers and stood, frowning as she looked in the direction Rita had gone. Rita was always so calm and steady. "Is she okay?"

"Pretty much so," Norma said, standing up. "But we could all use the opportunity to oxygenate our brains."

Outside, the warm, humid air pressed in on Yasmin, an oppressive embrace. She pulled her hair up into a high ponytail as the other two women started toward the park, then trudged after them.

After a minute, Rita dropped back to walk beside her, and Yasmin studied her face covertly. What had set her off in the center?

And right on the heels of that thought came her own worry: Would she be able to care about other people once she was in the grips of the disease, or heavily medicated to manage it?

Around her rose the cute cottages and tall Victorians of her hometown, fronted by lovingly tended little yards. Bougainvillea and yellow jessamine lined porches and picket fences, sharing their sweet fragrance. You had to watch your step: most of the sidewalks were buckled up from tree roots, because nobody in Safe Haven was quick to cut down the huge live oaks that lined the streets, providing shade and a home for the lacy decoration of Spanish moss that hung from the branches.

What would it all be to her once her illness got worse? Would she still get that warm, home-base feeling from walking through town?

She wondered whether Josiah still enjoyed the pounding waves and hot sand and open vistas that had drawn him to the beach all his life. Or was his joy damaged by the symptoms of his illness? Why hadn't she talked to him more about what it was like to experience delusions? She'd been trying to be sensitive, but in reality, she'd just left him to cope with his symptoms alone.

"I'm just plain freaked-out," Rita said suddenly, breaking into Yasmin's ruminations.

"Why?" She looked over, concerned.

A muscle jumped in Rita's cheek. "Yasmin, I don't tell most people this, but you might as well know that I have amnesia. There's a whole big chunk of my past that I don't remember." She paused, then added, "And I think part of it took place in Safe Haven."

"Amnesia?" Thoroughly jolted out of her own anxiety, Yasmin studied her friend. "That must be awful! I kind of thought it just happened in books."

"Nope." Rita kept walking, staring at the sidewalk in front of her.

"Wow." Yasmin leaned over and gave Rita a quick shoulder hug, wishing she could alleviate the older woman's pain in some way. "You seem so, I don't know, normal and together. I'd never have guessed."

"I'm a good faker." Rita's mouth twisted a little.

"Keep up the pace, guys," Norma said over her shoulder. "I want to hear all the gossip."

They both sped up so that they were walking right behind Norma again. "That must be so hard to deal with," Yasmin said to Rita. "How much of your life is…"

"Gone? Only about the first thirty years." Rita

glanced over at her. "I'm starting to get glimmer-ings, though."

"Like what happened in the center."

Rita nodded. "Yeah."

"Do you think you were a client there?"

Rita shrugged and lifted her hands. "I have no idea."

"Wow. That must make everything hard." They'd reached the edge of the town park, but it was de-serted enough that they could continue their con-versation. Most Southerners wouldn't venture out in the noontime heat. "Do you remember, like, your parents? Brothers and sisters?"

"Husband? Kids?" Rita shook her head. "None of it, before I found myself in Maine at age thirty."

"With a common-law husband who was crazy about her," Norma tossed over her shoulder.

"You're kidding!" Yasmin stared at the friendly waitress who had such a complicated life story.

"He'd found me around here," Rita explained. "Which is why, once he passed on, I decided to move back. Only it doesn't feel like back, most of the time. It all feels new."

"Do people know? Around here, I mean. Be-cause we have a pretty major sense of history here, and a lot of old people who remember everything that ever happened in Safe Haven. I could intro-duce you to—"

Rita waved both hands. "No, no. I… I have to

take this a little bit at a time. Despite what *she* tells me to do." She nodded at Norma.

"Even though it's basically wrecking her relationship with a good man. Jimmy," she added to Yasmin. Then she looked at Rita. "What? She's not going to say anything."

"I won't," Yasmin assured Rita. The fact that Rita and Jimmy liked each other wasn't exactly news, not to anyone with eyes in this town.

"Don't you give it another thought," Rita said. "I know you, Yasmin. You're the type to worry about other people. But I'm not going to become another problem on your plate. You have enough of your own to deal with."

"I won't. It's just... I care about you, you know?"

"You're a sweetheart." Rita pulled her over for a quick side-hug.

They swung along quietly for a few minutes. Her older friends had been right: she felt better from getting out in the sun, and even more, from spending time with friends.

She had a thought: maybe this was what it would be like to have a normal, mentally healthy mother. Someone who'd bully you into taking a walk because it was good for your health. Someone you could talk to, and, as you got older, they'd share their problems with you, too. So you could help each other, or at least give a shoulder to cry on. Younger helping older, older helping young.

Someone who'd be there for you if you got yourself into some big, big trouble, or found yourself with a terrible problem on your hands.

"Speaking of men," Rita said finally, "how are things going between you and Liam?"

"Must be convenient," Norma added with a wicked grin, "having him live right there on your property."

"I wouldn't call it convenient." Yasmin slowed, considering Rita's question. What *was* her relationship with Liam like? How was it going? Did they even have a relationship?

And if Rita was finding her relationship with Jimmy to be negatively affected by her amnesia… what would happen to any relationship between Liam and Yasmin, when it came to light that she suffered from the same condition Josiah had?

There would be no relationship, that was all.

Tears welled up and her throat tightened.

You knew you couldn't have a relationship. You'd decided that. You knew this issue ran in the family. You'd decided not to have kids.

But the reality was that when Liam had come back into her life, she'd started to hope. She'd started to care.

If she were honest with herself, she'd never stopped. But recently, since he was almost living with her, since he was helping her with Rocky, since he'd kissed her…she'd gotten attached. Again. Even more.

What was she supposed to do with that?

Her throat felt like a giant vise was constricting it, because the answer was nothing. She could do nothing.

"Hey," Rita said, putting a hand on her arm, making her stop walking. "You okay? Are things that bad with Liam?"

Yasmin blinked back tears. "He kind of pulled away from me again," she said. "I don't know why, but that's what it's always been like for us. We're not going to be a thing."

Rita looked at her sharply. "I thought you cared about him," she said. "It sure seemed that way. Do you think he's too damaged from his childhood to have a relationship?"

"No!" That was an odd thing for Rita to think, and Yasmin frowned at her, then started walking again, this time more slowly, and both Rita and Norma fell into step with her. "That's not it at all. I just… I have some issues that make it not very smart for me to think long-term with any man. The stuff I told you about before." She looked off across the greenery in the park. "If I had a relationship, if I thought long-term with any man, it would be Liam."

There. She'd said it.

If she chose any man—if she could—it would be Liam.

"Okay, look," Rita said to Yasmin. She indicated a park bench. "Sit down there and talk to Norma. She knows everything there is to know about mental health."

But Yasmin didn't feel especially comfortable with Norma, and she didn't want to confide in her. The woman might have a good heart, but she was brash and abrasive. What harsh thing would she say to Yasmin when she found out the truth about her?

Then again, nothing Norma said could be worse than what Yasmin was saying to herself.

And with these two women, pushy didn't even begin to describe it. They wouldn't let it alone until she did what they thought was right.

"Fine," she said, and sat down on the old green bench.

"I'm going to take a spin around the park," Rita said. "Back in fifteen or twenty minutes."

"That's a long time for a spin." Norma sounded amused. "Or wait. Is this when the guys play shirts and skins down at the basketball court?"

Rita's cheeks turned a pretty shade of pink. "Maybe they do. And maybe Jimmy said he's going to be playing. You got a problem with that?"

Norma lifted her hands, palms out. "No, no. I'm all in favor of love. And of handsome men with their shirts off."

"You are bad." Rita walked off toward the basketball courts at a rapid clip.

They both watched her, and then there was a minute of silence. It felt awkward to Yasmin, and she looked over to see if it was striking Norma the same way.

Norma looked perfectly relaxed. But then, Norma

had a background in counseling. She was probably accustomed to letting her clients find their own pace.

Yasmin stalled. "I hate to take advantage of your expertise for free. Isn't this kind of like how everyone goes up to a doctor at a party, and tells her all of their aches and pains?"

Norma cackled. "Believe me, I've had my share of people telling me all kinds of extremely private things at parties. But this is different. You're a friend."

The words, simple and direct, made surprising tears push at the backs of Yasmin's eyes. She blinked and swallowed. What was wrong with her? Was it PMS?

And now she felt bad about getting annoyed with Norma. She didn't have so many friends that she could afford to turn one down, even if Norma's personality was a little bit challenging. "I think I might have schizophrenia," she blurted out.

Norma let out a bray of laughter. "You? I don't think so."

Yasmin lifted her chin, her good thoughts about Norma fading. "I have like five out of seven of the symptoms," she said.

"What, on Wikipedia?"

Heat rose to Yasmin's cheeks. "Yeah."

Norma shook her head. "People self-diagnose all the time thanks to the wonders of the internet," she said. "Ninety percent of the time, they're dead wrong."

She looked ready to dismiss the whole subject, but Yasmin suddenly didn't want to. So she didn't like Norma a whole lot. Who better to confide in, than someone she wasn't likely to spend a lot of time with in the future? "My brother's been diagnosed," she said. "And my mom has some mental health issues, as well. My understanding is that it's genetic, or at least, that there's a genetic component. Am I wrong about that?"

The smile slid off Norma's face. She closed her eyes for a quick moment, then opened them, looked at Yasmin and patted her arm. "I'm sorry. Sorry about your brother, and sorry not to take you seriously."

"So... Given that and the symptoms I've been having..."

"Tell me your symptoms." Norma's jokey exterior had vanished, and in its place was the face of a seasoned professional. Even her workout clothes didn't detract from her intensity.

So Yasmin told her about the voices, and the forgetfulness and depression and confusion. Norma nodded through the whole story, her expression thoughtful.

"So... What do you think?" Yasmin gripped the edge of the bench, the splintery wood digging into her palms.

Norma hesitated, then spoke. "Look, this isn't

my specialty. And it would be ridiculous to make a diagnosis on a park bench. If you're worried about having any mental illness, you should see a professional in a professional setting."

"So you do think I have it." Yasmin had thought she felt the worst she could feel, but now she realized she had only scratched the surface. Because the serious look in Norma-the-psychologist's eyes had her stomach plunging.

"Actually, I don't." Norma tucked a foot under her thigh and turned, facing Yasmin more directly. "Yes, it's a possibility. And yes, you're still within the age limits of diagnosis for women. So getting tested would be a good idea."

Yasmin nodded, lifting her shirt out to let the slight breeze cool her sweaty stomach and chest.

"But I've never seen a case where the patient knew, in a lucid state, that he or she had it. People with schizophrenia, their delusions seem real to them. Whereas you're aware that that voice was a voice, not a real being with authority over your life."

"But then, if it wasn't a delusion, what was it?"

"I don't know. It could have been a dream. Could have been someone playing a trick on you. Your brother and your foster child live with you, right?"

Hmm. Rocky had become her foster child in people's eyes? Yasmin tested the notion—*I have a foster son*—and found she didn't mind it. "Yes, they live with me, but I can't imagine either of them playing such a mean trick."

"It does seem strange. It was probably a dream." Norma nodded decisively. "Listen, I really do think you should see somebody professional. Not because I think you have schizophrenia, but because I think you're struggling with a lot of things. And depression affects a lot of women. You could be headed down that path, and there are great medications that can help with it."

"Seriously? You think it's just my depression coming back?"

"You had it before?"

"Just a mild form, when I was a teenager."

"Then yes. That would be my guess." Norma shrugged. "If that. You could be just a little overwhelmed by your life right now. Happens to a lot of people."

Rita came power walking toward them along the blacktop path, her face pinker than ever. "Should I take another lap?"

"No need." Yasmin patted the seat beside her, feeling like she was one hundred pounds lighter. Mild depression or simply being overwhelmed, those she could cope with. She'd make an appointment with her doctor when she got back to the office.

But for a professional, Norma, to tell her it was unlikely she had the major mental health issue she'd feared made the whole world brighter and clearer and more beautiful.

Rita perched on the edge of the bench. "I'm not going to pry into what you talked about," she said.

"Pry away." Yasmin leaned back and let out her breath in a huge sigh. "She thinks I probably don't have what my brother has."

"Oh, honey," Rita said. She pulled Yasmin into sweaty arms for a quick hug. "That's what I thought, too, but she's the professional."

Yasmin looked over at Norma. "Thank you. I feel worlds better."

"And you're going to see someone?"

"Yes, Mom." She wrinkled her nose at Norma.

The older woman laughed. "I never had kids, but I've mothered a bunch of them. Welcome to the family."

Rita stood up. "If we're done here, I really need to get home. Need to take a shower and clean up."

Norma raised her eyebrows. "What's your hurry? I didn't think you had anything to do today."

"Now I do." Rita gave Norma a pretend glare. "And it's not your business what it is."

"Whee," Norma crowed. "Someone has a date!"

Rita put her hands over her face, laughing. "There is no keeping anything from you. Yes, I have a date with Jimmy." Her face went serious. "And I have a feeling it's going to be a make-or-break one."

As they walked through the sweltering heat, as they parted to go their separate ways, Yasmin's heart felt full.

Maybe she wasn't terribly, terribly sick as she'd feared.

And maybe she had a couple of good new friends.

CHAPTER FOURTEEN

THAT NIGHT, Rita opened the door to her apartment and swallowed hard.

Jimmy stood there, pretty much filling the doorway. He wore a light blue dress shirt tucked into jeans, sleeves rolled up. With his dark complexion and brown eyes, he was…devastating.

"I brought wine," he said. His voice was extra husky. And the way he was looking at her warmed her down to her toes.

"Come in." She felt like a high school girl. "I… should I open this?"

"I'll have a glass if you will," he said. When he handed her the wine, his fingers brushed hers.

She could barely catch her breath.

They'd had a rough stretch, she and Jimmy, after he'd gotten jealous that night at the Seaside Villages event. He'd acted cold at work for a couple of days, and she'd ignored him, too, because she didn't like him acting like she'd done something wrong. To her, that smacked of a kind of control she hated.

But he'd caught her after the lunch rush one afternoon and told her he was sorry for walking out that night, had admitted his jealousy in a charming way and also admitted he had no right and had acted immature.

There was nothing like a man who could apologize. She'd forgiven him instantly. And accepted his invitation to go out with him that same night.

Now, she was trying to gather the courage to tell him the truth about herself, but maybe there was another way this night could go.

"What's cooking?" he asked. His eyes lingered on her, increasing the vibe between them, but he didn't bring it to the surface or make a move.

"Come on back to the kitchen."

He followed her, closely enough that her cheeks went pink. She leaned down to open the oven and came up with the casserole dish of potatoes, her face hot from the oven and from his attention.

He smiled, but didn't make a comment, and his smile got broader when he saw what she'd cooked. "Are those scalloped potatoes?"

She nodded. "I know, it's too hot. But I have good AC. And I felt like comfort food."

And I know that meat and potatoes are the way to a man's heart.

"Just like my mama used to make," he said.

"Uh-oh. I can never live up to Mama." But as she put the casserole down on the trivet on the counter, a question stabbed into her.

Did her boys have any memories of the foods she'd cooked for them?

Jimmy pulled up a stool at the counter and took over the wine-opening for her while she got out the salad she'd made. He poured them both full glasses and then handed one to her.

"Salud." He clinked his glass against hers, his eyes warm.

Her heart fluttered like a bird, beating its wings in the cage of her chest.

She and Jimmy worked together most days of the week, and they'd gotten together a few times outside of work.

Tonight seemed different, though. She could get lost in those soulful eyes. But there was something she needed to focus on, something she was forgetting…

"The steaks!" She'd put them on just before he came. She rushed out to her balcony, grabbed the spatula, and flipped them over, then switched off the electric grill. They'd finish up cooking from the heat. Hopefully, their one side wasn't burnt.

"Want me to finish those up for you?" he asked.

"Sure." She flashed him a smile. "I already know you look good in an apron." She knew, because he sometimes threw one on and helped in the kitchen if they were busy or someone called off.

She admired that in him as a boss. He didn't just order people around; he got his hands dirty.

And there was something about a man who cooked.

He kept his eyes on hers as she handed him an apron. As he looped it over his head. Then he laughed a little, the sound husky, and shook his head. "I'm out of practice with this," he said.

"With what?"

He checked the steaks and then pointed from his own chest to hers and back again. "This. You're the first woman I've dated in, oh, three years."

So he considered them as dating, considered this a date. Interesting.

She didn't know a lot about his romantic history, but once he'd mentioned a divorce three years ago.

She felt good that he wasn't just running around with anyone and everyone. Especially since he could, if he wanted to. She'd seen how the ladies looked at him at the restaurant. He was a catch, for sure.

But she wasn't sure she'd know what to do with him if she caught him.

For that matter, he just might throw *her* back if he found out the truth about her.

She turned away from his way-too-appealing smile and went inside to get the table ready.

Once they'd eaten—or at least, Jimmy had eaten, Rita had just picked at her food—and drank a glass and a half of wine each, she started to clear. When he stood, she waved a hand. "Sit. I'll just get this off the table."

"Nope." He put a hand on her arm, and it felt like it left a warm imprint. "You work hard doing this kind of thing in your day job, you shouldn't have to do it at home while I sit there like a customer. I want to help."

So he carried in dishes and put them on the counter, right beside where she stood at the sink, rinsing them off and putting them into the dishwasher. Once he reached around her, and the warmth of his big body radiated, Rita caught her breath, her body heating. It made her remember she hadn't been with a man for more than two years herself, ever since T-Bone had gotten too sick for any kind of a relationship but that of a caregiver and patient.

Was she ready to start something up again, though? She enjoyed her freedom, not having to answer to anyone. Not having to reveal her deepest secrets.

Jimmy seemed to sense her ambivalence, and he didn't push. Clearly, he wasn't just helping with the cleanup to get physically close. He actually finished carrying in the dishes, put the extra food away and wiped off the table, so that the end result was a kitchen she wouldn't have to clean later.

She was wiping her hands when he came and leaned against the counter, a good foot away from her.

In his hand was the bottle of wine and two glasses. "Should we finish it off?" he asked, his eyes steady on hers.

"I… I don't know."

"What don't you know?" He let a little smile tug at the corner of his mouth.

She sought for words. "I want to be thinking straight," she said, "but I'm a little nervous."

He put down the bottle and glasses. "Come here," he said. He leaned back against the counter, legs wide, and pulled her close.

She relished the feel of his body against hers, undeniably. But mostly she wanted the security of his arms.

She should tell him the truth about herself. Maybe he was strong enough to take it.

Or strong enough to push you away.

"What do you want to do?"

Or maybe they should just… She leaned against him a little harder and he lifted her chin and kissed her.

And then she wasn't thinking anymore. She was just feeling his firm lips against hers, that male roughness of his skin, his obvious desire for her.

The fact was, he knew very well what he was doing. Despite any recent period of celibacy, he clearly had done his share of kissing. He was an expert.

Was she going to take him to her bed?

Was she the kind of woman who did that?

She pulled back a little and looked up at him. He was breathing hard and so was she.

"What do you want to do?"

"What I want to do and what I should do are two different things." She let her fingers stroke the back of his neck.

He ran a thumb along her jawbone, making her shiver. "What do you want to do?" It was the third time he'd asked the question. The magical third time, like in fairy tales.

"Can't you guess?" She couldn't help but look at his face, his lips.

He nodded, paused a minute, ran a hand around the collar of his shirt. "It might be the same thing I want to do. But," he added, "I can tell you're not feeling sure about it. So the other question is, what do you feel like you *should* do?"

That was the joy of an older man, that he could restrain his impulses. She could, too. "I have something I should tell you. Before…we do anything else." She stepped away from his warmth and all her fears came rushing back in.

Kissing him had been amazing, and she wanted to do more of it. And she'd really be bereft if Jimmy dumped her for what she was about to tell him.

She swallowed hard. "Come out onto the balcony," she said, and headed out, her hand behind her, pulling him along.

The grill had cooled down and so had the air, on the front of a storm. They sat, and then Jimmy half stood and moved his chair closer. "I don't want to be so far away," he said, and her heart melted all over again.

She looked out over the town, letting the breeze cool her warm cheeks. The sun peeked through clouds on the horizon, pink and gold and orange.

His hand intertwined with hers, but loosely. "What do you need to tell me?"

If he'd been at all patronizing, smiling, not taking it seriously, she wouldn't have been able to continue. But Jimmy was a good man, and he respected her intelligence; he'd made that obvious. If something was of concern to her, it was of concern to him.

What a great partner he would be.

"It's about Liam, and Cash, and Sean," she said.

He frowned as he put the names together. "What about them?"

"I...look. Have you ever known anyone with amnesia?"

"Amnesia?" He tilted his head. "Man, I thought this was going in an entirely different direction."

"Like…"

"Like, *Jimmy, I have this STD…*"

She snorted. "I've been with one man in twenty years, and he was faithful as the day is long. We're good there."

"I am, too," he said, "just so you know. But back to amnesia." He shook his head. "Nope, I know almost nothing about it. Well, wait. There was a guy in Vietnam who got knocked in the head. He had some short-term amnesia where he didn't even remember his own name. It went away, from what I heard, a few months later."

"It can do that," she said. "Every case is different."

He looked at her, eyes narrowing a little, waiting.

"Mine lasted twenty years. *Has* lasted. I still have it."

His eyes widened and his hand tightened. "Tell me."

So she did, starting from the time she'd woken up in Maine, and then going to everything she'd pieced together from what T-Bone had told her, and ending up here, now.

"I've been getting inklings while I've been here," she said, "and I... I heard a few things from Abel."

"Abel, our cook?"

She nodded. "He remembered me. From before."

"Wow."

She drew in a breath. Now or never. "And what he remembered was...that I had three boys with me when I came to Safe Haven. I've spent some time trying to piece things together, and what it all comes back to is the O'Dwyer boys." She looked him in the eyes. "I think they're my sons."

"What?" He stared at her. "Your sons, but you don't remember them? Do they know?"

She shook her head. "I have no memory of them. Zero. But I know they were abandoned in town by their mother at just about the time T-Bone found me, unconscious beside the highway outside of Safe Haven. Their ages are right for what Abel said."

He shook his head slowly. "What a story."

Did he mean he thought she'd made it up? But no, that wasn't in his face or voice. She struggled on. "So you see, I feel like I have to know who I am before I can…" She did what he had done, pointing first at her own chest, then at his, then back again. "Before we can really be together. And Jimmy," she added, putting a hand on his arm because he'd opened his mouth to speak, "you should know that I might have abandoned them, might have done something awful so that they were taken away from me."

He ignored that, or seemed to. "Why don't they recognize you?"

She shrugged. "I was a mess when T-Bone found me. I needed a lot of plastic surgery. I'm a redhead now, and believe me, it's not natural. Plus, I'm twenty years older." She frowned. "Abel recognized me, but he was an adult when he met me, and he's the kind of person who really looks at you. Where kids… I don't know. I think they *feel* Mom as much as look at her."

"Wow." He blew out a breath, leaned forward and took her hand in both of his. "I am so sorry that happened to you. Was there never any evidence about who might have done it?"

"I don't know." She bit her lip, looking out at the sun as the last sliver of it dipped behind the horizon. "T-Bone didn't stick around for me to look into it, didn't even tell me the truth about where he found me for years."

"Why?"

"He thought I might have been a prostitute, or a criminal, or involved with drugs and dealing. And it's true. I might have been."

This time, he seemed to take in what she said. His lips pressed together a little and he held her gaze. Then, slowly, he started shaking his head. "No. That's not the Rita I know."

The idea that he'd simply believe in her, rather than question her character, brought a sudden tightness to her throat. She swallowed, unable to speak.

"I don't think basic values change," he went on. "You must have been desperate in some way, either that or you were the victim of some horrendous random crime."

"You don't hate me for it."

His eyebrows came together and he shook his head, reached out to squeeze her hand. "No, I don't hate you for it. Of course not. You can't help what happened to you. I feel…not sorry for you, exactly, but a lot of sympathy." He pulled out his phone. "But I do think you need to tell them."

"What are you doing?" she asked, alarmed.

"I'm inviting them all to get together," he said.

"Now?" she squeaked out.

He shrugged. "Why wait?"

"No." She leaned forward and put her hand over the one he held his phone in. "No, don't."

He stopped scrolling on his phone, looking at her steadily. "You want to stay in this limbo? You want *them* not to know?"

She bit her lip. "No. No, but I'm so scared."

He nodded. "Sure you are. Anything hard is scary. But you can do it."

Her heart pounded so fast she felt like it was going to jump out of her chest and fly away. "I... I don't know if I can."

"I'll be right beside you," he said, "if you want me to be." He turned his hand over, squeezed hers.

She drew in a huge breath. "Yeah, okay. And I want you to be," she said. "But the text should come from me."

AN HOUR LATER, Liam walked into the Palmetto Pig and looked around for Rita. What could the waitress need, that had her finding his number and asking him—and Sean and Cash—to meet at the Pig ASAP?

The place was about half-full, par for the course on a weeknight. He smelled burgers cooking, something fried...maybe he'd order himself a late dinner as soon as he'd figured out what Rita wanted. The Pig's food wasn't exactly organic, but it did hit the spot.

There she was, at a table in the corner, away from the music and pool table. With her was Jimmy Cooper, the diner's manager.

Cash had already let them know he was out of town on a business deal and couldn't come. As Liam headed toward their table, a text pinged in from Sean. Running late, nothing serious. Be there soon.

So it was just him for now, and Liam hoped it wasn't a social call. Despite his good afternoon with his brothers, he was still in a mood over Yasmin and her late-night visitor. He didn't feel like making nice.

"Liam." Rita got up and looked like she wanted to hug him, which was weird. But then she sat down again, and Jimmy nudged out a chair for Liam with his foot, and he sat down.

"Thanks for coming," Rita said, her voice sort of nervous. That made Liam look at her more closely and notice she was crumpling and uncrumpling a napkin in her hands, and that a fine sheen of sweat coated her forehead despite the icy air-conditioning. "Do you know…are your brothers on their way?"

"Cash is out of town," he said, "and Sean just let me know he's going to try to come, but later."

She nodded, glanced over at Jimmy, who gave her a reassuring smile.

Okay, so not a social call. "What's up?" he asked.

She drew in a breath. "I always did think you were the one I'd like to tell first," she said.

"Tell me what?" She sounded all emotional, like there was something heavy on her mind.

"Liam, I think you're…" She broke off. "Oh, I can't even say it."

A strange, prickling feeling started in Liam's fingers. "Whatever it is, just tell me," he said. He'd gotten confessions in all kinds of places, but he'd be surprised if Rita had committed some kind of crime. She was a nice lady.

"I think you're..." She swallowed convulsively. "I think you're my son."

Liam stared at her, his mind a complete blank, although the prickling sensation continued. Had he heard her right? "Did you just say I'm your son?"

She drew in her breath, bit her lip. "See, I have amnesia," she said. "But I recently found out that I was here in Safe Haven, just about the time that you and your brothers lost your mom."

This. Did. Not. Compute. It had all the makings of a bad TV movie. And Liam felt like he was watching it on TV, rather than really living in it. "You mean...wait. Do you *remember* me, or something?"

Slowly, she shook her head back and forth. "No. I'm sorry to say, I don't."

"Then how..." He broke off. "What..." He couldn't think what to ask. "Maybe you'd better just tell me the whole story."

She went into some long explanation of how she'd been found by some trucker, a blow to the head, beaten up, remembering nothing. How she'd only recently learned, with the trucker's death, where he'd really found her.

Liam watched her mouth making words and her eyes getting teary, and he couldn't process it. He'd wanted to find his mother for years, put a lot of time

and effort into trying to locate her through the resources he had available as a cop.

He'd imagined what it would be like to find her:
the tears of joy on her part, her pride in what he'd
become, her apologies for not being able to come
back and rescue them when they'd been kids. Her
stories about their childhood. Her explanation for
everything that had happened.

Other times, he'd imagined finding her grave-
stone.

What he hadn't ever expected was to meet his
so-called mother in the Palmetto Pig, and to feel
nothing.

And to have her remember nothing about him.

"Hey, what's going on?" Sean pulled out a chair
and sat down next to Liam, across from Rita. "I
got here as soon as I could. It sounded important."

Liam found that he was taking slow, calming
breaths, something he'd learned to do as a kid and
honed in his police work. Calming yourself down
was a crucial skill. He normally didn't use it in a
bar, with friends and family...with his supposed
mother...but he needed it as he watched Rita swallowing and looking at Jimmy and then at Sean, wiping sweat from her forehead with a napkin.

It was going to take her forever to blurt it out
again. "She's our mom," Liam said to Sean. "Or at
least, she thinks she is."

Sean's head jerked around to face him, and then
he looked at Rita. "What?"

Rita blew out a breath, smiled at him. "Thanks, Liam," she said, and took his hand.

He pulled it away. He didn't know this woman.

She swallowed and transferred her attention to Sean. "I've had amnesia for twenty years, still do," she said, "but what little I know points to me being the woman who left you boys here in Safe Haven." She launched into the same story she'd been telling Liam.

Sean was tilting his head to one side, staring at her, recognition dawning in his eyes, a smile tugging at the corner of his mouth and then breaking wide. "I always thought there was something a little familiar about..." He looked heavenward, shaking his head, pressing his lips together. Tears welled up in his eyes.

Rita watched him, her own eyes filling, tears running down her face.

Liam felt as cold as ice.

Sean looked at her again, and then he was out of his chair and over beside her, pulling her up and hugging her hard. "I never thought I'd see you again!"

She shook with sobs, and people throughout the Pig gave them curious stares. Pretty embarrassing, having his incredible hulk of a brother crying over some middle-aged woman in a bar.

Jimmy looked over at him. "It's a lot to take in," he said.

Liam nodded and looked away. His own throat

felt tight, but not with the kind of joy his brother obviously felt.

Instead, he felt like a dream he'd been carrying for years was disintegrating inside him.

"I'm so sorry," Rita sobbed into Sean's chest. "I don't know what happened. I can't… I can't remember any of it." She looked up at him.

Sean helped her back into her chair and knelt beside her. "Our dad pushed you into his truck," he said. "It happened right after we'd all moved into the women's center, which was a full-on shelter back then. We went out to do some shopping and he found us. He took you." Sean was speaking gently, holding Rita's hand.

Liam felt faintly nauseous.

"I'm so terribly sorry," she choked out. "I didn't take care of you boys the way a mother should. I… It's going to be a process, but I hope you'll let me get to know you."

"Of course!" Sean glanced at Liam and then at Rita. "We want to get to know you, too."

Dark turmoil churned inside Liam, because he *didn't* want to get to know this woman. He didn't believe for one minute that she was their mom. More like an imposter.

As soon as he'd tripped on that idea, it felt right. Yes, that had to be it: she was faking them for some personal gain. He'd heard of these scams plenty of times.

He stood and cleared the thickness out of his

throat. "Do you have any identification?" he asked her.

She looked up at him and the smile faded from her face. "I do," she said slowly. "But it's nothing that's going to stand up to investigation. My husband—" She broke off. "There's so much to explain."

"Yes, there is," he said. Now that he'd figured out that she was an imposter, he felt better. More in control. "We'll need to run prints and do some investigating. In the meantime…" He looked at Sean. "You need to make sure you don't give her any personal information, nor lend her money. I'll let Cash know the same, since he's got more to lose."

Sean put a hand on his arm, but Liam shook it away, impatient with his brother for being so easily scammed.

Rita was looking at him with a deep sorrow in her eyes, and for a minute, he felt like he could see his mother there. Trick of the imagination, obviously.

"Come to the station tomorrow," he said, trying to look at her like any other petty criminal, impersonally. "I'll start an investigation."

He'd bet his life savings, such as they were, that she wouldn't show.

THE NEXT MORNING, Liam came out of his house dressed for work, but early enough to take Rio for a good walk.

He wished he could just walk forever and postpone the possibility of his fake mother coming to the station to make stuff up and try to convince him of it.

Yasmin opened the door in a bathrobe, handing Rocky a biscuit and glass of orange juice as he burst outside. She looked over at Liam's apartment, and when she saw him and Rio, she gave a hesitant little wave.

Of course she was hesitant. She'd cheated on him. Deliberately, he turned away without returning her greeting, covering up his own immaturity by kneeling to adjust Rio's harness.

Rio jumped at him, knocking his head into Liam's cheekbone, hard. Automatically, Liam's hand went to his face, and he dropped Rio's leash. The dog bounded away to Rocky.

Even his dog wanted nothing to do with him.

Stop acting like you're Rocky's age. He straightened and headed toward the porch steps where Rocky sat rubbing Rio's sides and feeding him pieces of biscuit. Liam looked up to see if Yasmin would scold him, but she'd already gone inside.

"Look, Liam! Look what he can do!" Using the biscuit pieces as food rewards, Rocky got the dog to sit, lay down and then roll over.

"Smart dog!" Rocky hugged Rio and buried his face in the dog's neck, laughing.

Liam felt some of his tension lift, felt his shoulders loosen. Kids and dogs, the innocent souls of the universe. You couldn't be unhappy around them. And he felt good that he'd encouraged Rocky to train the dog. It made the boy proud and gave Rio some needed training. Win-win.

All of a sudden, Rio took off through the yard just as Liam registered a car, going by slowly. He stood to look while Rocky yelled, "Come, Rio, come!"

The dog jumped and leaped at the fence as the car, a nondescript white sedan that looked like a rental, passed slowly by. Liam couldn't see the driver, only the woman in the passenger seat, someone he didn't know.

Rocky was running toward Rio. "I'll get him," Liam called to the boy. He gave a piercing whistle—that was the one thing he *had* taught Rio—and the dog spun out of his leap and ran back to Liam.

Rocky, though, didn't stop; he hurtled out through the gate and ran toward the car. "Mom! Mom!"

But the car sped up and disappeared down the street.

Rocky chased it for a moment and then turned and ran back, panting. "That was my mom! We have to catch her!"

"Your *mom*?"

"It was her! Can we go after them?"

"Come on," Liam said grimly, and Rocky and Rio jumped in the back seat. By the time they got out of the residential section and onto Safe Haven's main street, though, the white car was nowhere to be seen.

"I know it was her, I know it!" Rocky was half yelling, half crying. "She saw me. Why didn't she stop, if she saw me?"

Liam didn't know how to answer. Losing your mom was heartbreaking, obviously, but this mom seemed to have made that choice on purpose. The face Liam had seen wasn't anguished, and there had been no physical struggle to get to her child.

Not like his own mom, who'd been forced into his father's truck, at least according to what Sean had seen.

Rita? No, Rita *wasn't* his mom.

Liam rubbed a hand over his face as he turned the car back toward Yasmin's. He had to take Rocky home, get him settled and then go to work. Had to talk to a woman about proof of whether she was *his* mother.

And he had to step up his investigation of what was going on with Rocky's mother. Before she broke her child's heart into even more pieces.

CHAPTER FIFTEEN

YASMIN HAD JUST finished mopping her kitchen floor—her way of working off the stress of seeing Liam and having him act as cold as an iceberg—when there was a pounding on her back door.

"Be careful!" she cried just as Rocky burst in, skidded on the damp floor with muddy feet, and then ran into the living room, crying. Rio galloped after, mulch and mud from his big paws making splattery footprints.

"Hey!" she half yelled, then "Hey…" trailing off, as the sound of more crying came from the front room.

She turned back to close the door, and there stood Liam.

Her heart flipped over and she sucked in a breath as her whole body melted. So tall, so impossibly handsome in his uniform…and so grim-faced. "What's going on?" she asked.

"We saw his mom." Liam parked his hands on his hips and looked back toward the street, frowning.

"What? Where?"

Liam waved a hand in the general direction of downtown. "Driving by. She was in the passenger seat. Slowed down like she was trying to see her son, but when she did see him—and me, in uniform—the car sped up, drove off. We tried to follow, but…" He spread his hands. "They were gone."

Yasmin bit her lip, looked toward the living room where Rocky's sobs were subsiding, and then turned back toward Liam. "What in the world is going on? Did it seem like she was being coerced to stay in the car?"

He shook his head. "I saw her, too. I just didn't realize who she was. She looked like she was searching for someone. She looked maybe a little upset, but not scared."

"So she's alive and she's in the area. That's something." It was a lot, actually, but what did it mean? Had she seen something on the night of the murder that could be incriminating? To her son, to Josiah, to someone else?

Where was she staying, and what was her plan?

Liam cleared his throat. "Look, Yas, I have to go to work. I'm sorry to dump him on you. Sorry about your floor, too, but can you…" He gestured toward Rocky.

"I'll handle it. See what I can find out."

"Thanks." He was looking at her for longer than their discussion warranted, and a storm seemed to brew behind his sea-blue eyes. Then he turned, sharply, and walked out the door.

Which…of course he did. Because that was how it was with her and Liam. They didn't work things out, they didn't argue, they just walked away.

And that was good and right, she reminded herself. If he didn't walk away from her, she'd have to walk away from him. She'd done it once, but she didn't know if she'd have the strength to do it again.

Like a lovesick girl, she rushed over to the window to watch him get into his car and drive away, her heart squeezing painfully, her stomach dropping as she watched his taillights disappear.

If I could be with any man, it would be Liam.

That was what she'd told Rita and Norma, much to her own surprise. And it was still true. But she wasn't going there. No matter how much her inner teenager longed to throw caution away and jump into Liam's arms.

Then, because she *wasn't* a girl, but an adult woman with responsibilities, she walked back across her now-muddy kitchen into the living room and sat down on the floor beside Rocky and Rio. "Liam said you saw your mom."

Rocky didn't answer, but instead jumped up. "I think he needs to go out," he said, gesturing toward Rio. He tugged at the dog, who obligingly followed him back through the kitchen once again, and out into the backyard.

But he wasn't getting rid of Yasmin with that old

trick. She followed him, sat down on the porch step and beckoned. "So you saw your mom. That must have been pretty intense."

He looked over at her, his forehead wrinkled. Then, seeming to realize that she wasn't going to let up on him, he nodded.

"Are you sure it was her?"

"Yeah," he said, and then hesitated. "At least… well, I'm… I'm not sure, not now. I thought it was her, but…" He looked away.

She studied him. "Are you telling the truth?"

"Yes!" He scooted away from her and grabbed Rio's rope toy, waving it in front of the dog until he grabbed it. "It might have been her, but it might not have been, I don't know."

There was something Rocky wasn't telling her. Had he made up the sighting, or wished it into being? Was he trying to make her and Liam think his mom would be back soon, so they wouldn't make him start school next week?

"It probably wasn't her," he said, tugging at the rope toy.

Yasmin ignored that comment. "Could she be staying somewhere around here, and wanted to check on you?" She frowned. "Although if that was the case, why wouldn't she stop?"

"Because she's scared!" The words seemed to burst out of Rocky, and then he added, "or something." He got very busy playing tug-of-war with Rio.

Rocky definitely knew more than he was saying about his mom's disappearance. But what exactly did he know?

The dog growled fiercely. Rocky let the rope toy go and Rio shook it hard, and then Rocky said, "Rio, drop it."

The dog dropped the toy and sat.

Rocky produced a treat out of his pocket. "Good boy!"

Even in the midst of her confusion about Rocky's mom, Yasmin was impressed. "You taught him that?"

Rocky nodded. "He's real smart. He just didn't ever get trained before."

Yeah, and maybe Rocky could identify.

Suddenly, there was a lot of yapping outside the fence, and Rio raced over. The yapping intensified, and then at the same time, both Yasmin and Rocky saw the open gate. "Rio, no!" Rocky called as the dog raced through it.

More high-pitched yapping and Rio's deep bark. "Call off your mutt!" came a familiar and very unwelcome voice.

Mitch Mitchell.

Rio was circling and nosing Mitch's shih tzu, and the little dog jumped and barked fiercely. But both tails were wagging, and the little dog went into a play bow, and Rio rolled onto his back, tongue hanging out to one side. Whew. Not exactly a dogfight.

"That beast could kill Daisy!" Mitch grabbed for

the end of the little dog's leash, which he had apparently dropped in the excitement.

"Rio! Come." Rocky spoke with authority.

Rio turned instantly and ran to Rocky's side, the little dog nipping at his heels.

"You'd better call off *your* dog," Yasmin said, fighting a chuckle.

"It's not a joke to have a big mutt like that running wild." Mitch kept grabbing for his little dog's leash, but she danced away each time he got close.

Again, Yasmin restrained a giggle. "Look, I'm sorry my gate was open, but thanks to Rocky, our dog is well trained." Then she mentally replayed what she'd said. *Our* dog.

She was thinking of Rio as belonging to the three of them.

It was a short step away from thinking of Rocky, Rio and Liam as her family.

Rocky was focused on Rio. "Sit," he ordered the dog, and he obeyed, his tongue lolling out in a laugh. "Stay." He backed slowly away from the dog, one hand up like a stop sign.

Rio sat, ears alert.

Without losing eye contact, Rocky knelt, grabbed the end of the shih tzu's leash and handed it to Mitch, who took it with an ill-concealed curl of the lip.

"Okay, boy," Rocky said to Rio, and the dog ran to him for a good belly rub.

That feeling that rose up in Yasmin had to be like

what a mother would feel: pure pride. How many thirteen-year-olds would be able to train an unruly dog and be polite to an unpleasant man so early in the morning? And to top it off, after a mysterious sighting of his missing mother?

Mitch stomped on down the street, tugging his dog and muttering about reporting Rio.

"Can he do that?" Rocky asked.

"He can try, but no one will take him seriously. Not now, not the way you've trained Rio. That was impressive."

Rocky beamed. "He still makes some mistakes, but he's doing really well."

"So are you, as a dog trainer. And as for mistakes…we all make some." Yasmin felt like she was reminding herself at the same time she was reminding Rocky.

She'd made mistakes in how she'd dealt with Liam, but he'd done the same, and that was just life.

Maybe he couldn't handle the way life was, due to his chaotic upbringing. Maybe he could change. Maybe he'd accept her with her limitations.

But no. She wasn't going to speculate about the "what-ifs" again.

They walked back inside, and Rocky helped Yasmin clean up the kitchen floor, and then she fixed him French toast, even though she'd already given him something to eat earlier. He was growing so fast he could eat whatever he wanted; she couldn't, but nonetheless, she made herself a plateful, too.

Even though she was trying to watch her weight, it seemed like a good time to have a treat.

As she poured another river of maple syrup over her last few bites, Rocky looked across the table at her. "Did you know there was someone in the house two nights ago?"

She blinked. "What do you mean?"

"Somebody broke in," he said through a mouthful of food. "I heard him. I heard him talking, and there were footprints on the ground outside the house."

Yasmin stared at him, her heart skittering a little. "This happened Friday? And you're only now telling me?"

"Sorry. I guess I forgot." He pushed his last bite of French toast around on his plate. "Liam didn't act like it was very important."

"Liam knew and didn't tell me?" She gripped the edge of the table to keep from pounding on it. What was *wrong* with the two of them? She was the homeowner. Wasn't it her right to know what happened on her property? "So let me get this straight," she said. "You heard an intruder in the house. Walking around and talking."

"He wasn't really talking, more like whispering." Rocky shrugged and carried his plate over to the sink.

And Yasmin sat, watching him rinse his dishes and put them in the dishwasher, and processed what he had said.

Someone had been in her house. Someone had been here on the night she had heard the voices. Someone whispering in a way that other people could hear.

Now she heard voices, all right: like a heavenly choir. Because maybe those voices she'd heard saying all the awful things to her hadn't been in her head. Maybe they'd come from somebody trying to fake her out. Though why anyone would do such a thing she couldn't imagine. No one knew she feared mental illness, or almost no one.

Thank You, she whispered to the heavens. If she didn't have the disease...if her fears were wrong... Wow. Just wow.

Be sensible, she told herself. *This is a teenager reporting on something that happened in the middle of the night.* She needed to cool off a little and then probe for details in a friendly way, find out more about what he'd heard and what he'd seen.

"Okay if I watch some TV?" he asked.

"Sure, go for it." Even though he'd bounced back amazingly, he'd still had a rough morning. She couldn't add to his upset by piling on a bunch of questions. She had to think of him first.

It was only when she was washing the mixing bowl that she took the next step in reasoning it all out. If the voices had come from a real person, voices saying unkind things to her, who could it be? Who would do that?

After all, Josiah had told her that his voices didn't

tell him bad things. He had said his voices were good.

Which, if that were the case, meant that Josiah didn't have anything to do with the dead man. On his own, he'd never come up with the idea of harming anyone. She knew that for sure.

But maybe the voice she'd heard in the night *did* relate to the crime.

She cast her mind back, trying to remember what the voice had sounded like, what it had said exactly. If only she'd written it down. If only she'd had the sense to get herself fully awake, and turn all the lights on, and look around her room, she could have caught the whisperer in the act.

Except the whisperer might be dangerous. And he'd been in her bedroom. Goose bumps rose on her arms and a prickle ran up and down her spine. How unsafe was that?

And what could possibly be the motivation? To make her insecure, to silence her? From saying what?

The only other motivation was that someone was trying to make her feel crazy.

The question was, who?

THE NEXT EVENING, a Monday, Liam walked from his cruiser to the junior-senior high school with a strong sense of déjà vu. Did you ever forget that smell, the janitors' chemicals never quite able to scrub away the teen sweat? Did you ever forget that high, almost hysterical sound of kids' voices greeting each other at the start of a new school year?

In truth, he was glad to be giving this presentation tonight, glad for any extra work he could take on, because it kept him from thinking about his own concerns.

It was looking more and more like Rita was telling the truth; she was his mother. Which just stuck in his craw, because they felt nothing for each other. But her story, such as it was, had checked out. There was some shaky stuff in her background—she'd had to use a fake ID—but she'd explained why she'd done it and it wasn't for criminal reasons. She'd been worried that whoever had beaten her up—according to Sean and to his own memory, their father—would be looking for her. So she'd taken on a new identity for safety, and because she didn't remember her old one.

As she'd talked, explaining things without expecting him to fall head over heels in love with her just because she said she was his mom, he'd started to believe her. But she'd been a poor excuse of a mother, letting all that happen to her when she had three boys to take care of. Surely she could have found a way out if she'd tried.

He glimpsed Rocky walking in with Yasmin, and a wave of sympathy passed over him. Rocky didn't have friends to greet; he was stuck walking in with an adult, not even his mother. And Yasmin hadn't bargained for doing the real work of parenting a teenager when she'd invited Rocky to stay with her just a couple of weeks ago.

She looked great in her close-fitting, above-the-knee summer dress, greens and blues like the ocean and her eyes. Just flip-flops on her feet, but her toenails were painted gold and…was that a toe ring?

Liam's body tightened and he swallowed.

"We're about ready to start," Mr. Smith, his ex-landlord who also happened to be the school principal, said. "Thanks for doing this for us again."

"No problem. I like it." And the fact that the guy had evicted him didn't affect the fact that he felt like kids listened to him well, like he could relate because he remembered the challenges of the teen years with particular clarity.

Principal Smith spoke for a while, welcoming students and parents, letting them know a few changes in the schedule for the new year, the progress of the construction project on the new wing, because the school was growing.

"But this is primarily a safety program," he said, "so without further ado, let me introduce Officer Liam O'Dwyer, who's going to talk about safety issues specific to middle and high school."

Liam launched into the talk he did every year, updated for new trends in social media bullying and internet-related crime, new challenges on the local drug scene. But there was a lot the same, even the same as when he'd been in school, about the risks of dating the wrong person or getting involved with the wrong friends. He always gave a particular push to dating violence and other risks that plagued young girls, because oftentimes, this was where it all started, in adolescence and in school.

He wondered if that was where Rita's problems with domestic violence had gotten started. Had someone beaten up on her when she was a kid or a teenager, made her think that was how love was supposed to feel?

He tried to stay focused on his subject, not Rita. And not on Yasmin and Rocky seated on the left side of the auditorium. It was tough not to look at them, to wonder what Yasmin, in particular, was thinking of his talk and of them. Rocky, he could almost guarantee, wasn't thinking about Liam's words at all; he'd be more upset and worried about the difficulties of being the new kid in school.

That was confirmed afterward when he joined the two of them, walking toward the students-only part of the presentation, run by the guidance counselors. When Liam approached, Rocky almost visibly cringed.

The only thing worse than being the new kid, here with your mother figure who wasn't really your mom, was being associated with a cop. And from what he understood, the area where Rocky had lived with his mom was deep country, fifty miles and a whole world away from Safe Haven. Rocky must feel out of place.

Trying to be sensitive to the boy's feelings, he

fell back and talked to a couple of teenagers who'd been involved in a citizens' ride-along they'd run last year. Their conversation got animated, so when his group caught up with Rocky and Yasmin in the crowd heading toward the cafeteria, Liam introduced the kids to Rocky, told them he was new. They were nice kids, and they soon found a common interest in dogs and actually had a half-decent conversation.

Liam passed his old locker and, as he always did, banged on it with his fist, right in the spot where he'd dented it all those years ago. Back then, he'd never have thought a kid like him could become the cop at the front of the auditorium. It just went to show you how much things could change, and not always for the worse, either.

As the kids filed away into the gym, he was left standing with Yasmin.

She glanced up at him. "That was nice. I'm glad he can get to know a couple of kids before the first day."

"It's important. I remember all too well."

She nodded, looking distracted, and drew in a breath. "Hey, Rocky told me that there was someone in the house the other night."

"What do you mean?"

"He said that he heard someone walking around and whispering, and found footprints outside a window. He said you knew about it."

He tilted his head, looking at her, trying to figure her out. "Uh-huh," he said slowly. "I saw the footprints. Saw the guy, too."

"What?" She said it so sharply that several people near them stopped their conversations to look their way. "You actually saw some guy lurking around my house and didn't tell me?"

He squinted at her. "It was Buck," he said. "Figured he was there by invitation."

"Are you kidding me?" Now she was looking at him like he was nuts. And then concern grew in her eyes. "Buck was in my house?"

He shrugged a little. "I *thought* it looked like him. It was late, and he was climbing down the trellis from your room."

She put a hand on her hip. "So let me get this straight. You thought I had a nighttime male visitor, and instead of having him come in the front door like a normal person, I had him climb in through my window?"

"It seemed weird," he said, "but…" He waved in the direction Rocky had gone. "I figured you didn't want Rocky to know. Maybe even Josiah."

She ran her fingers through her hair, making it even wilder and curlier than it had been before. "I can't believe this."

It was dawning on Liam that her reaction was 100 percent sincere. Which meant Buck *hadn't* been in her bedroom…at least, not by invitation. "If it wasn't Buck, then who? How could someone get in?"

"I'm not letting go that assumption you made, Liam O'Dwyer, just because figuring out who did it is more urgent."

He ignored her comment, his adrenaline racing, because if it hadn't been Buck, then someone else must have broken into her house. "Do you have a security system?"

She snorted. "Half the neighbors have keys. Rocky and Josiah are in and out. We don't usually lock the house."

"Did you *hear* anything about what I was saying about safety, even in a small town like Safe Haven?" He took a step closer, frustrated. She didn't seem to realize that there was a murderer unaccounted for, who'd already killed one person in town.

She stood her ground. "The horse is out of the barn, Liam! Who got into my house and whispered really weird stuff to me?"

"Whispering stuff?"

"Uh-huh. Telling me I was crazy, and a horrible person. And fat."

"We need to make a report," he said. "Look for prints in your house, develop a list of people who might have something against you and start checking out where they were. I can take the report, or someone else if you'd rather."

"Well, considering the voices told me to send Rocky and Josiah away and stay away from you…"

"What?" He put a hand on each of her upper

arms, the better to glare at her. "And you didn't tell *me* that?"

"I thought it was all in my head! I thought I'd developed schizophrenia!" Tears rose to her eyes and he ushered her away from the crowd to a table at the edge of the cafeteria. "That's why I really needed to know there was someone in my house. It's not good news, but it is."

Liam pulled napkins from a dispenser and handed them to her, and she wiped her eyes. His mind was racing. Who had been in Yasmin's house? Had it really been Buck? But why would he have whispered such mean words to her?

"Excuse me," Principal Smith said. "Can I talk to you a minute, Liam?" He looked apologetically at Yasmin. "I'll just keep him a minute."

She waved a hand. "I have to go, anyhow. We'll talk," she added to Liam, and was he wrong to see that as a promise...in a good way? Yes, definitely wrong, because his focus needed to be on her safety.

"Listen, Liam," Principal Smith was saying. "I made a mistake, and I want to set it right. I shouldn't have evicted you from my apartment building."

Liam shrugged. "It's okay. My dog *had* gotten too big for the place, according to the rules. Though you'll be glad to know he's getting better trained."

Smith shook his head. "I was told some things that influenced me in that direction, and I should have known better than to listen to gossip."

Liam didn't get it. "Someone was gossiping about me?"

The older man nodded.

"Can I ask who?"

"Someone I thought I could trust. But I realized tonight how much you always do for the schools, and even my evicting you didn't make you turn down the invitation. You're a good man, Liam." He looked Liam in the eye and added, "I'm not sure I can say the same about your colleague. Buck Mulligan. He's the one who as much as told me to evict you."

Buck Mulligan. There he was again. As he thanked the principal and walked back through the school, the image of Buck's face and name revolved through his head like a mug shot.

What did Buck have to do with the craziness happening in Safe Haven?

WHEN YASMIN PULLED into her own driveway later that night, she saw a woman standing at Liam's door.

Her heart turned over. Tell herself what she might, she cared for Liam and didn't want him to be with someone else. Yeah, he was infuriating—especially with not mentioning that he'd seen an intruder climbing down from her bedroom window—but his relief that she wasn't with Buck had been gratifying.

She was still flummoxed about why someone would whisper crazy-making ideas to her. So flummoxed that she couldn't think about it anymore. Instead, she focused on the woman, who was knocking on Liam's door and standing on tiptoe to look in through the door's small glass windows.

Yasmin had gotten the impression that he cared for her, from how he'd talked to her in the school cafeteria, but now he had a late-night female visitor. His truck was in the driveway, so at any minute he'd be coming out to greet her.

Fine.

"I'm gonna go watch TV." Rocky unfastened his seat belt and opened the door.

"Wait," she said, and almost to her surprise, he did.

"There are cookies on top of the fridge," she said. "Grab some on your way, and let Rio out."

"Sure!" He ran toward the house. This event had been stressful for him. No teen liked starting a new school. But at least he'd met a few kids. Thanks to Liam.

Liam, who still wasn't opening his door. Odd.

The woman turned slowly around and came down the steps of Liam's apartment.

Rita? What was *she* doing there?

Without a glance in Yasmin's direction, the older waitress headed along the sidewalk toward downtown, shoulders slumped.

Yasmin got out of the car and Rio ran to greet her, then bounded around the yard. As she stood watching him, waiting to let him back inside and enjoying the cool air, Liam came strolling around the edge of her house.

"Hey," he said as if showing up out of the darkness at nine thirty was the most natural thing in the world.

"You just missed Rita, and what are you doing?"

He glanced in the direction Rita had gone. "Yeah, I know. I was kind of hiding. But also kind of checking over your house. You've got a couple of windows that would make it really easy for someone to break in."

She shook her head back and forth. "You're avoiding Rita?"

He nodded. "That side door's lock is pathetic, too."

She sat down on the top step. "Why are you avoiding Rita?"

Liam blew out a breath, sat down on the bottom step and leaned back against the pillar. "If you have to know," he said, "she's my mother."

"She's what?" Yasmin's hand flew to her mouth. "Oh, Liam, really? That's fantastic! Tell me everything."

He shrugged. "Not much to tell. She got knocked out by our dad, lost her memory, got picked up by a trucker and moved to Maine, and came back here to see if she could figure out her past."

"She doesn't remember you?" Yasmin thought of Rita, how she'd seemed so worried and upset at the center the other day, and her heart hurt. For Rita, and for Liam.

Liam shook his head.

"Wow." She studied him. "But you believe she's your mom."

He nodded slowly. "I checked things out. Looks like she's telling the truth. And she doesn't seem to be trying to get anything from us, at least for now."

"And you're avoiding her because…"

"Because she was a terrible mother! She didn't take care of us, didn't do the tough work of raising us. So now she wants to come back and play grandma to Sean's kids, and he's letting her."

"Sean accepts her?"

"She and Sean are having a love fest." He rolled his eyes.

"But, Liam," she said hesitantly, "she didn't beat *herself* up or give herself amnesia. Don't blame her."

"She shouldn't have gotten us into that situation in the first place," he said, his voice indignant. "A good mother would have left him as soon as he got abusive, protected her kids."

"Oh, Liam." Yasmin sighed. "No mother's perfect. Look at mine."

"True," he said, "but your mom can't help the way she is."

"Can yours? Is it her fault she had that susceptibility for whatever reason?"

He shrugged and looked away. "I don't know."

"Give Rita a chance, Liam. Just talk to her. Let

her in a little. She's a good person. She volunteers at the center, and she's trying to understand her past."

"I'll take it into consideration," he said, sounding grumpy. But as he stood, he reached over and gripped her hand. Just for a second, but it felt emotional. "See you tomorrow," he said.

"See you." She watched him walk across the lawn and marveled at the complexity of life.

CHAPTER SIXTEEN

THE NEXT DAY'S shift change started out as usual. Liam was officially done, but had a few more things to clean up, so he was still at the station. Buck strolled in a few minutes late and propped a hip on the edge of Willa Jean's desk, so he could ask her what had gone on today.

Anyone else would have asked Liam—he'd been here and on the streets all day, since the chief was out—but Buck made a point of semi-ignoring him.

Liam heard the clatter of Willa Jean's printer and waited for her complaint about it. Right on time, it came: "This thing is from the 1990s, and it's going to die on me any day. Don't come to me crying the blues because your important report didn't get printed. I've been telling you we need a new printer for years."

Buck walked over toward the printer, did a double take and grabbed the papers. "Don't print that out."

What was Buck trying to hide?

"Sorry," Willa Jean said. "I forgot." She rolled her eyes at Liam.

He half smiled at her and looked around the station. Beat-up as it was, he loved this place. The old tile floor, speckled white with the occasional olive green tile, someone's 1950s version of decoration. Fluorescent lights reflected off the floor and the gunmetal-gray file cabinets. The whole station was permeated by the nose-prickling scent of disinfectant.

"Hey, I just got a text," Willa Jean called out to both of them. "Ramirez has been having stomach pains, so he went to the Express Doc out on the highway. Turns out they want him to go to the ER. He'll be out for a few days, at least."

"Diabetes or something else?"

"They don't know yet."

Liam frowned. He'd go visit the chief later tonight or tomorrow, see if he needed anything. "Keep me updated if you hear anything else, will you, Willa Jean?"

"I'll take over for him," Buck said, his voice casual. "I know most of what's going on around here."

Liam gave him a look. "I'm acting chief. It was put in the organizational structure when it was reviewed two years ago."

"That was supposed to change," Buck said. "We already started the paperwork."

Liam's stomach dropped. Could that be true? But no. Chief Ramirez wouldn't have made a change like that without telling Liam. Still, Buck's boldness surprised him. "No need for a coup just because the chief's got a stomachache."

"I'll talk to the council about it," Buck said with a challenging stare.

Liam watched him swagger out of the station. Mulligan was so cocky these days, almost like he knew he already had the chief job tied up. Maybe he did; maybe he knew something Liam didn't. Certainly, he socialized in different circles than Liam did.

But something about Mulligan didn't compute, especially if he was the man who'd sneaked into Yasmin's room and tried to play crazy-maker with whispering voices. And there was no maybe about the fact that he'd turned Principal Smith against Liam, helping to get him evicted.

Although that had backfired on Mulligan, because Liam had ended up living over Yasmin's garage, thus getting closer to her.

Could Mulligan's quest for the chief job have pushed him over some kind of edge?

"See you later, Liam," Willa Jean said as she got her purse out of her bottom drawer. Then she beckoned him closer.

"I'm not supposed to print out what's on my screen," she said in a low voice, "because Buck doesn't want it to be common knowledge. But with Chief Ramirez down, seems to me it wouldn't hurt if someone else took a look."

Liam didn't like the sound of that. "Something you want to talk about?"

"Nope," she said. "I just forgot to turn my computer off. Wouldn't be a problem if someone sat in my chair to turn it off for me." She gave him a wink and walked out the door.

Liam walked over to her desk and sat down. He ought to find out what Willa Jean was talking about, what Buck didn't want printed…he guessed. He didn't like even the hint of impropriety, considering how he'd grown up. On the other hand, he wasn't naive, and he knew a lot went on behind the scenes of even the cleanest police department.

His shot at chief was looking more and more difficult to achieve, but he should at least know what was going on.

He moved Willa Jean's mouse and the screen brightened up. An email from someone named Geena, thanking Buck for forgiving her parking ticket and offering to get together again, anytime.

Liam shook his head and closed the email. It wasn't in the least surprising that Buck traded favors regarding minor traffic violations, especially if the perp was pretty. Liam didn't approve of it, would put a stop to it if he were chief—yet another reason Buck didn't want him to get the job—but it wasn't big enough to report.

He closed the email and was about to turn off the computer when he noticed the note that had come in right after the one from Buck's lady friend.

Forensic ID—more info was the subject line.

The only forensic ID that was likely to come into this department, right now, was the underwater victim. But so far, there'd been nothing, according to Ramirez.

Without a second thought, Liam clicked on it.

Rec'd yr query. Latent lift labeled ABC was matched to the right index finger of William Baker, recently of Channing, South Carolina.

William Baker. The name was common and meant nothing to Liam.

Uneasiness gnawed at his belly and the hairs on the back of his neck prickled. Buck must have made an ID, then confirmed it with a print.

But who was the guy? And why had Liam—and the chief, apparently—been kept out of the loop?

Liam scraped a hand over his face. He'd have called Ramirez to discuss it, but the man was in the hospital.

He paced through the station, thinking. On the wall beside Ramirez's desk was the printed commendation from the State of South Carolina: on Ramirez's watch, crimes in Safe Haven had declined every year for ten years.

Liam wanted to be the chief who'd continue that trend.

But Buck was gaining ground by whatever means he could, including hiding information that could help solve a murder. His being chief wouldn't lead to Safe Haven being a better place. The opposite, in fact.

Liam didn't like to snoop. But some occasions justified it. Decision made, he walked over to Buck's desk and started flipping through the paperwork. He'd just come upon a report from the DMV, identifying the submerged car as belonging to William Baker, when he heard the door open. He glanced up and registered Buck coming in but didn't stop what he was doing.

"Looking for something?" Buck asked. His voice was casual…or at least, he was trying to make it sound so.

"Just seeing if there's anything else the rest of us should be in on."

"What are you talking about?"

Liam looked up, made direct eye contact. "Why didn't you let anyone know that body and the car had been ID'd?"

Buck looked away as he leaned back against Willa Jean's desk. "Stop trying to play in the big leagues, O'Dwyer. There's a lot you don't know."

The attempt to put Liam down didn't work. "I can see you're hiding things about this investigation," he said. "What I don't understand is why."

"That's because you're still on the outside of what's going on in Safe Haven."

"Is this all about your becoming chief?" Liam stood, slowly, and something made him be conscious of where Buck's weapon was, where his own was and where Buck's hands were. They shouldn't be enemies, they were colleagues, but it was feeling less and less that way.

"As a matter of fact, it's not," Buck said easily. "I'm in charge of that case, and there are some developments you don't need to know about."

"And why's that?" Liam's blood was starting to boil, but he kept his voice calm.

Buck lifted an eyebrow. "Because you're pretty close to one of the suspected perps. Maybe two of them." He strolled out of the office. "Later, my friend."

Liam stared after him. Buck thought he was close to a couple of perps, did he? Which of his close people—Rocky, Yasmin, his brothers—could Buck be wanting to implicate? And why?

THE NEXT DAY Yasmin finally felt like her work was getting back to normal. She'd counseled two women, one by phone and one in person, on strategies to make changes in their lives. She'd written up case notes and then started a new grant application.

As long as she kept researching and writing the grant, she could avoid thinking about Liam. But the moment she stopped for a break, her mind went there and stayed.

It had felt so good to be with him at Rocky's school orientation night, and she'd admired his way with the high school kids. On the other hand, she couldn't believe that he'd thought she would have

Buck sneak into her bedroom at night. The very notion was appalling.

First, because she had no desire *at all* to sleep with Buck. And second, because some real human male sneaking into her bedroom was extremely creepy. Who could it have been? Who would have that crazy-making agenda?

Liam had seen the outline of the guy and had thought it was Buck. Maybe. But that didn't make sense.

Deep in thought, she lost track of her work. She was just pulling her mind back into it when her phone buzzed. She was shocked to see that it was almost lunchtime.

It was Miss Vi. "You'd better get down to the library," she said. "Josiah is in trouble."

"I'll be right there." She grabbed her purse and rushed out the door.

Waiting at one of the few traffic lights in town, she realized what she wanted to do, although she felt funny about it. Before she could come up with excuses not to, she texted Liam about what Miss Vi had said. "Could you meet me there?" she asked.

When she reached the library, she found Josiah pacing in the small, glassed-in classroom. She hurried through the door, and only then did she realize that Buck was leaning against the chalkboard at the front of the room. He held up a hand. "Can it wait, Yasmin? I'm conducting an interview."

Buck was interviewing Josiah? Since when did he work extra hours to solve a case? "About what?"

"That's confidential, unless he chooses to disclose it to you."

"He has special needs, you know that, Buck!" She wished she hadn't been so desperate to talk that she'd shared his diagnosis with Buck, especially the way things had turned out. But knowing that, Buck ought to follow procedure all the more. "Doesn't he have the right to have a lawyer here?"

"He does." The voice came from behind her. Liam, and she practically sagged with relief. "What's this all about, Buck?"

Buck held up a hand like a stop sign and shook his head. "Josiah can have a representative here, but I'm not at liberty to disclose what this interview is about."

"I'll disclose it," Josiah said. "I didn't kill that man."

Yasmin's stomach twisted into a million knots.

She'd suspected Josiah herself, at one point, because of the way he'd run into the center wanting to hide that night. But she just couldn't believe that Josiah had it in him to kill someone. It wasn't in his DNA. "Of course you didn't kill anyone," she said, walking over to grasp her brother's hand. "And you don't have to answer Officer Mulligan's questions if you don't want to. If you need a lawyer, we'll get you one."

Josiah shook his head back and forth. His forehead wrinkled, his eyes nearly crunched closed, he looked shaken and miserable. A hot rage built inside Yasmin that this had happened to her brother. He didn't need accusations like this. He suffered enough already.

"We all know he's sick, Yasmin," Buck said. "People with schizophrenia are violent, and it's not even his fault. I'm sure a jury would take his condition into consideration."

Yasmin wanted to press her hands over her brother's ears to keep him from hearing the hurtful words. How she wished she'd never confided in Buck about Josiah's diagnosis. But they'd started seeing each other soon after Yasmin had learned about Josiah and had realized she could develop the disorder herself. She'd been desperate for someone to talk to, but Buck had been a terrible choice. He'd had little sympathy, and now he was throwing the information around in front of Liam and whoever else might be listening. She wondered how many people he'd told. "He would never do anything violent," she said firmly.

"She's right," said Miss Vi, who had showed up in the doorway behind Liam. Now she walked all of the way in, hands on hips. "I've worked with this man for months now, and I know his personality. He doesn't have a violent bone in his body."

"Why is this interview turning into a social hour?" Buck threw up his hands. "A little professionalism, please. Liam, could you take them out?"

Yasmin wrinkled her forehead. Buck talked to Liam as if he were his boss, but she happened to know they were on equal footing, and Liam was by far the superior officer in terms of competence.

"If we're talking professionalism," Miss Vi said, "I'd like to see you display a little bit more of it. Have you ever looked at the statistics about crime and mental illness? People like Josiah are far more likely to be victims of crimes than perpetrators."

Buck made a disgusted sound, picked up his tablet and pointed it at Josiah. "Obviously, I'm not getting anything done here. I still want to talk to you, but now doesn't seem to be that time. I'd like for you to come into the station."

Yasmin was still holding her brother's hand, and now she reached up to put an arm around his shoulders. "He's not coming to the station if I have anything to do with it."

"He's not the only one having delusions around here. Think about that." Buck gave her a meaningful look and then stormed out of the room before anyone could answer his rude remark.

Why had he said that? Because he *wanted* her to think she was having delusions? Had he been the one who'd whispered things to scare her, after all? But why?

Josiah just shook his head, looking impossibly weary.

Yasmin gave her brother a quick hug and then sat down in one of the classroom's chairs, feeling like she had been through one hundred emotions today. "I'm so sorry that happened to you, Joe," she said. "Miss Vi, can he have the rest of the day off?"

Miss Vi frowned. "He might be better served by staying here, keeping busy," she said. "Besides, I need his help with a computer problem I'm having. Josiah, you can leave if you really want to, but I'd appreciate it if you would stay for the rest of the day."

Josiah looked at Miss Vi as if she were holding out a lifeline. "I'll stay."

"Come on, then. We have work to do." She gestured for him to follow and walked out of the room like a queen.

Josiah didn't look to the right or the left. He just followed.

That left Yasmin in the room with Liam, and even though she wanted to keep any connection between Josiah and the murder away from him, she was still relieved that he was here. She propped her cheek on her fist and blew out a breath. "Wow."

The next moment, she felt warm hands on her shoulders, gently kneading. "You did a good job speaking up for your brother, but you're really tense," Liam said, his voice a low rumble. "You need to relax."

They were big hands, strong hands. And she remembered from their time together how extremely competent his hands were, how they seemed to search out the aching muscle or the knot in her back.

His touch felt like heaven, but she needed to keep herself grounded, so she forced out a laugh. "I don't think I know the meaning of the word *relax*," she said. She was waiting for him to question her about Josiah and any connection there might be with the murder, but to her surprise, he didn't mention it. Instead, he massaged her shoulders for a couple of more blissful moments, and then put his hands on the sides of her upper arms, gently lifting. "Come on," he said. "It's lunchtime. Let's grab sandwiches and take them to the beach and forget about all our cares for a bit."

"You're serious." She stood, and his hands were still on her upper arms as he stood behind her. When she turned, she was close enough to smell his slightly musky cologne, and her senses seemed to pull her closer to him as if he were a magnet.

His gaze dropped to her lips. "On second thought, we could just stay here and make out in front of everybody in the library," he said. A smile tugged at the corner of his mouth, but his hands had tightened on her arms and his eyes had darkened. "You know I'd like nothing better. Even though it might ruin my reputation."

That made her laugh, because she knew he was really more worried about her reputation, and that neither of them could afford to get caught kissing in the library.

"The beach would be nice, but I think you'd be

pretty hot in your uniform, and I need to get back to work, too. But… I'll take a rain check."

He didn't let go of her. "After work tonight?" His gaze was intense.

She shouldn't. She knew she shouldn't, but her whole heart cried out for this man. "Sure," she agreed, her insides doing cartwheels, even as her mind wondered how she could justify it. She was pretty sure it was a huge mistake.

CHAPTER SEVENTEEN

AT LUNCHTIME ON Wednesday, Rita walked with Jimmy toward La Florentine, an elegant tourist restaurant right on the water. It was their first really fancy date.

She should have been happy, but instead, her insides churned.

"I'm so glad you got things figured out with your sons," he said, taking her hand and squeezing it. "This date has been a long time coming, but you're worth waiting for."

No, I'm not. She smiled over at him and discreetly pulled her hand away.

It didn't deter him. He put an arm around her. "I feel really lucky that you walked into the café when you did. I'd given up hope of finding someone I could respect and care for in my golden years."

His arm felt warm and strong, strong enough to support her, and a part of her longed to just sag into him, relax and let the relationship flow. But her heart told her otherwise. She wasn't ready.

"I don't feel exactly the same," she said, easing away from his arm.

"What?" He looked over at her, his smile fading just a little.

"It's just… I don't feel all fixed, you know? There's still a gap of twenty years. There's still this huge chunk of my life that's lost to me."

"But you know who you are now. You have your sons."

"I have Sean," she corrected. "Cash, we talked by phone and it was just…meh. He didn't really react. And Liam's actively angry about the whole thing."

"Even when your story checked out?"

She nodded. "He believes I'm his mom now, but like he said, I didn't…" Her voice caught and she took a breath to steady it. "I didn't raise them or protect them or take care of them. I didn't do any of the things a mother is supposed to do."

"And you don't remember anything, so you can't defend yourself."

"It's indefensible!" Her throat tightened again. The breeze off the sea couldn't cool her warm face.

"You're looking at this all wrong," he said. "Taking the blame for something that isn't your fault. The O'Dwyer boys—men, you have to remember they're men—will come around."

She wanted to believe him, to believe that she could just move forward in a carefree way. But the pinched, hurt look that had been on Liam's face haunted her. "Look, maybe this date isn't a good idea."

"Rita." Jimmy walked forward more slowly now, at her side, no longer trying to touch her. "I've been patient."

"You have been. And you were a huge help the other night. You didn't judge me, and you helped me tell Liam and Sean the truth."

"Right. And now, I want you to build a life here. Be a grandma to Sean's kids. Be friends with Norma and Claire and Yasmin." He paused. "Do things with me, have some fun together, see what grows."

"It's not that easy." They were almost to the boardwalk now, walking past the shopfronts where tourists and townspeople strolled the sidewalks and went in and out of the shops.

He put a hand on her arm to stop her from walking into the more crowded area. "It's not that complicated, either. Women overthink things."

She swallowed the giant lump in her throat. "I don't know if I'll ever be whole. All carefree and ready to jump into a relationship."

He threw up his hands. "It's been months, Rita. I can't wait forever. *We* can't wait forever. We don't have all the time in the world." He drew in a slow breath, let it out. "Look, I'm in my fourth quarter. I want to make it as good as I can, and I finally feel ready to move on after my divorce. I'd really like to do that with you, but if you can't..."

"If I can't do it on your schedule?"

He held up a hand. "No. Uh-uh. It's been all on your schedule, and that's fine, but there's a limit."

"I understand that," she said reluctantly. He *had* been more than patient, and it was no wonder he couldn't do that forever. Most men wouldn't have waited as long as Jimmy had.

Her chest ached, but she couldn't, wouldn't, submerge who she was and how she felt. Not after everything she'd been through. "I guess, then, it's not going to work."

He put his hands on her shoulders and looked directly into her eyes. "For real? You're going to turn your back on everything we could have?"

"It's not fair to you to keep stringing you along," she said. "Honestly, I don't know if I'll ever be ready, ever be healed. And I'm too old to just cave in and fake it."

Their eyes stayed connected for a long moment, until Rita felt her own start to well up with tears.

He must have noticed it—how could he not? "Aw, Rita," he said, and pulled her into his arms, not too close, just a friendly hug. "Come on. This lunch date's a bust, but I have one more idea." He tugged her arm to get her to turn a corner, away from the boardwalk. Then he walked beside her down a residential street as she tried to get herself together. He was *such* a good man, and she cared for him more and more. But this barrier, this feeling of worthlessness, wouldn't let her be free and wholehearted with him.

"Here we are." They were standing in front of the Safe Haven Women's Center.

"Why'd you bring me here? I don't have a volunteer shift today," she protested.

"I'm bringing you here as a client. You were abused, and you're not recovering from it. So maybe you should take advantage of all the counseling and support groups they offer."

"I don't need—"

"You need something. Maybe they can help you." He paused, then added, "I can't." And then he backed away.

Wait, she wanted to cry. *I can do it, I can fake it to keep you.*

She could, but she wouldn't. "Thank you for everything you've done for me, Jimmy," she choked out.

He wasn't facing her, he was half turned away, but she could see his eyes squeeze shut. He nodded.

Then he walked away.

She watched him, her chest aching, her throat impossibly tight. What was wrong with her? Was everything wrong with her, like her son Liam thought? She wrapped her arms around her middle, hunched over, trying to hold herself together.

A car pulled up to the curb, and a woman got out and stood staring at the women's center. Through tears, Rita recognized the woman who'd been at the festival with Buck.

She should greet her, offer to help, but she didn't

have it in her. She stood, swallowing hard, trying not to lose it.

She was relieved when, finally, the center's door opened and Yasmin came out. Yasmin could help the woman.

"Rita?" Yasmin took a few more steps and reached Rita's side.

"Hey," Rita choked out.

"Are you okay? You're not okay." Yasmin took her by the hand.

"There's someone who needs help, a client." Rita turned to gesture toward the woman she'd just seen.

But both she and her car were gone. So was the slight distraction the woman had provided, and Rita felt her face start to crumple.

"Hey. What's wrong?" Yasmin drew her into a hug.

At which point Rita let her emotions go, and Yasmin pulled her inside the cool, welcoming women's center.

LIAM PUSHED THE rest of the elegant chocolate dessert over to Yasmin. "Here. You finish it."

Not that the dessert wasn't delicious. But watching Yasmin savor it was even more enjoyable. She took small, delicate bites, and closed her eyes with each one, and smiled.

And Liam was a goner. He wanted to make her smile like that for the rest of his life.

She opened her eyes and caught him looking. "I really shouldn't. You eat the rest."

"Why?" he asked, although he knew what her reason was going to be. Women. They had the strangest ideas.

Right on schedule, she said, "It'll ruin my diet. This dress was a little tight."

He outright laughed. "Are you kidding me? It fits you perfectly. And you look perfect." He meant it. Yasmin was a real woman with curves, and he liked her that way.

As a matter of fact, he liked almost everything about Yasmin. Her concern for others that led her to work so hard at the women's center and help her brother and Rocky, too. Her brains—any conversation with her made him want to go read up on whatever they'd been talking about. And the sparkle in her eyes that hinted at her fun, witty, sensual side.

She was an amazing woman and he'd think later about what that might mean, but for now, he just knew she needed a break. So when she'd finished the last forkful of chocolate decadence cake and he'd taken care of the check, he took her hand and tugged her toward the restaurant's back doorway that led onto the boardwalk. "Let's take a walk," he said. "It's only nine thirty. Way too early to go home."

She glanced down at her shoes—high-heeled, strappy sandals—and then shrugged and held on to his arm while she slipped off first one, then the other. "What about you?" she teased. "Those shoes look more like Cash's style. Not made for salt water and sand."

"Cash made me buy them, and you're right." He sat on the edge of the boardwalk to take them off, and his socks, and roll up his pant legs. "Think we can leave our shoes here?"

"It's *Safe* Haven," she said. "I heard the police force is really great."

He grinned at the comment and held out his hand for her to take.

They walked down to the water. The days were getting a little shorter now, and the moon had risen in the deepening twilight, making a silvery path on the water. A light breeze blew the humidity out of the air. And Yasmin's hand in his felt better than anything he'd felt in a long time.

"Can we start over?" he asked, then wished he hadn't been so abrupt. She looked up at him quickly, then just as quickly, looked out to sea.

"I don't... I don't know if we can," she said. "I..." She trailed off, biting her lip. "There's a part of me that wants to, a big part, but I just don't think it'll work."

He waited, but she didn't continue speaking. Didn't tell him the reason for her hesitation, that barrier that was always there with her. He'd thought he'd breached it, tonight, but he'd obviously been wrong.

Pain cut through him, because despite their improved relationship, she still didn't want what he wanted. She'd go on a date, but not get serious with him, not try to make it last.

Grow up, he told himself. *She's entitled to want whomever she wants.* "Is it Buck?" he asked, and then wished he hadn't.

"Liam!" She stopped walking and spun to face him, hands on hips. "For the last time, I have zero interest in Buck Mulligan, okay? It's not that. Even when it *was* that, it wasn't."

"What's that supposed to mean?" Sounded like some complicated female justification that wouldn't hold water with men, whose minds were simpler.

"Look, come on. Let's walk." This time she took his hand and the lead, pulling him along.

The sand was still warm from the day's sun, and the waves made a rhythmic backdrop, but for all that, Liam wasn't at ease. Was she going to feed him a line?

He'd felt so close to her tonight. And it wasn't just tonight. Their weeks of living so close together, of working with Rocky, of sharing their lives, had given their friendship a depth and richness it hadn't had before.

All that would be destroyed if she tried to fake him out and let him down easy now. "Just be honest with me, Yas. Whatever it is, be honest."

She gave him a sideways glance. "Are you ready for this? Because I *want* to be honest. *And* I want to be happy, but it's...a complicated story."

"I can handle it," he said, even while he wondered if he could.

"Okay. First, Buck," she said. "Liam, I knew if I told you the real reason I wanted to break up, you'd never have let me do it. The only thing that would work with a guy like you was another guy."

He winced, because it was true. He'd have argued hard against anything but that. "So you *didn't* care for Buck?"

She shook her head, a little rueful smile tugging at the corner of her mouth. "Can you even imagine our conversations? We have nothing in common."

"Sometimes conversation isn't what a guy like Buck is after." He kicked at the sand.

"Right. And when he found out he couldn't get what he was really after from me, he lost interest. But by that time, you'd already gotten furious and cut me off." She sighed. "Mission accomplished, and faster than I could have dreamed."

Something twisted hard at his stomach then. He didn't like the pain he was hearing in her voice. Had he caused it? "Sounds like you didn't want me to take your bait so quickly."

"I didn't, but I did."

"Why?"

She drew a toe through the sand, face downcast. "Because… I knew how much you wanted kids."

He studied her, then touched her chin. "Hey. What does that have to do with anything?"

Her chin trembled. "Schizophrenia has...it has a genetic element," she said, her voice breaking.

"But you don't have schizophrenia."

"Yet." She swiped her knuckles under her eyes. "It starts later in women."

Understanding broke over him, a wave of it. "That's why that intruder was able to scare you so bad."

She nodded, swallowing hard, obviously trying to keep it together. "Right," she said. Then she paused, rubbing the heel of her hand over her chest, and looked out to sea. "And even if I don't get it, I could pass it along to kids. Liam, it's a horrible illness. Josiah is managing pretty well, but it's been such a struggle for him. I don't want to have kids who might carry the gene for it."

She still wasn't looking at him, which gave him a chance to process what she'd said.

She didn't want to have kids. Or rather, judging from the sadness in her voice and posture, she wanted to, but she'd decided against it.

It gave him pause. One of the things he'd wanted to do was have kids with Yasmin; it had been behind all the homemaking activities they'd done together. Starting a family, raising them together.

But there were other ways. He tested the notion of adoption and found he didn't dislike the idea. "I wish you'd told me the whole truth," he said. "If you couldn't have kids, we could have adopted. I mean, I wasn't raised by my biological parents. I was raised in the system, and there are still a lot of kids there who need homes."

She looked up at him then, her eyes brimming with tears. "You mean it, Liam? You'd give up... you'd have given up...biological kids for me?"

He nodded slowly. "Yeah. I would've." He put his hands on her shoulders. "And you know what? I still would."

He waited until he saw relief and happiness in her eyes and lowered his lips to hers.

CHAPTER EIGHTEEN

LIAM'S KISS FELT like soothing rain, washing away Yasmin's anxieties and fears for the future, adding a hope that despite everything, they could be together. She wrapped her arms around him and let the warmth of his embrace carry her to a warm, joyous place. A place even better than where they'd gone before, because this was so hard earned.

When he deepened the kiss, though, something nagged at her, some unfinished business that she needed to deal with before she could truly relax into his arms. She twisted a little away and he immediately let her go, just keeping one hand on her arm.

His eyes on her were so warm. She wanted to treasure that. Because she knew, now, what she needed to tell him. "I...there's something else."

"What?" His voice was indulgent.

"The night of the...the murder." She swallowed. "I was afraid to tell you, but Josiah was there."

"What? Where?"

Her heart lurched. Best to get it all out at once.

"Rocky, too," she said. "They were…somewhere at the docks when it happened. I still don't know what they saw, exactly."

"You think they saw something?"

She nodded. "Yes, I do, because when they got to the center, they wanted to hide. Josiah did, anyway. Rocky was just kind of shell-shocked."

"And did you ask them about it later?" The warm, intimate tone of voice was gone; he sounded overly patient, like he was speaking to someone with a very low level of intelligence. It wasn't a voice she heard that often.

"I did try to ask them, but they wouldn't say anything. And you know, Joe, because of his illness, he's not always real clear on the distinction between what's real and what's delusion."

He took a step back from her, his jaw clenched, his eyes cold. "You realize this is serious. You should have told the police. Ideally, me."

She swallowed, nodded. "I was afraid—" She broke off.

He lifted an eyebrow.

Her phone buzzed, but she ignored it. "I was afraid that, you know, Josiah had had something to do with it. That his voices had told him to…but now I don't think so. Now I know his voices are mostly good, so I don't think…" She trailed off because he was shaking his head.

Her feeling of hope and optimism took a hit. It

didn't seem like he was going to be okay with all of this, after all.

He crossed his arms over his chest. "I thought you respected me as a cop, at least."

"I do, Liam!"

"You do," he said, "but not enough to tell me important information about a murder that took place in our town? In the end, you're still thinking I'm not worth it or good enough?" His voice rose at the end. "How am I supposed to keep this town together, help lift it up, if I don't have all the information?"

If you don't have control. Sadness filled her, because she understood his need for control given what he'd been through. "I'm so sorry, Liam. I should have told you, but I… Well, my first instinct was to protect Josiah."

"Rather than do what was right?"

Clearly, he didn't understand her reasoning. And maybe she'd been wrong in what she'd done.

Her phone buzzed again, with a text, and then his did, too. He pulled his out, so she did, too.

Miss Vi: Do you know where Josiah is? He was supposed to work tonight but he didn't show up and he's not answering his phone. And Rocky just came here looking for him.

Harsh ropes knotted around her stomach and her heart fluttered into a rapid pounding. It was hard to breathe. She looked at Liam. He was frowning at his phone, and then he punched a button and lifted his phone to his ear.

She did the same, made a call. "Miss Vi? What's going on? Can I talk to Rocky?"

A moment later, Rocky's voice came through the phone. "His stuff isn't in the bathroom," Rocky said. "And he's not at the library. I think… I think he kind of ran away."

She licked dry lips. "We'll find him," she promised the child, and herself, and ended the call.

Deliberately, she turned to look at Liam. He was frowning at her as he held up his phone. "I'm called in to work because Mulligan's sick," he said.

"That was Miss Vi," she explained. "Rocky's with her. And Rocky thinks…" She swallowed. "He thinks Josiah is gone."

"Gone?"

"He was researching ways to disappear," she said miserably. "I'm afraid he did it."

"Were you ever going to tell me any of this? Come on." He started walking double time toward town, and she half jogged to catch up with him. It was full-on night now, and the crashing waves no longer sounded rhythmic and peaceful. They sounded violent. A wind was blowing hard now, and clouds covered the moon.

How had Rocky gotten to the library this late at night? What was Miss Vi doing there after closing time? And where was Josiah?

Her certainty that her brother hadn't committed a crime was wavering, now that he'd done such a guilty-seeming thing.

They reached the boardwalk faster than she'd have thought possible, grabbed their shoes, and by mutual, unspoken agreement, headed for the car. "I'll drive you home. You get your car and go pick Rocky up, and I'll get to the station," he said. His voice was cold, but then he added, "I'll see what I can find out about Josiah, and you keep me updated, as well."

It was a far cry from the closeness they'd started to share, but it was the best she was likely to get.

Five minutes later, they were in front of her house. Liam turned the car off, but she put a hand on his arm. "You don't need to walk me in," she said. "I'm just going to grab an extra jacket for Rocky, and go get him."

And anyway, it might break my heart to spend even one more minute with you being so cold.

"You're sure?"

She nodded because she couldn't speak, got out of the car, and slammed the door shut. Forced herself to march away, march up the sidewalk to her front door. She gave Liam a little wave to show she was safe. There was a short hesitation, and then he drove away, tires screeching just a little. An angry sound.

She was fumbling for her key, eyes blurry with tears, when a voice from her porch swing almost made her jump out of her skin. "Hey, Yasmin, need to talk to you."

It was Buck.

AT THE STATION, Liam read Jenkins's half-baked reports of the day's activities, looked at Buddy's notes and prepared to go out to complete Buck's shift.

He needed to focus on his work, not on the fact that Yasmin hadn't seen fit to tell him a huge number of things she'd known about the night of the murder. Not on the fact that she hadn't trusted him to have sympathy for Josiah, to run a fair investigation, to find out the truth.

Of course, he wasn't in charge of the investigation. Maybe she was right not to trust him. His own department, his own chief, hadn't.

But those thoughts dissolved when he saw old Mr. Bennet walking down Main Street in his bathrobe. His daughter, Marcy, must be frantic. Liam called her and then drove Mr. Bennet home.

"You're the best," Marcy said, hugging him as the old man sat down in a rocker on the front porch as if it were noontime. "I'm so glad you know everyone in town and look out for the ones who are struggling."

Where else did a police officer get hugged for doing his duty?

And he was good at his duty. He was a Safe Haven cop, and a successful one. Better at the range of duties encountered in this job than Mulligan was, or Jenkins, or even Buddy, who'd been at it for thirty years and was getting tired.

If he wasn't good enough for the council to choose him as chief, if he wasn't good enough for

Yasmin to trust to be fair to her family… Those were the council's issues, Yasmin's issues.

But something about that analysis didn't sit right.

Yes, the council had issues. And yes, Yasmin did, too. But what about him?

He'd been so quick to believe Yasmin had chosen Buck over him that he hadn't probed into why she'd ended their relationship. And he'd been quick to believe that the council would choose Buck over him, to a point where he hadn't even tried to talk to Ramirez about all the things Buck was doing wrong.

It was insecurity. His own insecurity, and he felt like way less of a man to admit it, except that admitting you had a problem was the first step toward solving it.

His heart still hurt for what could have been. And his mind reeled with what Yasmin had told him tonight, about Buck, and about the reasons for her breaking up with him. Against his will, sympathy started to build. She'd never had it easy, despite her family's wealth. And now, with Josiah's diagnosis… with being uncertain about what he might do under the influence of his delusions…and with him wandering off like this, she had to be totally stressed.

As he drove past the docks, he did his habitual visual sweep and hit the brakes. Someone was down there. He used his searchlight and realized it was a boy. And a dog.

He parked and got out. "Rocky! It's way too late

for you to be out. Didn't Yasmin come and get you at the library?"

"We left. Didn't see her."

Rio trotted over and nudged Liam's leg, but didn't jump up. Rocky's good training. "What are you doing here?" he asked Rocky.

"Me and Rio are looking for Josiah. He's gone!"

Liam tilted his head to one side. "He's probably around, right? He likes to walk." He frowned at the boy. "More to the point, it's after ten o'clock. Too late for you to be out. Come on, I'll drive you home."

And going home would give him the chance to check on Yasmin, reassure himself that she was okay and probably find Josiah safe in his own bed by now, too.

As they drove the short distance to Yasmin's place, Rocky talked on, a teenage mix of how hungry he was, what tricks Rio had mastered today and the fact that Josiah's toothbrush and shaving cream were missing from the bathroom.

Liam's concern boosted up a little at that last revelation. They pulled into the parking space in front of Yasmin's cottage and he walked to the door with Rio and Rocky. They knocked, and then Rocky grabbed the key from under the doormat.

Just where anyone in the world could find it. Liam shook his head.

"Yasmin?" Rocky called. "Hey, Yasmin!"

No one answered.

Rio bounded in, checked his food bowl and ran

through the house, tail wagging. Thirty seconds later he was back in front of Liam and Rocky, panting.

He hadn't found Josiah, or Yasmin, either.

Liam scrolled through his phone to her name and tapped it, but his call went straight to voice mail.

Worry started at the base of Liam's spine and worked its way up his back. Where would Yasmin be at this hour, if not here? Something was wrong.

"Look," he said to Rocky, who was ripping open a bag of tortilla chips, "I'm on duty, but I think I'll call Jenkins, see if he can come in and cover for me." He kept his voice casual, not wanting to alarm the boy.

But Rocky turned in the middle of pouring salsa into a bowl, causing a big blob to drip onto the counter. "You never call off work. That's what Yasmin said."

"I am tonight." He made the phone call and Jenkins was perfectly agreeable, excited even, about coming in to cover a night shift.

Liam pulled out a chair across from Rocky, who pushed the bowl of salsa and bag of chips his way. He took one, dipped it. "So who are Yasmin's best friends? She's probably with one of them. Claire, do you think?"

Rocky nodded. "Or Rita. She's been spending a lot of time with Rita. In fact, I think she said Claire's out of town."

Great.

The last thing he wanted to do was go to his so-called mother's apartment, but Yasmin didn't answer her phone. So he put Rio in his crate in the back of his truck, and he and Rocky headed across town to Rita's place.

Rita's face broke into a huge smile when she saw Liam. Then, she glanced at Rocky and at Liam's face, and her smile faded. "What's up? Want to come in?"

Liam updated her on their search for Yasmin "and Josiah," Rocky threw in, making Rita turn to Liam with a frown.

"Sit," she told them, grabbing her phone. "You can bring the dog in, by the way." She called Norma, then Claire, and on that call, relief crossed her face. She clicked off and came over, perching on the edge of an armchair across from the couch. "Claire thinks she's at a party," Rita explained. "She's going to call her friend who's hosting it and check. She said she'd call me right back."

That didn't sound like Yasmin, especially if she was worried about where Rocky had gone. And she hadn't mentioned anything about a party when they'd been together earlier tonight. He hoped Claire was right, though, because he didn't like to think of her out looking for Rocky and her brother alone.

Rita put on a late-night cartoon channel for Rocky and draped an afghan across his feet. She put down a bowl of water for Rio. Then she beckoned Liam into the little dining nook off the kitchen.

She opened the refrigerator, held up a pitcher. "Iced tea? Beer?"

"Tea's fine. Thanks." Liam watched her deft movements in the kitchen and reviewed her calm way of handling Yasmin's absence, her easy hospitality.

That's my mother.

He let the words repeat across his mind, trying them on.

But hostility kept nudging at him. *Yeah, your mom who didn't take care of you, who abandoned you.*

She plunked a glass on the table in front of him, pushed a sugar bowl his way. "I don't sweeten it," she said. "I'm from the North." Then she bit her lip, and added, "at least, what I remember about myself is from the North."

Liam took a sip and studied her. "I don't like it sweet myself," he said. "You really don't remember this place?"

She shook her head. "Glimmerings, that's all. Same with my life before we all came here, which means I've lost all of your baby years."

But while Rita wasn't finding her memories, Liam's were all coming back to him. He remembered his mother, more and more. Remembered how she'd taken them fishing and made them study, how she'd had a ready laugh.

How that laugh had gone underground whenever their father was home.

"I really feel for Yasmin," Rita said. "I hope she's out having fun. She's told me a little about what she's been dealing with, while I was volunteering at the center. She's been trying to stand by her brother and a child." She nodded toward the front room where Rocky was. "She has an impossible situation."

He nodded slowly. "She does," he said. "I wish she'd shared some information with me, that's all."

Rita studied him shrewdly. "Could she do that, and be sure of being understood?"

The question hung in the air.

It was a question that hit home. The way a mother's question would.

He'd been judgmental of Yasmin from the start, he realized. Judging her for being with Buck, when in truth, she'd done it to try to protect him. Judging her for not revealing that Joe and Rocky had been at the docks on the night of the murder, when, again, she'd been doing it to protect her brother and a child who needed to depend on her.

Nothing she'd done had been for selfish reasons. She was loving, protective, caring. And as soon as he found out where she was, he was going to her, party or no party. He was going to apologize for the condemning way he'd acted and see if he could get her to forgive him. After that...well, one step at a time.

Rita was looking steadily at him, a sympathetic

smile on her face. "If you need to do some thinking, I can leave you alone."

"I've judged you, too," he said, blurting out the sudden realization. "I'm sorry." He couldn't call her mom, not yet, but when she reached a hand across the table, he took it and squeezed.

It was a start.

After that, they both went into the front room and watched the cartoon while Rocky dozed on the couch. It wasn't long before Rita's phone buzzed.

She listened, frowned and asked a question. Then she clicked off the call. "She's not at the party," she said to Liam, looking worried. "It's awfully late. If she's not there, where is she?"

CHAPTER NINETEEN

YASMIN LOOKED OVER at Buck's handsome profile, comfortable and confident driving his SUV, and then at the wooded bayou around them. So dark. So mysterious.

Was Josiah really out here? It wasn't his kind of place.

And Buck wasn't his kind of guy. "Why did he come out here with you?" she asked. "He's not normally supersocial."

"I picked him up hitchhiking," Buck said. "Talked him into chilling out a couple days at my country place." He smiled over at her. "I figured I'd better try to let you know. He's not exactly competent on his own."

The disrespect in Buck's tone grated, but she *was* thankful he'd brought her brother here rather than leaving him to take his chances with anyone who might pick him up off the side of the road and take advantage of him.

They pulled up to Buck's place, a fairly new,

two-story white house with a porch overlooking a lake that faded into the bayou on the other side. She reached for her door—she really wanted to see Joe and she didn't want to be in the car with Buck anymore—when he put a hand on her arm.

"Hang on a minute, Yas," he said. "There's something you should know."

His words and his tone made dread pile on top of her like heavy weights. "What is it?"

"There's no easy way to say this." He was staring straight ahead toward the lake. "You know that body they found in the car by the docks?"

"Yeah." She held her breath.

Buck's eyebrows drew together and he patted her shoulder. "I'm sorry to have to tell you this. It looks like Josiah is responsible."

The weights bore down on her. "I don't believe that, Buck! He's not violent."

"Unless he's provoked," Buck said. "He might have been trying to protect someone, or the guy might have said something that made him angry. By all accounts, he was a lowlife."

"You know who he was?"

"I do." He glanced over at her. "Rocky's stepfather."

"What?" Her voice screeched high but she didn't stop to modulate it. "He moved to California!"

Buck shook his head. "No, he didn't."

"The guy who's been abusing Rocky's mom and winning her back, all these years?"

"I told you, a lowlife." He turned to face her. "Look, maybe we can come to some agreement."

Blood pounded in her ears. "What kind of agreement?"

"I don't want to see Josiah prosecuted, any more than you do. I'm willing to overlook some evidence if you and Josiah just keep quiet about it. If you can keep him quiet about it. I know he's not reliable on his own."

The temptation was there. It was what she'd been doing, right? But something about this didn't ring true.

"You're an officer of the law," she said slowly. "Why would you be willing to overlook a murder?"

He was opening his mouth to answer when another car pulled up beside them. The door opened and a woman got out.

Yasmin's mouth fell open and she flung open the passenger door and scrambled out. "Lorraine! What are *you* doing here?"

"What are *you*?" Lorraine asked.

Now Buck was out of the car, too, looking from one to the other. "Come on up onto the porch," he said quickly. "We all need to talk."

"I want to see Josiah," Yasmin said.

"In due time. He's fine." Buck spoke so casually and offhandedly that Yasmin believed him, and she nodded, feeling dazed. Lorraine was here?

"How long have you been in the area?" *And aren't you at least a little concerned about your son?*

Lorraine shrugged. "A few weeks."

They sank into chairs on the porch. Buck went inside and came back with a tray, passing out open bottles of hard lemonade.

Yasmin put hers down without tasting it.

Lorraine took a big draw on her bottle. "I've been staying out here, trying to lay low," she said, "because I think I'm in trouble for killing my ex."

"*You* killed your ex?" Yasmin stared. "But I thought…" She looked at Buck, confused. "Who was it who hit him over the head? And put him in a car and drove it into the ocean?"

"I don't remember a whole lot about it," Lorraine said, frowning. "I'd been drinking, to be honest. But I know we got into it physically, and the next thing I know, Buck's hustling me into his car." She squeezed his arm and smiled at him. "He's an old friend, and he always takes good care of me."

Buck smiled and nodded. To Yasmin, it looked completely insincere.

Her mind raced. The way Buck was acting lined up with him being the person who'd whispered things to scare her. What was his endgame?

"But the more I think about it…well, I don't know what happened. And isn't there some kind of clause, anyway, for women who beat up their abusers? So I was thinking." She looked at Buck fondly. "I appreciate what you've done for me, and all, but I miss my kid." She turned to Yasmin again. "I made him drive me by your house a week or so ago, to make sure he was okay, but seeing him just made me miss him worse. And I know I can't leave him with you forever. I think I ought to just confess everything and face the music."

"Wait," Yasmin said, her mind reeling, "are you sure you killed him? And Buck knew that, thought so too?" She turned to him. "Then why were you telling me that Joe was the one who killed him? And where *is* Joe, anyway?"

There was a noise at the screen door into the house, and they all turned. Josiah stood there, a silent shadow.

"Joe!" She stood, rushed to him and opened the door, wrapped her arms around him. "I was so worried!"

Josiah extracted himself from her hug but left an arm around her and guided her back out onto the porch. He looked bedraggled, wearing the same clothes he'd been wearing yesterday, his eyes sunken. Had he been taking his medicine?"

He nudged her. "Yes, I took my meds," he said too quietly for the others to hear.

"You always could read my mind. Oh, I'm so glad you're safe."

His head tilted to one side as if listening to voices no one else could hear. "We're *not* safe," he said.

She bit her lip. He was still having his delusions.

"And it's only since I got out here and met Lorraine and thought it all through," he said, his voice clear and rational, "that I figured out the truth. At first I thought Lorraine did it, and Rocky thought so, too. But she didn't." Josiah looked straight at Buck. "*He* killed the guy."

Before Yasmin could react, Buck took two steps toward them, face furious. "Who's going to believe you?"

Yasmin stared at Buck, and at Josiah, and everything fell into place. The reason for Josiah's anxiety and Rocky's fear; the reason Buck hadn't pushed the investigation forward; the reason he was trying to blame Joe. She looked over at Lorraine and saw the same realization dawning on her face. "If they don't believe Josiah, they'll believe us," Yasmin said, and Lorraine nodded agreement.

Buck turned and saw them exchanging looks and his lip curled into a snarl. "No one will believe you either," he said to Lorraine. "They all know you cheat and lie and drink." He nodded toward his boat, docked down at the lake. "Come on," he said. "Let's go for a ride."

Josiah, Yasmin and Lorraine all stood their ground. "We're not going for a ride," Yasmin said.

Buck grabbed Josiah with a roughness she hadn't known he was capable of. "And you," he said to Yasmin. "I know you won't go anywhere without your precious brother. So come on, man. You're the pied piper gonna lead your sister back to…wherever the pied piper leads people to."

"Don't go with him, Joe," she said.

"He has a gun."

Josiah said those kinds of things all the time, but this time, it was true. Buck held a gun pointed straight at Josiah's head.

"Put it away," Yasmin said, trying to keep her voice from shaking. "I'll come, just put it away."

"I don't think you're really in any position to call the shots. Come on." Roughly, he jerked Josiah toward the long wooden dock below his place.

"Get help," Joe said to Yasmin.

"Can you?" she mouthed to Lorraine. Because she didn't think her brother had a chance of surviving if she didn't go along.

Wasn't sure she had a chance of surviving, either. Wherever Buck was planning to take them couldn't be good. But she was going to try.

She was strong, she knew that now. And even though she'd made mistakes, she still wanted all the happiness she could squeeze out of life.

Buck was untying his big, powerful fishing boat, flicking the gun to point at Josiah every few seconds. His movements were jerky, manic.

Oh, this wasn't good. Not good at all. If they got onto the boat and went into the swamp, their chances of survival would decrease dramatically.

Although, if they *didn't* get on the boat, Buck might very well shoot them and let their bodies fall into the swamp. Either place, they'd be unlikely to be found.

They were out of options.

Rocky would have Lorraine, who was even now

squealing off in her car. She and Josiah would be together, in death as they'd been in life. And Liam...

Oh, how she wanted the chance to hold him, to be with him, to try to explain. One more time, she wanted to see him laughing with his brothers, or patiently teaching Rio, or explaining to middle-schoolers the consequences of their actions.

He was a man who held family and community at the core of his being, who valued it above all else. A truly good man.

The woman who gained his heart would be lucky, indeed.

She'd had the chance to be that, but her own feelings of not deserving happiness had ruined it, had made her push him away in an unforgiveable way. Yes, she'd been trying to sacrifice herself for him, but why? Had he asked her to do that? Had it helped him at all?

"Get on the boat," Buck said, pulling her arm roughly.

Liam, where are you?

She let go of the dock and let Buck force her into the boat.

LIAM LOOKED AROUND at Rita and Miss Vi, all frustrated in Rita's apartment. He'd talked to the state police, who couldn't do much yet. He'd alerted Buddy in their own department, and he'd called his brothers to come. Sean had the twins alone and couldn't leave them, though he was looking for a sitter so he could help. Cash was on his way.

Keeping it together was a challenge, because he had the sense that Yasmin was in danger. She wouldn't have just left town with no notice, and she always answered her phone. Something was wrong.

And he had to remain calm no matter what. He was the cop. "I still think we have to find Josiah," he said. "That's where Yasmin is. That's *who* she is." She'd help her brother despite whatever risk to her own safety.

But they'd followed several false leads. Miss Vi knew Josiah well, and it had been right to consult her, but her ideas hadn't panned out.

Rocky had fallen asleep, but now he sat up on the couch and rubbed his eyes, looked around. "Did we find Yasmin and Josiah yet?"

"Not yet, honey, but we will." Rita went and sat beside him, and to Liam's surprise, Rocky allowed her to put her arm around him.

It hit him then: Rocky had lost his own mother, and now he'd lost the woman who'd stepped in as a mother figure to him. A trauma for any kid.

But Rocky was made of pretty stern stuff. After accepting a glass of orange juice from Rita, he sat forward and asserted that whatever they were doing, he didn't want to be left behind.

"We can keep using my place as a home base," Rita said. "I'll stay here with Miss Vi and we'll wait for Jimmy, keep track of Rocky."

"I think that's a good idea," Liam said. He had all the respect in the world for Miss Vi and Rita, but for serious investigating, he was worried he'd be too preoccupied with protecting them to focus on the search.

The doorbell rang, and when Rita opened it, she went still. Jimmy walked in. "Thanks for coming," she said, her voice breathless. "We're trying to figure out what to do."

"No problem." But he sounded cool, distant. Something must have gone down between them, but Liam had no time to focus on that now.

Cash walked in behind Jimmy. Good. His brother was a great resource, strong and smart.

They quickly brought Jimmy and Cash up to speed. Cash turned immediately to Rocky. "Tell me everything you know about Josiah and what might have happened to him," he said.

Good thinking. Liam hadn't paid enough attention to the boy and what he might know, but the truth was, he spent more time with Josiah than anyone else.

"I know a few things," Rocky said, but he turned away from Cash's intensity, his face closing.

Rita came over with a big bag of chips and some sour cream dip, and put them on the table. Good maternal thinking. A boy like Rocky, growing the way he was, needed constant nourishment.

Liam reached for patience to connect with the boy. With Yasmin involved, he wanted to rush out, look for her and fight his way in to save her, but that wasn't good police work. They first had to find out where she was. Running around crazily was the opposite of how to find out.

He felt wildly out of control and he hated that. But he knew what it took to be a great cop, and panicking wasn't it. "Anything you remember will help," he said to Rocky, keeping his tone casual. "You've probably spent more time with Josiah than any of us. Did he say anything about places he wanted to go?"

"He talked about places he *didn't* want to go," Rocky mumbled around a mouthful of potato chips.

"Like where?" Liam passed him a can of Coke and reminded himself that the story would come out at its own pace. You couldn't hurry people; that just made things worse. So when Cash looked ready to explode, Liam asked him to go check on Sean.

"Buck invited him to come visit his place. On some lake? Joe didn't want to go but he thought I might like to try fishing, so he said he would. Only Buck didn't want to take me, so then Joe said no."

Liam looked at Rita. "He has a big house over on Five-Mile Bayou," he said.

"Yeah," Rocky said, gulping cola and getting more animated. "They were talking about disappearing, and I listened to them, because I want to be a cop one day, too."

That gave Liam's heart a little squeeze. "What did you find out?" Still calm; no rushing, and as

Cash came back into the room, Liam willed him to keep quiet and listen.

"Buck said he had a good starting point for it, a place on the water. But Joe still said he didn't want to go."

"Maybe he changed his mind," Liam said slowly.

"It's the only lead we have." Cash grabbed car keys. "I remember that place. Went to a party out there once. Let's go."

"I want to come," Rocky said. "And I want to bring Rio."

Cash shook his head. "No, buddy, it wouldn't be safe."

"I've been training Rio like a police dog," Rocky said stubbornly. "He can help. And so can I."

"If you stay in the car, okay." Liam ruffled the boy's hair. "I mean it, though. No running around or putting yourself at risk."

"I won't," Rocky promised.

Cash looked at Liam like he was crazy. "We may as well have everyone come," he said. "Jimmy? Rita? How about Miss Vi?"

Rita patted his arm. "Cool down. The three of us will wait here and be a central spot for people to call and share information."

"Thank you," Liam said. "Let's go."

"I hope you know what you're doing," Cash said, but didn't argue with him. Liam couldn't have explained why he thought bringing the dog was a good idea, but intuition was a big part of police work, and that was what he was running on.

Ten minutes later they were making the half-hour drive to Buck's country place: Liam, Cash, Rocky and Rio. Cash was driving—well, but way over the speed limit. They didn't talk much. Liam vacillated between thinking the whole thing was a wild-goose chase and worrying they wouldn't get there in time.

What was going on with Buck? Liam had always thought of him as smooth, maybe a little less than ethical, but certainly not dangerous. More and more, it was looking like he had things to hide.

If he was behind breaking into Yasmin's house and trying to put insane—literally—notions into her head, then something was seriously wrong. Wrong, and dangerous.

That had been a blind spot, Liam acknowledged to himself. Because he and Buck were rivals for the chief job, and because Liam felt at a disadvantage to Buck's country club background, he'd missed important signs.

Now, he had to hope his own insecurity hadn't put Yasmin at risk. He was never, ever letting that happen again.

"Up there," Cash said. "What is that, a car?"

"That ran into a tree," Liam said grimly as they pulled up to it. At the steering wheel was a woman slumped forward, and Liam's heart went into his throat. He ran to the car and opened the door.

It wasn't Yasmin, and the woman had a strong

pulse. Relief washed over him, and then, as they tried to ease the woman out of the car, he realized she looked familiar.

"It's my mom!" Rocky cried just as Liam recognized the woman who'd driven slowly by Yasmin's house.

Rocky tugged at her. "Mom! Mom, it's me!"

"Be real careful. She could have some injuries," Cash said, but gently. He glanced at Liam. "No matter what, you still love your mom."

When you were a kid, yeah, but now?

They eased the woman out onto a blanket Cash had in the back of his SUV, and she began to murmur, her eyes flickering open.

Strange, choking noises came from Rocky, interspersed with one word, repeated: "Mom. Mom."

After making sure the woman was basically okay, Liam and Cash stepped back by mutual agreement. Liam had a lump in his throat, and looking over at Cash, he suspected his brother felt the same.

They didn't know what it would be like to find your mom as a kid because they never had. "We have to try to connect better with Rita," Cash said, and Liam knew just what his brother meant.

"Hey, police officer," Rocky's mom gasped out. "You gotta go save Yasmin and Joe."

"You know where they are?"

"Buck's taking 'em out on his boat," she said. "And he doesn't mean anything good. Pretty sure he put something into my drink."

They loaded Lorraine into the car, in the back beside Rocky and Rio, and then Cash drove like crazy while Liam called Rita. He updated her on the situation, and she agreed that she, Jimmy and Miss Vi would wait to hear more and would contact others in the community who might be able to help, including Chief Ramirez, now home from the hospital.

Fury rose in Liam as he listened to Lorraine's muddled description of what had gone down at Buck's place. Corruption had no place in this town. His back straightened and he focused hard. They'd save Yasmin and Josiah, and they'd free Safe Haven of the poison that was Buck Mulligan. There was no alternative.

"Rocky," he said as they approached Buck's place. "You and Rio need to stay in the car and help your mom. You can watch, but don't come out. Stay on the phone with Rita and Jimmy and Miss Vi. Let them know what's going on. Understand?"

"But I want to…"

Liam turned and gave him a full-on glare. "What's Yasmin going to say if I let you be in danger?"

Lorraine croaked from beside him, "He's right, son. This is adult business. Besides, I need you here with me."

Rocky's eyes flickered back and forth from Liam to his mother and back again. Tough when you didn't know exactly who was your authority figure, but that was life for some kids. He'd been there.

They parked on a dirt road in a thick stand of pines. Buck's place glowed white through the trees. "There's a dock just down there, if I remember right," Cash said, pointing. "Let's go through the woods to there and then circle up toward the house."

Rio let out a yelp when they left the SUV, but Rocky calmed him instantly. And then Liam and Cash were creeping through the swampy pines. Like when they'd played as kids, or escaped consequences for bad behavior as teenagers, but now the stakes were high.

The dock was splintery and decaying, at odds with the pristine house. Showed that Buck wasn't a real low country person. He didn't prioritize the connection with the water.

Movement up near the house caught Liam's eye, and he put a hand on Cash's arm and nodded toward it.

Mulligan was coming out, scanning the water, with a weapon he wasn't authorized to have at the ready. But something was wrong with how he looked, and it only took a minute for Liam to realize the man was soaking wet.

Liam pulled his weapon, holding it low but ready, and Cash did the same. That didn't surprise Liam; his brother did some of his business dealings in dangerous places and he was a crack shot.

Jerking his head to one side, Liam indicated for Cash to separate off toward the house. Hopefully they'd cut the man off and take him down without a shot fired. Even though he deserved injury and more, if what Liam suspected was true, he'd still try to take the man in unscathed.

They were about to do a standard distract-and-capture when the sound of a boat's motor came from the water. Buck obviously heard it, because he straightened and turned that way. "Coming back here. I knew y'all would. Crazy man pushing me out of the boat…you're gonna pay for that." And then he was muttering dark threats of which Liam could only understand a few words.

Liam knew who was going to be in the boat before he saw them, and his heart sank.

Yasmin and Joe, standing beside each other. Joe used to be an expert sailor and boatman, and obviously still remembered how. Yasmin sat close beside him, talking intently. But how steady they were mentally was anyone's guess.

Liam broke cover. "Stay away," he called, coming out into the open and waving his arms, gesturing for them to stay out of Mulligan's range. Then he turned and stared the man down, weapon still ready.

"What the… I'm going to kill you," Mulligan snarled. "Always messing with my plans."

What made it worse was that Yasmin and Josiah just kept on coming.

Mulligan walked toward the water's edge.

"Stay back," Liam ordered.

"Can't believe you think you'd do for chief. Naive. People know they can work with me."

"What do Yasmin and Josiah have to do with that?" Liam genuinely wanted to know, but he also wanted to distract Mulligan so that Cash would have time to do...something.

"They wouldn't have had anything to do with it," Buck said grimly, "if Old Crazy, there, hadn't been where he shouldn't be when Lorraine and her idiot husband came into town."

Liam tried to process that. "Her husband who's in California?"

"Her husband who's *dead*, and if anyone deserved to die, it was that jerk," Buck said.

Understanding crashed in on Liam. "The guy in the car was Lorraine's husband. Rocky's stepfather." His head pounded with the shock, and the self-recrimination that he hadn't figured that out sooner.

There was no time to think about all the implications now. "Did you do it on purpose?" Liam asked, hoping to distract Buck.

But he ignored Liam, still walking toward the boat. Getting closer.

"I hate to have to shoot you, but I will," Liam said. Buck was close enough, now, that Liam could smell nervous sweat coming from the man.

Then everything happened at once. Cash burst out from under the docks and feinted like he was going to board the boat, but with some kind of hand signal, Joe leaped off the deck and they both landed on Buck, taking him down. That freed Liam and he turned to Yasmin, but then there was the sound of a shot and Buck took off running.

"Wild one!" Cash said. "We're fine!"

But Buck was turning, taking aim at Josiah. Yasmin leaped in front of her brother, and then Liam dived in front of her.

"Buck's scared of dogs!" Yasmin screamed.

A dark shape hurdled through the air: Rio, leaping at Buck and knocking him to the ground. Rocky yelled something. Cash and Liam, Yasmin and Josiah all ran toward the man, boy and dog.

And together, they overpowered Buck.

RITA SPENT THE next day helping to do damage control. She'd never liked Buck Mulligan, but she wouldn't have pegged him for a criminal mastermind. "He just didn't seem that smart," she said to Yasmin, who was parked on Rita's couch with a big cup of hot tea.

"I agree, but there's smart and smart." Yasmin's voice was husky, strained; apparently, she'd done a lot of screaming last night. "I guess he was the dumb-like-a-fox kind. He almost got away with all of that. He sure had Chief Ramirez fooled."

"How do you mean?"

Yasmin lifted her hands in a palms-up position. "Apparently he told the chief a bunch of lies about Liam. Got him to believe that council would blame him and his legacy in Safe Haven would be ruined if he backed Liam over Buck."

Rita shook her head. "And Buck turned out to be a killer. Although the actual murder seems to have been an accident. Right?"

"Uh-huh. Buck was trying to help Lorraine— apparently they'd had a relationship years ago and still cared about each other—and he just got out of control, hit the guy too hard. If he'd come forward and confessed right away..." Yasmin sighed. "Among other things, Joe wouldn't have had to go through so much."

Rita's heart tugged. God willing, Yasmin would never experience the mental health issues her brother faced, but she seemed to feel every nuance of the pain he went through. "How's he doing?"

"It could be a setback." Yasmin sighed. "His doctor insisted he go to the hospital for twenty-four hours of observation. But I'm almost thinking he'll end up better than before. He felt good that he could help Cash take Buck down, and he actually pushed Buck out of the boat and drove it, which I could never have done. It was like some of his old self came back. I hope it stays."

"Is Rocky doing okay?"

"Yeah. He suspected the victim was his stepdad, because he and Joe saw a lot of the fight. He was afraid his mom had killed his stepdad, though, so he was more worried about what would happen to her. The stepdad... Rocky won't miss him."

Her voice trailed off at the end, and she sounded drowsy, so Rita didn't press her for more information, including about what might be happening between her and Liam. She wanted to know, and wanted to help both of them, but they'd been through way too much. Liam was busy at headquarters, writing up and interviewing and explaining, and would be for a while. And Yasmin had basically collapsed after everything had finally settled the night before.

Rita was still holding inside herself, like a delicate glass of happiness, her joy about one thing: Liam and Cash both seemed ready to have some kind of relationship with her. Like their older brother Sean, who'd been a rock throughout these crazy two days. It would take time, and who knew where it would all end up, but they'd both hugged her and apologized for being distant and said they wanted to talk when the situation with Buck got resolved.

She'd just pulled a blanket over Yasmin, who'd already dozed off, when there was a quiet rap on her front door.

When she opened it, there was Jimmy. Hope flared inside her.

He looked just as handsome as the first day she'd met him. Shaved head, muscles, tattoos…he was a sexy guy for sure.

But now, she knew more about him, knew of his compassion and tenderness, his patience and passion.

What was more, she felt worthy of being with him now. No, she didn't completely know who she was or what had happened in her past, and that might always remain a mystery, shadowy and shrouded. But in the warmth of the Safe Haven community, working side by side with Yasmin and Liam and Sean, she'd started to believe that she must have done her best. Maybe she didn't have to be down on herself forever to make up for whatever wrongs she'd done.

There were people like Josiah, who suffered so much more than she did, and worked so much harder for happiness. And there were kids like Rocky, desperate for any connection with their moms. She'd rediscovered her children and was starting to build something with them. For now, it was enough.

Like Jimmy had said, she wasn't getting any younger and neither was he. She put a finger to her lips and gestured toward the front room. "Yasmin's sleeping, but do you want to sit on the balcony, talk a little?"

He nodded, without smiling. Uh-oh. Maybe she felt like she deserved happiness, but it was very possible that she'd blown her chances with Jimmy. Was he here for a final goodbye?

As she led him through the kitchen toward the balcony, though, she caught a whiff of something sweetly floral and fragrant. At the balcony door, she turned to look at him, but he just lifted an eyebrow.

Still no smile, but his hand was behind his back.

On the balcony, he pulled it forward. Red roses... at least two dozen, in what looked like a crystal vase. "These are for you," he said.

She pressed a hand to her mouth. Buried her nose in the flowers and inhaled their fragrance. And then set them down and turned to him. "Thank you. Does...does this mean we have a chance?"

"Do you want one?"

She tilted her head to one side and nodded. "I want it more than anything. I'm sorry for what I've put you through."

"And I'm sorry for being impatient. I can't imagine what this has been like for you, coming to Safe Haven to figure out your past."

"I haven't figured it out, not entirely," she said, "but you've made it better than I could have imagined."

He opened his arms. "Come here."

She walked into them, and he held her as the low country breeze cooled her face and warmed her heart.

CHAPTER TWENTY

A WEEK LATER, Yasmin perched on the edge of her desk at the women's center and looked around at the women gathered here. Rita, Norma and Claire: they'd all become closer friends through the challenges they'd faced together.

Even Lorraine, who was technically still a client, was here because she'd said she wanted to help.

"We're going to do whatever it takes to keep this place running smoothly," Miss Vi said. She was already way overcommitted at the library, but when she'd realized what all had happened with Lorraine and Buck and Yasmin, she'd decided she needed to put in some hours here, as well.

Her focus was on building a small library at the center, of course. Building up one for women, in addition to the kids' one they already had. Miss Vi was putting together a list of books that were uplifting to women who were struggling with domestic violence or abuse, and she'd already started raising the money to purchase the books, along with shelving and lighting.

She'd also suggested that Josiah teach the kids, and maybe the moms, to play chess, since his work with the kids' chess club at the library was going so well. Even though Yasmin wanted most of the center's activities to be organized by women, she'd make an exception for Josiah. He loved teaching chess to kids and could wax eloquent about the benefits: thinking ahead, problem solving, good sportsmanship.

The others weren't quite so forceful as Miss Vi, but they were all helping with the center, even talking about getting it back to its roots as a live-in center. Norma was considering joining the staff part-time, as a counselor. Rita was committed to helping however she was needed; she freely admitted to being a jack-of-all-trades. And Claire wanted to do something for younger women, who tended to think of women's centers as being for married women with kids. Claire insisted that dating violence happened at every age, and she wanted teens and twentysomethings to know about how to spot it and avoid that type of partner.

Yasmin looked around the office and sighed. "I'm sorry it's so crowded in here," she said. "I wish we had a bigger facility."

"I wish it were residential," Lorraine said. "That might have kept me away from my husband. I just never knew where I'd stay if I cut him all the way off."

Yasmin bit her lip to stifle the critical words that wanted to come out. Lorraine had done something nearly unforgiveable in letting Rocky suffer as he had, but she was penitent, open about not having been a good mother, and supposedly, she wanted to raise him.

And Yasmin knew something she couldn't yet tell the others: Cash was thinking about making a big donation to the center. Which might mean that they *could* develop a residential program in the future, by building onto the church or by finding another property that would suit.

"I need some air. Let's go out onto the steps," Lorraine said, and the others agreed. As they walked outside, Lorraine tugged at Yasmin's sleeve. "Something's been bothering me," she said. "Are you going to report me to social services for what I did, neglecting Rocky like that?"

"I'm not sure. But I'd definitely like for you to consider staying in Safe Haven, where you can get the support you need."

"I'm already looking for apartments," she promised. "I want to do better, Yasmin. Honestly, I do."

"Hey, look!" Norma said in a falsely quiet voice. "The cops are coming! Somebody's in trouble."

"I'm outta here," Claire said.

"Me, too," Rita said, and Norma followed her. "Come on, Lorraine, breakfast at the café is on me."

Yasmin tilted her head to one side as she watched her friends hurry off. That had seemed odd.

Then she refocused her attention on the police car that had pulled up in front of the women's center.

She and Liam had spent time together during the past week, talking through what had happened. They'd worked out their differences, she felt. They even had plans for a date tonight, so what was he doing here now?

Liam got out, in uniform. He was holding a box from the café. "I brought you breakfast," he said, holding it out to her.

"Thank you." He was so thoughtful, and she had hopes that one day she might regain his trust. She opened the box. "My favorites!" Jean Carol's cinnamon rolls were to die for, and she normally limited herself to just one, but there were three here.

"Have one," he urged. Just as he had so many times when they'd dated before, and she was touched he remembered her favorite breakfast after all this time.

"Only if you will, too."

"Okay, if you insist." So they sat in the morning sunshine and ate their rolls.

"Split the last one?" he suggested.

"Oh, well, if you insist."

"I was hoping you'd say that." He ripped it carefully and handed her half on a napkin.

She picked it up, and something sparkled underneath. "I think there's…" She trailed off.

It was a ring. A diamond engagement ring.

She lost her breath. Slowly, she raised her eyes to his. "Liam?"

He shifted to the step below her and looked up. "Yasmin, I've loved you for so many years, and I've almost lost you twice. I can't take a chance on losing you for real and for good." He wiped a fine sheen of sweat from his forehead.

"Wait," she said. "What did you just say?"

"I said I can't take a chance—"

"No," she interrupted, waving a hand, staring at him. "The other part. You *love* me? Not just for old times or because I need help with my life?"

"No." He smiled then. "I hope I *can* help you with your burdens, and I'm glad I've known you forever. It'll make a great basis for a marriage." He tilted his head to one side, looking at her with eyes burning. "But only if you feel the same. If you love me, too, as more than a friend."

All the breath she'd been holding burst out of her in a nervous laugh. "Do you think I'd kiss a friend the way I kiss you?"

"I don't know," he said. "Maybe you'd better show me again."

He was kind of joking, she knew that, but she slid forward, her heart seeming to expand in her chest, her throat tight. She tangled her fingers into his dark hair and pressed her lips to his, trying to put all her love and caring into this one kiss.

It was Liam who finally broke it off, breathing

hard. "Will you marry me and let me protect you and help you and take care of you?"

She bit her lip to stop the tears. Nothing could stop the swell of emotions in her heart, though. "Liam…there won't be any kids."

"No biological kids, but there are other ways. Adoption, foster care. I'm open to either."

"I don't know if I might develop what Joe has," she said, her voice trembling, somewhere on the edge between fear and joy. "And I'll always have him to take care of."

"I like Joe, and that's fine," he said. "And as for you…we don't ever know what the future holds. But I just know I want to spend mine with you. Will you marry me, Yasmin?"

Very slowly, looking into his eyes, she nodded.

His eyes got shiny and he pulled her into his arms.

It was a few minutes later that she heard the voices around her and realized that her friends hadn't left at all. "It's all recorded," Norma said with satisfaction.

"And I took still photographs," Rita added. They, and Miss Vi and Claire and Liam's brothers, all gathered around Liam and Yasmin.

And Yasmin, who'd often felt lonely, knew that she had a community to care for her, and for her to care for, forever.

EPILOGUE

WHEN MA DIXIE brought out the Thanksgiving turkey, Liam couldn't believe the size of it. But it made sense, given that half of Safe Haven's population seemed to be here.

The little cottage on the bayou couldn't hold everyone, so they set up a long plank table outside. It was midafternoon, high sixties, sunny.

Liam had so much to be thankful for. He reached over and tugged Yasmin a little closer, still unable to believe that she was his for keeps. That after all, they'd be making a home together, a home where visitors could stay, big enough for Josiah as long as he wanted to live with them, probably big enough for them to foster some kids and maybe, one day, adopt a baby.

He and his brothers had been those kids who needed homes, had benefitted from the system. He wanted to give back, and Yasmin was totally on board with that.

He heard a muffled exclamation from the corner

of the living room. "I should have seen that," Pudge said. He and Josiah were leaning over a chessboard, and Josiah wore a small smile. "You son of a gun, you're going to beat me, ain't you?"

"Joe looks happy," Liam said to Yasmin.

She smiled. "He's doing really well on the new medication. That once-a-month injection has smoothed the ups and downs a lot. But speaking of happy, look at Anna."

Liam looked over at his sister-in-law. Sean had his arm protectively around her, and their twins, Hope and Hayley, were nudging their way into the love seat, piling on top of Anna.

"Careful," Sean said, and whispered something to the girls.

Hope clapped a hand over her mouth, and Hayley smiled and put an ear to Anna's stomach.

They were a picture of family joy, and... "Wait. Is Anna expecting?"

Yasmin lifted an eyebrow, a smile tugging at her mouth. "If I were a betting woman, I'd say yes."

He studied her face. Did she feel jealous, when she'd decided not to have children due to the family genetic heritage? Would it be hard for her to celebrate with Anna?

But her eyes were clear and serene. "I'm happy for her, don't worry," she said, reading his mind, and reached up to give him a quick kiss that shot warmth straight through him.

Their Christmastime wedding couldn't come soon enough.

The door opened again, this time bringing Rita and Jimmy, loaded down with food. He and Yasmin hurried over to help them carry in four pies and a giant tray of mac and cheese. "Are any of those pecan?" Liam asked.

"Two," Rita said, "and two peach." She gave him an easy side hug. "And just in case anybody doesn't like my cooking, we brought a box of Jean Carol's cinnamon rolls."

"Smart. Let me help you." He took a couple of pies out of her hands and headed toward the kitchen. They weren't exactly comfortable as mother and son yet, but they were both trying. And Liam was glad Rita had Jimmy at her side. They didn't seem in a hurry to make a long-term commitment, but from the way they looked at each other and the fact that they were almost always together, it seemed like they were a solid and very happy couple.

Norma, coming in behind them, did *not* sound happy. "You invited *him*? Seriously?" She was nudging Rita and nodding sideways at a tall, silver-haired man who was leaning over the chess table behind Pudge.

Rita lifted her hands, palms up. "It's not my party, it's Ma's," she said, her eyes wide and innocent. "You don't like the guest list, you'll have to take it up with her."

Norma snorted and turned in the opposite direction from the silver-haired man. Then she did a double take and touched Yasmin's arm. "Your mom's here?"

Yasmin lifted her eyebrows and nodded. "She really wanted to come down, and Ma Dixie said she always has room for one more. So far, so good."

"I'll go talk to her," Norma said, and headed over.

"Your mom seems like she's doing okay," Liam said to Yasmin. "And Josiah doesn't look like her presence is bothering him."

"He'll have fun with Hayley and Hope. And Rocky," she added as the teenager emerged from the back of the house. He and his mother were living here for the time being. Lorraine was helping with the house and yardwork, and Rocky and Pudge had bonded over their mutual interest in dog training. Several people from Safe Haven had brought their unruly animals out here for lessons.

Their moment of glory had come when Mitch Mitchell had brought his shih tzu, Daisy, for training. Rocky was too diplomatic, or too good of a businessman, to gloat publicly, but he'd certainly crowed to Liam and Yasmin about it.

The living arrangement was good for everyone. Lorraine seemed calmer, maybe benefitting from being in the presence of Ma and Pudge's healthy, happy relationship. She'd been through a lot, losing her abusive husband and getting under Buck's influence, but she was the type who'd always bounce back.

And Rocky was thrilled to be living with his

mom again. It was like Cash had said: no matter what your mother did or didn't do, you loved her.

"When's Cash going to find the right woman?" Yasmin asked. "He looks lonely."

Sure enough, Cash stood off from the group, gazing out over the bayou, a pensive expression on his face. Liam knew that expression, because he'd worn it himself, plenty of times. His stomach tightened in sympathy.

"It's hard for him to see Sean and me so happy," he said. "I mean, he's happy for us, but he doesn't think he'll ever be able to settle down with anyone."

"You O'Dwyer men don't make it easy," Yasmin said, standing on tiptoes to kiss his cheek. "But it's definitely worth it."

"You're worth it." He pulled her close, and even though they were surrounded by the buzz of family and friends, the singing of crickets and the laughter of children, she was the whole world to him. "I love you," he murmured in her ear, and drew her toward him for a lingering kiss.

* * * * *

*Read on for a sneak peek at the next
heartwarming book in the Safe Haven series,
Low Country Christmas,
from Lee Tobin McClain!*

CHAPTER ONE

On a late-November evening, Cash O'Dwyer locked the front door of his luxury condo and trotted down the steps, holding his phone to his ear to listen to the third message from his CFO in Atlanta. "Urgent that you return this—"

"Watch it!" The feminine voice was accompanied by a baby's cry.

Cash stopped with one foot halfway down to the next step and squinted at the woman who'd pressed herself flat against the railing, baby cradled protectively in her arms. He lifted a hand, palm out. "Sorry, sorry, ma'am, wasn't watching where I was going." He continued past them as he listened to the rest of his message. And then, as he processed what he'd seen, he clicked off his phone and turned back, shifting his focus from Atlanta and business deals to a very pretty young mother practically on his doorstep here in Safe Haven, South Carolina.

The woman was still on the landing, gently joggling the baby, whose cries were already dying out.

"Can I help you?" As he spoke, he checked the time on his phone. His brothers and their families would be waiting for him, the kids getting more and more impatient, the wives ready to strangle him. His pockets full of candy and little toys wouldn't make up for a night of fussy kids. He'd *told* them to go ahead without him, that he'd meet them at the holiday tree-lighting ceremony in the park, but his sisters-in-law had insisted that they all have dessert together first, at the Southern Comfort Café.

His sisters-in-law were big on tradition, something he and his brothers were pretty severely lacking.

Three messages flashed onto his lock screen. His sales manager, his brother Liam and his brother Sean's wife, Anna.

Above him on the landing, the woman hadn't moved, hadn't spoken. The baby, who looked to be a girl and about a year old, settled against her shoulder with a gurgley sigh. "Can I help you?" he asked again. These stairs led to two condos, his own and an older businesswoman. "Are you looking for Hillary?"

"No." She looked into his eyes and hers were strangely familiar. "We're looking for you."

A spark of anxiety climbed up his spine. He didn't like it. "Is it an emergency? What's your connection to me?"

Her eyebrow lifted just enough that he realized he sounded abrupt. Which was too bad, but that was how he was. Driven, impatient, materialistic. Not as bad as his father had been; at least Cash wasn't violent about it. But still. The old man must have known what he was doing, giving him the name of Cash.

It was no surprise that he didn't have a wife and kids the way his brothers did.

"It's…a long story," she said. There was anxiety in her voice. "Is there somewhere we could talk?"

He glanced at his phone again, the time ticking away. "Not right now, no." He tried to keep the irritation out of his tone. There were a lot of people in the world, especially in the South, for whom time had a different meaning than it did for him. People who didn't mind having drop-in guests because their schedules were flexible or nonexistent.

Cash O'Dwyer wasn't one of those people.

"Does the name Tiffany Gibson ring a bell?"

"Tiffany… yeah." Involuntarily, he smiled. He'd shared a very lovely week with Tiffany, when she'd vacationed in a beach resort adjoining Safe Haven at the same time he'd been spending a rare week in his hometown. "I do remember Tiff," he said.

"She's my sister." She was watching him steadily, like that was going to mean something to him.

But he and Tiffany hadn't spent their time together talking about their families. They hadn't spent their time talking much, period. He didn't think Tiffany had even mentioned she *had* a sister.

That must be why this woman's big gray eyes had looked so familiar. He didn't have time to piece together why Tiff's sister had showed up on his doorstep with a baby, but she probably had a sob story and needed money. That didn't even faze him anymore; as his bank account had expanded, so had the number of people who wanted to be his best friend. Couldn't blame 'em for trying.

But this one had a baby, which got to him. "Look," he said impulsively, starting down the stairs and gesturing for her to follow, "I'm late for this tree-lighting thing. It's a tradition, and there are kids involved, kids I can't disappoint. If you'd like to ride along, we can talk in the car. Or..." He frowned at the baby. "You can follow in your own car, if you'd be more comfortable."

"I came in an Uber," she said as she reached the bottom of the stairs, half knelt and picked up a car seat she must've left there. "I can ride along with you."

She'd come in an *Uber*? That meant she didn't have a car. Definitely a sob story coming, but two more messages pinged onto his phone and he didn't have time to deal with it. He just took the car seat out of her hands, opened the falcon wing rear door of his Tesla—a cool feature he didn't often have the chance to use—and slid it in. From his brothers, he'd actually learned how kids' car seats worked, so he fiddled with the never-used rear seat belts and strapped it into place, then stepped back to give her access.

"I'm impressed. Most guys can't do that." She bent over, carefully buckling the baby in.

Just as carefully, Cash tried to keep his eyes away

from her shapely rear view. He focused on the sound of the waves lapping just beyond the parking lot, the sweet-smelling winter honeysuckle that climbed a lamppost, the stars emerging against the velvet blue sky.

He loved it here, would have made it his permanent home if things were different. But he had never really fit in, and now that his two brothers were happily married and fathering families, he felt like even more of an outsider.

She cleared her throat as she walked around the car to the passenger side. "You said you were in a hurry?"

"Right." He held her door for her, closed it once she was inside.

His brothers were going to think he was an idiot for bringing some stranger along to their family gathering. But he'd learned from experience that ignoring people who thought they had a claim on you could make for all kinds of harassment. And this one had shown up just when his family was demanding his immediate presence. So what choice did he have?

HOLLY SAT FORWARD in the front seat and turned to look at the baby, quiet and peaceful. Little Penny, at one year old, couldn't appreciate the incredible acceleration of the space-age car, its silent engine. Nor the fact that the driver was wearing a beautiful summer wool suit that fit his tall, muscular form perfectly.

Holly herself did notice, but she wasn't impressed. Sure, money was nice; in fact, she had a pretty major shortage of it herself, and wouldn't mind solving that problem.

But Cash O'Dwyer had acted like she and Penny were impediments in his journey to more important activities and people. That bothered her, especially given what she knew.

He'd lowered the windows partway, and the smell of salty ocean blew into the car on a warm breeze. "You familiar with Safe Haven?" he asked. Again with the rich, sexy baritone. The man had everything going for him.

But she *wasn't* attracted to him. Holly was known for keeping to herself, avoiding relationships, especially close ones with men.

"I'm not at all familiar with Safe Haven." She looked around at the tree-lined streets full of people strolling along, browsing the shop windows. It was well over fifty degrees, sweater weather to someone from the North, but the people here wore leather or wool jackets, scarves and boots. "First time in the state, actually," she added.

Lots of small groups stood chatting. It looked like a friendly town, just as Tiff had described it.

But could she live here? Make a life here?

She was opening her mouth to begin the difficult conversation they needed to have, when Cash pulled into a diagonal parking space in front of an old-fashioned diner.

"Uncle Cash!" Two little girls, probably six or seven, ran toward the car. "We've been waiting forever!"

"Let me just check in with the family and then we'll talk," he said to Holly. "You need help with the baby?"

"I've got it," she said. It would give her another minute to enjoy the fabulous vehicle. And figure out a little more about the man she hoped would help them.

As she pulled the baby out, trying not to wake her—thank heavens Penny was a good sleeper— more voices joined the two eager, childish ones around Cash. Propping the baby on her shoulder, Holly knelt to pick up the diaper bag and her purse, taking her time so she could watch her target.

Two dark-haired men, one wearing a police uniform, the other in work clothes, were pounding him on the back. They were laughing, giving him a hard time about being late. A toddler lifted his hands, and Cash swung him up high, making him chortle, and then settled the child into the crook of his arm.

The two identical-twin girls were boldly sticking their hands into the pockets of his suit jacket.

"Hey, you little bandits," he said, laughing down at them. "Why would you even think I have candy for you?"

"Hope! Hayley!" A woman holding an infant just a bit smaller than Penny leaned down. "No begging!"

The biggest of the three brothers—for they were brothers, she could see now, all dark-haired and blue-eyed—knelt and talked quietly to the twins, and they nodded and stepped back from Cash, one of them with a lower lip pushed out.

"Aw, give 'em a break," Cash said. "It's Christmastime." He reached into a pocket and pulled out two tiny gold boxes. He grinned winningly at the twins' mom. "Never too early to get them started on Godiva."

"Cash!" The woman laughed and shook her head.

"Don't worry," he said, "I brought you one, too." He fumbled in his other jacket pocket and handed her a slightly bigger box.

Standing there with a smile on his face, a toddler in his arms, giving extravagant gifts to people who obviously adored him, Cash O'Dwyer was so breathtaking that Holly swallowed and looked away.

"He's a good guy," said a female voice next to her shoulder.

Startled, Holly turned to see a curvy woman with multiple long braids. "That's…good," she said. She was hoping Cash was a good guy, because she needed him to step up.

"I'm Yasmin," the woman said. "Married to the cop." She nodded toward the brother in uniform. "Foster mom of the toddler he's holding, and for little Gino to warm up to Cash is so awesome. He was afraid of everything and everyone when he came to us." Without taking a breath, she added, "What's your connection to Cash?"

"I... Oh, well, I..." What was she supposed to say, when she hadn't had the discussion she needed to have with him yet? "Friend of a friend," she said.

"And who's this little cutie?" Yasmin leaned in to see Penny more closely, touching her tiny foot.

The less information she shared, the better, at this point. "She's Penny, and she's one year old."

"Adorable."

A waitress came out of the diner—actually, it was the Southern Comfort Café according to the sign—and beckoned to Yasmin. "Can't hold the table much longer," she called across the crowd.

"Everybody inside," Yasmin yelled, and the whole group trooped into the café.

Holly bit her lip. This was a family gathering and she was completely out of place. And Cash was clearly at the center of the family, so he couldn't bail on them now.

She should have made arrangements for a business meeting with him, and she'd tried, but his secretary had set up a series of barriers that were almost impossible to breach, unless you disclosed your business.

Which Holly wasn't willing to do.

A hand touched her elbow, accompanied by the faintest whiff of spicy men's cologne, and Holly's stomach clenched with awareness. Cash. She turned to him. "Hey," she said, working hard to keep her voice cool and professional, "if we could just set up a meeting next week—tomorrow would be even better—I'll head out."

"In an Uber?" He frowned at her, one eyebrow quirked.

She nodded.

"No." He shook his head. "Come in and have some dessert. You haven't lived until you've tasted Abel's pies. And then things will settle down and we can go off in a corner and talk about whatever it is you came to talk about. And then I'll get you where you need to go."

"You don't have to do that."

He tilted his head to one side and met her eyes. "What kind of gentleman would I be if I let a lady find her own way home after dark?"

She sucked in a breath. This guy was a very skillful flirt, and the fact that he'd flirt with a woman holding a baby made him seem like an actual nice guy. No wonder Tiff hadn't minded doing what she'd done.

Firmly, Holly pulled her mind away from the distasteful realities of her sister's short life. She tried for a different excuse to avoid the convivial group heading into the café. "It's a family gathering. I don't want to intrude."

"You won't be." He took the diaper bag from her and put a hand on the small of her back. "Look, they're already pulling up an extra chair and high chair. You'll hardly be noticed."

But Holly had seen the speculative way Yasmin looked at her. She had the feeling she *would* be noticed.

It was inevitable in a small town, which was why she wasn't real fond of them. But to fulfill her sister's wishes, she'd make the sacrifice and live here. Getting to know some people would be a good way to start. "If you're sure," she said.

His hand on her back increased its pressure, just a smidge, and heat suffused her chest. "I'm sure," he said in a husky voice.

You need him for cash, just like his name. Anything else will get you deep into trouble.

LATER THAT EVENING, Cash joined with his family singing Christmas carols as they waited for the giant, ancient live oak tree to be lit, as it was every year in mid-November. It was the town's traditional kickoff to the holiday season.

Holly seemed to be having an okay time, but they'd never gotten the chance to talk because his nieces and nephew wouldn't leave him alone. And he had to admit, he loved it. He'd shut down the whining of his CFO for the night. Because what good was owning the company if you couldn't take a night off to hand out candy to a bunch of kids you loved? He knew he was too work-focused and impatient, could never be a good father, but he was determined to excel as an uncle. You didn't have to be the biological parent to help and influence a kid. He was living proof of that.

He glanced over at Holly now and noticed that she'd stopped singing and was shifting the baby to her other shoulder. He'd brought Holly here and he hated to see her looking so tired. Typical thoughtlessness on his part, but he'd do his best to fix it. "Let me hold her for a while," he said. "You've got to be tired."

She tilted her head to one side and studied him as if evaluating his worth as a baby-holder. "Okay," she said, "if she'll let you. She's picky."

"As a lady should be." Gently, he lifted little Penny out of Holly's arms.

The weight of the child settled something in him, felt good. The baby studied him with round blue eyes and then yawned, and when he patted her back, she leaned her head against his shoulder and sucked her hand.

Cash's heart expanded about three sizes.

Holly looked surprised. "She doesn't go to everyone."

He refocused on the here and now. "I'm a baby whisperer," he said casually, brushing off the often-paid compliment. "Listen, they'll light the tree any minute now. After that, we can have our talk and I'll take you back to your hotel. Where are you staying?"

She named a small inland town, not exactly known for tourism, and a motel he'd never heard of.

"How'd you land *there*?" Cash mostly met women

who wanted luxury. Holly was different. Or maybe desperate.

"Cheaper," she said. "I don't know how long we'll need to stay."

Aha, desperate. But he didn't have time to think about it because the tree lit up in a blaze of white lights. Gasps and oohs and aahs went through the crowd, and then as more and more lights came on, kids started shouting.

"So pretty," Holly said. "Look, Penny, pretty!"

The baby stared and waved chubby arms. And for just a moment, he felt like he and this woman and this baby were a little family, doing a holiday tradition together, and his chest tightened with crazy longing.

It must be the Christmas season that was making him soft and emotional. He had to toughen up. The crowd was dispersing, all the little ones needing home and bed, and he handed the baby back to Holly and hugged everyone goodbye.

"Don't stay away so long next time," Yasmin, Liam's wife, said sternly.

Anna, Sean's wife, nodded. "The girls miss you when you're gone," she said.

They made it sound like he lived here, but he didn't. He lived in Atlanta. It was just that, with all the weddings and babies and family events in the past two years, he'd spent more and more time here.

Finally, he broke away and ushered Holly toward the car, hitching her diaper bag over his shoulder to lighten her burden a little. Funny how she'd seemed to become part of the group in just this one evening. He was a little reluctant to spoil the sweet holiday, family feeling with a conversation about whatever she wanted from him.

But that was ridiculous; best to get things out into the open right away. "So what did you want to talk to me about?" he asked. "Sorry it took so long, took up your evening."

"No, it's okay," she said, smiling up at him as she shifted the baby from one arm to the other. "I'm glad to find out a little more about you and your family."

A strange uneasiness gripped him. "Why's that?" he asked.

She nodded down at Penny. "Because she's part of the family, too," she said. "She's your daughter."

Don't miss Low Country Christmas
by Lee Tobin McClain!

Welcome to Safe Haven, where love—and a second chance—is just around the corner...

Order your copies today!

SPECIAL EXCERPT FROM

Love Inspired.

Paralyzed veteran Eve Vincent is happy with the life she's built for herself at Mercy Ranch—until her ex-fiancé shows up with a baby. Their best friends died and named Eve and Ethan Forester as guardians. But can they put their differences aside and build a future together?

Read on for a sneak preview of Her Oklahoma Rancher *by Brenda Minton, available June 2019 from Love Inspired!*

"I'm sorry, Eve, but I had to do something to make you see how important this is. We can't just walk away from her. It might not be what we signed on for and I feel like I'm the last person who should be raising this little girl, but James and Hanna trusted us."

"But there is no *us*," she said with a lift of her chin, but he could see pain reflected in her dark eyes.

The pain he saw didn't bother him as much as what he didn't see in her eyes, in her expression. He didn't see the person he used to know, the woman he'd planned to marry.

He had noticed the same yesterday, and he guessed that was why he'd left Tori with her. He'd been sitting there looking at a woman he used to think he knew better than he knew himself, and he hadn't recognized her.

"There is no *us*, but we still exist, you and me, and Tori needs us." He said it softly because the little girl in his arms seemed to be drifting off, even with the occasional sob.

"There has to be another option. I obviously can't do this. Last night was proof."

"Last night meant nothing. You've always managed, Eve. You're strong and capable."

"Before, Ethan. I was that person before. This is me now, and I can't."

"I guess you have changed. I've never heard you say you can't do anything."

He sat down on a nearby chair. Isaac had left. The woman named Sierra had also disappeared. They were alone. When had they last been alone? The night he proposed? It had been the night she left for Afghanistan. He'd taken her to dinner in San Antonio and they'd walked along the riverfront surrounded by people, music and twinkling lights.

He'd dropped to one knee there in front of strangers passing by, seeing the sights. Dozens had stopped to watch as she cried and said yes. Later they'd made the drive to the airport, his ring glistening on her finger, planning a wedding that would never happen.

"Ethan?" Her voice was soft, quiet, questioning.

He glanced down at the little girl in his arms.

"What other option is there, Eve? Should we turn her over to the state, let her take her chances with whoever they choose? Should we find some distant relative? What do you recommend?"

He leaned back in the chair and studied her face, her expression. She was everything familiar. His childhood friend. The person he'd loved. *Had* loved. Past tense. The woman he'd wanted to spend his life with had been someone else, someone who never backed down. She looked as tough, as stubborn as ever, but there was something fragile in her expression.

Something in her expression made him recheck his feelings. He'd been bucked off horses, trampled by a bull, broken his arm jumping dirt bikes. She'd been his only broken heart. He didn't want another one.

Uplifting romances of faith, forgiveness and hope.

What she knows will change everything...
at *Redemption Ranch*.

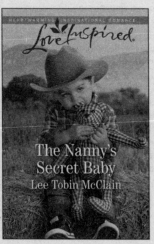

Arianna Shrader's new nanny gig is more than a job—it's an opportunity to bond with the infant boy she gave up to her sister for adoption. But widower Jack DeMoise doesn't know she's not just his child's aunt. As Arianna grows closer to the ranch veterinarian and his son, can she find a way to reveal her secret...and become a permanent part of their family?

Available August 2019, wherever books are sold!

LIBPA0619

Get 4 FREE REWARDS!

We'll send you 2 FREE Books <u>plus</u> 2 FREE Mystery Gifts.

FREE
Value Over
$20

Both the **Romance** and **Suspense** collections feature compelling novels written by many of today's best-selling authors.

YES! Please send me 2 FREE novels from the Essential Romance or Essential Suspense Collection and my 2 FREE gifts (gifts are worth about $10 retail). After receiving them, if I don't wish to receive any more books, I can return the shipping statement marked "cancel." If I don't cancel, I will receive 4 brand-new novels every month and be billed just $6.74 each in the U.S. or $7.24 each in Canada. That's a savings of at least 16% off the cover price. It's quite a bargain! Shipping and handling is just 50¢ per book in the U.S. and 75¢ per book in Canada.* I understand that accepting the 2 free books and gifts places me under no obligation to buy anything. I can always return a shipment and cancel at any time. The free books and gifts are mine to keep no matter what I decide.

Choose one: ☐ **Essential Romance**
(194/394 MDN GMY7)

☐ **Essential Suspense**
(191/391 MDN GMY7)

Name (please print)

Address   Apt. #

City   State/Province   Zip/Postal Code

Mail to the **Reader Service:**
IN U.S.A.: P.O. Box 1341, Buffalo, NY 14240-8531
IN CANADA: P.O. Box 603, Fort Erie, Ontario L2A 5X3

Want to try 2 free books from another series? Call 1-800-873-8635 or visit www.ReaderService.com.